SLIP ON
A FAT LADY

SLIP ON A FAT LADY

Philip Norman

W H

HEINEMANN : LONDON

William Heinemann Ltd
LONDON MELBOURNE TORONTO
JOHANNESBURG AUCKLAND

First published 1970

434 52300 3

TO GILLIAN

Printed in Great Britain by
Northumberland Press Limited
Gateshead

1

Some friends of Mother had invited them out to Christmas lunch. Mother herself loathed cooking: when Moorman first came home from the R.A.F. his fingernails and the clefts in his nose grimy, he could tell she was in the beginnings of a bad mood simply at the thought of getting his lunch. First he had to go all around the town to buy a cabbage and potatoes and a packet of damp, white sausages.

If they hadn't gone to this woman's for Christmas lunch, Moorman's three-month business career might never have begun. In his excellent memory, the occasion always smouldered in dark reds—place mats and bulky, red paper napkins, the splendid ruby colour of the hostess's black eye when she whipped off her sunglasses—and the bad words used still rang about his head sometimes. 'Gin and tonic baby.' 'Mealy-mouthed old mare.' And then someone threw a Lazy Man's Bar, a presentation cabinet of Max Factor shaving lotions, right across the dining-room.

As they set off for Lorna's in the van, Mother had

described their hostess as 'a very, very worried and frightened woman.' Moorman also remembered how her rather slow choice of words had cheered him up. She appeared to be making an effort to talk to him. His blood raced. He wondered if he should ask her for the £900 on the way to Lorna's. Then, with the van turning in and out of the streets of a large village, her marked friendliness had increased. Pointing to several driveways, she said how peculiar the people around there were; religious maniacs with a lot of money. But that, Moorman knew, was a bad turn in the conversation. He could never ask her for money if she was on the subject of a religion she disliked, particularly Catholics.

He bit his lip and arched himself up in the passenger seat to get a grip on the linings of his trouser pockets. He writhed in the morning's bright cold. The wind whipped and flicked the trouser legs of an old religious maniac out walking. At a junction, two little boys sword-fenced with bamboo stick shrimping-nets. Moorman was well aware that he smelt of Cooper's Fresh Air. He'd sprayed it all over himself in case his stay with Mother was already making him smell of fish and chips. He had chapped lips, which made him feel dirty all over—Christmas morning.

Lorna kept the Woolpack near Waterlooville. Her guests were her old mother, her daughter Clare, Mother and Moorman, an old friend of Lorna's who was a captain in the Durham Light Infantry and, to begin with, Lorna's boyfriend Bambus the master chef. *He*, mother repeated contemptuously, was simply an adventurer, he 'smelt of bed' when he had once opened the Woolpack door to speak to her out of licensing hours; but Moorman had rather a soft spot for him, based mainly on his attractive name. Also, Moorman was envious of his clothes, the beautifully-made suits with waisted jackets; the deep green ties and pocket handkerchieves, specially made up, at Lorna's expense, from bales of green silk paid for by Lorna. Often (Mother continued bitterly) the master chef would just stick his hand in the till, take three or four hundred pounds and vanish to a health farm in Bedfordshire. But at the time, all Moorman remembered of him was that he was pencil-bearded and very stout, with a head of brilliant black curls; that, like Lorna, he was a native of Cirencester; he looked as if he might knock you down, but would suddenly confound this impression by picking up a kitten to make a fuss of it.

'I think it'll be a free-for-all today,' Mother raised her voice, 'but still . . .' This note of apology in her voice, Moorman remembered, cheered him up even more; and it occurred to him that, if the Christmas Day at Lorna's turned out really horrible, she might try to make it up to him by lending him that £900 necessary to take up Leslie Langdon's offer. At any event, she would probably throw the cheque at him. This gave Moorman confidence; he even thought he might find a girl at Lorna's; but then the sight of the filthy van window returned him to feeling awkward and flabby, with a sensation of black toast in his throat. He grew nervous of meeting the others in Lorna's party, especially the army officer. If anyone could see right into him, his weakness, his cowardice, and so forth, it would be an army officer; the army officer's gaze would soon kill any pretence at a literary education, and would (Moorman gripped the linings of his pockets) smoothly take in his two-button Hepworth suit with its coat shoulders ruined by weak wire servicemen's hangers.

Worst of all, he could smell the Cooper's Fresh Air

on himself as well as the fish and chips on the uncured lynx fur cape worn by Mother; worse than *that,* the shirt she'd given him for Christmas was collar size 15½ instead of 15. It was white Terylene with a faint, almost invisible silver stripe. If Moorman pulled his tie to its proper tightness, the collar bunched up at the back, and in the end the tie knot became as thin as a matchstick with all the pulling. He remembered how the possibility of the £900 receded when they were almost at the Woolpack. Moorman leaned over to try to see his tie-knot in Mother's driving mirror and she, furiously, knocked his knee out of the way of the gear stick. 'Always *looking* at yourself,' she snarled. That was true; he strained his eyes to catch his reflection in shop-windows. He stared miserably into mirrors for hours. But should she have knocked his knee out of the way quite like that—his first Christmas home from the R.A.F. and he almost twenty-five? He was close to tears.

An absolutely delightful pub, the Woolpack was situated at a little crossroads with a war memorial in the middle; it stood among harmonious elm trees and the willows at the foot of its beer garden touched the water of a lake. Once, old fellows had risen from the nettly ditches round about, to eat hard-boiled eggs and home-made cake and bread pudding in Peggy's tap-room; Young Conservatives had driven out, barking, from Southsea and Havant to the Woolpack on Sunday mornings, but all that had been before the master chef's arrival. He (Mother said) had coarsened the establishment. Moorman remembered all the details. In the tap-room, much to the horror of the old fellows, the master chef had put a mynah bird named Pepi and a Harrison Marks calendar, each naked girl being identified in biro as a specific member of the local British Legion Women's Section. The lounge-bar walls he had crowded with such unnecessary objects as square-toed Cromwellian boots, copper shoe horns and a blunderbuss which the master chef warned customers not to touch in case the concealed spring bayonet cut off their heads. In addition, Moorman remembered with some admiration, the master chef had off to a fine art the terrorizing of Lorna's cash customers. He told nervy milk stout drinkers that he was an assistant hangman. He warned women with dogs against his own boxer ('I warn you—a killer. Now I've told you.') and certain other people had failed to return after the master chef had offered to smash them over the jaw with his personal, private, glass ashtray.

The Woolpack's lounge bar, when Moorman followed Mother in at about one o'clock, was deliciously orange and warm and thickened by celebration Manikins. A roar and rumble of spontaneous welcome greeted any new arrival. Moorman's eyes immediately darted around the room to try to see himself in a mirror. There was one behind the bar but the inverted spirit bottles and measures prevented him from seeing anything but the strangled knot of his tie. When the customers parted for them, there was a metal bowl of punch steaming on the bar, the ladle sliding here and there in it. The master chef stood a little further down, next to a Stilton cheese enfolded by a napkin. His fingers rummaged in it for porty bits. He had on khaki drill trousers and a pink shirt that showed the outline of his vest. Lorna was clearly determined to put on an impression of close harmony—she wore pink satiny trousers that almost matched his shirt, and hugged and kissed a great many bystanders including Mother and

Moorman. But as he accepted two warm wineglasses full of the fruit-bumping punch, Moorman noted the master chef's expression with interest; particularly the terrible frowns he directed at Lorna's behind, which was far from attractive.

Otherwise, she was quite good-looking. She had honey-coloured hair, a full mouth, and kept her nails well. There was a faint shampoo aroma. She was about the same age as Mother; they had been girls together in Clapham Old Town; but the real difference was that Moorman could imagine Lorna with no clothes on. Mother in a state of undress meant Mother in bloomers, a vest, a foul mood. Moorman had a feeling that, if he put his hand on a bar stool, Lorna might sit down on it. She asked how the shop was doing and Mother began to describe the chicken barbecueing machine she hoped to install there. Then Lorna threw herself into the telling of a wartime anecdote that became more and more unctuous and sentimental.

'The Plough! Uncle Ted!' Lorna cried. 'Ah. Mention my name in there! Oh, he was such a cute old man. How he used to wind up that old car of his, old banger. Remember his old Vauxhall car? Towards the end, you know, cranking it up got too much for Uncle Ted and he sometimes used to faint in the yard. We'd find him out there in the . . . in the . . .' she laughed uproariously, 'in the morning. "Oooo", he'd say, "pint o' mixed, dear." And how about when he went out to start the Vauxhall and found a dead body lying in front. He came back in the bar as white as a ghost. You can imagine. Some old drunk, I suppose, who'd fallen on his head. The cops had to let him go, though. His engine was stone-cold.'

They stood, drinking this warm, sour punch, in a

Christmas-morning crowd, different from a Sunday-morning crowd in that it formed much larger semi-circles, as if waiting for someone to recite, and there was this suspicion of brand-new white shirts, like Moorman's, and of brand new sheepskin gloves lying on the settee cushions. The sights and scraps of talk Moorman remembered from that morning had, as usual, seemed to illuminate so many of his own discomforts. That, mainly, was why he had such a remarkable memory for dialogue, for the precise expression used: so much of it seemed to relate to him. For example, that popular fat man who, flaring his nostrils over a sherry, had said, 'Ah, Tio Pepe. That and soap on a woman's neck are the two sweetest smells in the world.' Moorman knew he would never have either the confidence or quality of voice to make a remark like that. When he raised his own voice, it bleated. And he overheard another man saying, 'You see, if my fire's plugged in, I can't have the T.V. on.' Wasn't that precisely his own home situation—mixtures like Swiss roll, chocolate, crisps, and lime-ade spread out on a counterpane in front of an unreliable electric fire? At Mother's succession of flats there had never been an electric fire without at least one bar broken.

'No, but Uncle Ted could be a wicked old devil,' Lorna continued, peering coquettishly through a glass flecked with lemon. Moorman could remember every word. 'Uncle Ted. Uncle *Ted!* He had an old pal named Frosty.

'Frosty used to work in Horne Brothers opposite Leicester Square tube. Isn't that funny, we never did get to know what his first name was. He'd got a house he'd built himself—spent weeks pebbledashing it at the front—in Orlando Road, up there by the police flats, that he'd bought when some investment of his realized, and he and Uncle Ted were always together down from the Plough. "I want a large gin for my friend, Frosty, and a large gin for myself . . ." Remember the two of them? And were you in there the night that A.F.S. chap came in wearing a tin hat and tells everyone it could withstand any knock? So Uncle Ted says—Cheers, Tom. Cheers, Nor. Happy Christmas—so Uncle Tom says to this fellow, "Suppose I hit you." He says, "It ought to withstand it." So Uncle Ted, egged on by Frosty, says to him, "I'll have a go then," You'll never guess what Uncle Ted picks up off the floor . . .'

Moorman had watched for the start of the disagreement and his attention was now rewarded. Next to Lorna behind the bar, the master chef was busily telling a joke to someone a great deal further down the room, about a poor woman who was to be shaved by her husband before an operation. Gradually his words drowned Lorna's, and confused her.

'So any rate, see, her husband gets his cut-throat razor out of the drawer and says to her, "Now, darlin', you've seen me use this enough times, haven't you? Every morning like?" She says, "Yes".' The force of the story, related in a deep and melodious West Country voice, had drawn the master chef's listener right along the bar on his elbow, and now he almost wept with laughter. He seemed to be the army officer, as he was dressed very formally. He leaned right over the bar, put an arm round Lorna's shoulders, quivered and bayed: 'Oh, God, Oh, crikey! Listen to this, Lorn. Listen to your old man. Have you been listening? It sounds ab-sol-ute-ly dis-*gusting*.'

Moorman actually knew how this story ended. The laugh came when the teller suddenly twisted his mouth, and, very deliberately, when the army officer (presumably) was laughing into her ear, Lorna twisted her mouth and said, without any interest: 'This is the one when the husband asks her "can you go like that?" Right?' She added: 'Look, try not to keep putting your fingers in the cheese. *Dear*. You were the one that wanted to blow six pounds ten on a cheese-scoop, so use it and not your fingers, because it's enough to put everyone off.'

'Don't you start giving out with bloody instructions. Keep your bloody remarks to yourself, see? Will you? Do you hear? Scoop your bloody self. You just try putting on that boot face with me and . . . and . . . and . . . while you're at it you can stop your slanders about Sandra Draper or I'll pay you.'

Lorna was talking to Mother, her back to the master chef: 'No washing up or anything like that,' she said. 'Sleep all afternoon if you want. Really have a nice, quiet day.'

'Oi've bloody seen you bent in huddles with that old charlatan, Mrs Hufford, that bloody twaddler, your friend. You wait, if I see her in here . . .' He made his voice suddenly brief and serious. 'Look, Lorn, if I'm going to get playful while you're out shopping, it won't be with some bird in long knickers from down the village, you may depend. See? I'll do a lot better than that. My Dad always said, "Never poop on your own doorstep," and I don't, see? Do you hear? I can tell you that for nothing. Ask Bernie there.'

'I don't care what you do, long as I don't have to be present. I don't care what he does, Bernard.'

'Bernie, tell this stupid cow something.'

'I told you,' Lorna said hoarsely, 'I don't *care*. Past caring.'

And what Moorman remembered particularly was Lorna's incredible way of adding, with such appalling timing as to make the £900 seem almost there already, packed in his wallet:

'I wish you'd picked something a bit nicer, that's all . . . if you must *do* half the village.'

The master chef stepped forward, grabbed Lorna, whirled her round, and gave her a hearty push back against the bar, slopping the punch vigorously about. The preceding discussion had concerned the master chef's partiality to a slice on the mat and his choice of partners for this purpose. It was a side of his character that Mother hadn't really dwelt on; she preferred a nice, strong cup of tea to anything sexy; but Moorman had a feeling all the time that the master chef played dirty games. Besides, he had since learned from Leslie Langdon (who'd spent six months in the Savoy kitchens, filleting oranges) that there'd been a certain chambermaid with whom all the master chefs used to take turns in the deep freeze: cold, pink carcasses, cold breath puffing.

Lorna lay back against the bar for a few seconds, and then, quite unreasonably, she pulled out her lower lip to see if it had been cut, and after that, snatched off her sunglasses and turned her eye on Mother, Moorman, and the army officer.

'I don't care, let 'em all see my black eye. Things what you do after they've gone, damn, damn you.' The eye's purple, in fairness, meant it was almost better but Moorman remembered how he'd shuddered and gripped the linings of his pockets: at that time, a year before he met the stoutest Italian girl in the world, he truly loathed the idea of thumping women around. He also remembered with some interest, how the master chef had said nothing in reply to this, had simply wiped his big fists on his sides and had begun to prepare a Pimm's No. 1, slicing up the fruit painstakingly, arranging it along a cocktail stick balanced along the rim of the goblet, with a cocktail cherry at each end. The army fellow assisted Lorna through the gate from the bar, through which she had to crawl as the dish of punch rested on the counter flap, and, having given vent to a number of deep sobs and whispered blasphemies into Mother's ear, she was able to continue her story: Uncle Ted, it turned out, had smashed the A.F.S. man with a small table but had done no damage to the man's head.

At about three o'clock, the last of the customers cleared from the Woolpack, leaving it surprisingly neat and tidy; the army fellow ran after someone who'd left behind a revolting little Tyrolean hat. Now two more people joined the circle round Lorna on her stool. The master chef was still behind the bar, drinking brandy quickly. Now here were Lorna's old mother, who also knew Mother from the Clapham days, and the army fellow's fiancée. She wore a purple and white check knitted dress with mauve beads and said nothing at all (otherwise Moorman would have remembered it). The uneasy peace had remained. Mother talked quite brightly, even bringing Moorman into the conversation: only a slight 'Oops' caused him to grip the linings of his pockets when the master chef, with a sudden and warlike movement, swept the punch bowl upwards from the bar by the handles, narrowly avoiding an impact with Lorna's old mother's chin.

Moorman went out to the Gents. Softened by his six or seven glasses of vin rosé, he allowed the jet to play over the porcelain rim and about the pipe-joints. It had been funny how exposure to a crowd of unmitigated oddities like Lorna's friends and family had toned down his worrying dread of Mother. Really he began to feel that he would get the money easily, even by charm, and the first piece of capital he had ever in his life owned, would quickly multiply, with Leslie Langdon's guidance; and, after all, he *had* an education, he'd read *Samson Agonistes,* and Wordsworth's Prelude (books one to seven) and had this memory for quotations which a certain sort of girl in fly-away spectacle frames tended to admire. Moorman put his hands behind his back, pulled his stomach in, arched his pelvis and tried to compose a poem. Tiring of this he returned to the bar, looking in on his way at the little dining-room. For a moment, with a slight sinking of his heart, he'd thought perhaps the actual eating would turn out to be normal. The table and high-backed chairs were carved intricately. The reds from the table decorations settled on his memory. But where were the wines, the exclusive-looking bottles with foil to be shaken off? He remembered, too, that the crackers had about them a slightly hysterical look. They were red and fluffy, in fact excessively fluffy, like oven-gloves, strung tautly in their box. Then, turning from the doorway, Moorman bumped into the army fellow who had obviously just gone upstairs and darted down, having changed his jacket for a brick-coloured, crew-necked pullover, which forced out at right-angles the knot of his regimental tie. It was a great relief to see that he was at least as big a prick as Moorman himself. Both of them grinned palely at one another, rolling their eyes.

Although neither had really been introduced to Lorna's old mother, she welcomed them back; in her gingery wool suit, full of whisky and orange, turning on the top of a stool with nowhere to rest her feet, she was like everyone's old mother at Christmas. She'd put one arm round the army fellow, another round Moorman and drawn them close. 'My two boy friends,' she said.

'Now you look to me a nice, sensible chappie. Nice hair, nice suit—oh! nice woolly on now. It's very aristocratic, don't you think?' she demanded, gripping the army fellow's wrist and scanning his features, 'Say, don't you think my Clare's grown up lovely?'

He did.

'But I want to ask you something. No, she's really made a *life*, really made a . . . where is she?'

'She's out.'

'No, dear, listen to an old bird, eh? Gurk! Oo. Windy-pops.

'No,' she continued, 'I want you to ask me, I mean, tell me something. Unless I'm just a naughty old girl mixing all me words up. Tell me if I am. Say, tell me if I am. Shan't be offended. I will! Tell me something, dear.'

'All right,' the army fellow replied, trying to sound debonair, trying to make her consider him and refer to him in future conversations as a *nice* chap. 'What?'

'Well, why . . . Naaaw. Can't. It's just me being a nosey old faggot.'

'No, go on, dear.'

Peggy's mother stabbed with a finger towards his fiancée, who was being very quiet, looking very beaky and sad with a Babycham; but so plain. She quickly looked the other way. 'You know, you can't keep it from me,' the old lady said roguishly. 'She's got a wing on, I mean, wig. She's wig-headed. Now be quite candid. She has, hasn't she? Got a wig on? Garn! I can see the blessed pin. You can't fool an old bird like me with wig-heads. Don't know how they think they fool anyone. Now what's a nice chap like you doing out with her?'

Swivelling his pint tankard around in his hands, the army fellow struggled to find a reply; and Moorman, with a little thrill, had realized that, despite the fish shop, the van, his suit, his shirt, Mother's height, Mother's lynx, its crisp, dead, batter smell, the fact that he'd never *ever* seen her in the nude, he and Mother were the most normal people in that gathering, which was something he had no idea how to react to.

At this point, a door had slammed in the kitchen regions where by now both Lorna and the master chef were looking after the lunch. The old lady said, 'Hel-lo,' and to Moorman's alarm put down one leg from her stool, exposing a long, pink shimmering, elasticated knicker leg which she immediately sheathed again. 'That sounds like my little Clare coming back.'

The army fellow said he was afraid Clare was in Lorna's bad books for going out on Christmas morning.

'Well, it's Christmas. What's the good of Christmas without a bit of fun? No, listen, boys (old wig-head—Ha, ha, no, naughty old me!) Clare's made good, made a *life*. She's got her Grampa's brains. "Hetty," he used to say, "I'm rich enough to dress how I like and eat how I like." And little Clare thinks like me about . . . things, you know. *We* could be mother and daughter, us two.'

'With your looks, I agree.' Inwardly Moorman applauded his delivery of that remark.

'Oooh, you, none of that sauce.' Lorna's mother turned round to Moorman. 'Clare gets in trouble here for one very good reason, you see, dear. She's just like her Nanna. She appreciates her privacy. Shut and lock your door—Safe! Do you see? You're a sensible boy. How she used to love coming up to me when she was a little girl, and having early morning tea with me on my big pillow. Of course she thinks nothing of *him*,' continued the old lady. In the palm of her hand she held, like a rare slug, a bit of Stilton she'd gouged out of the cheese but apparently forgotten about; and her eyes narrowed just like Lorna's—Lorna's pliant eye. '*Naw,* nothing. Nothing. She's told me it. It's a hold he's got. Wicked. Ooooh, he's a bad man.' Then she plunged away to another topic, as tight old ladies do. 'Eh, now look, tell me something. I'm not deceived, you know. She 'as got a wig on 'er 'ed.' Lorna's old mother spoke up in unabashed and researchful tones. 'I'm quite sharp when I like. She *is* a wig-head, eh?'

The quiet girl in purple sobbed once, quietly, just as a very large labrador will only bark once but with feeling, and vanished upstairs. Then, before her fiancé could go after her, before even his round, pale, pleasant, perfectly shaved face had even properly registered her flight, another girl came recklessly through the bar, brushing tables and also ran up the stairs to the living quarters, hump, thump, prump. Moorman had time to notice only that her hair was blonde and pinned up, that he'd never forget she wore a suède coat reaching almost to her ankles. And simultaneously there came from the kitchen region a scream succeeded by a number of sustained hoarse sounds as if someone with a full mouth was undergoing torment.

Lorna's mother put down her crumbly bit of Stilton, laid her hand on her heart: 'Oh, God. It's started. . . .'

'Calm down, old love,' begged the army fellow. 'It's only a bit of mother and daughter jealousy you don't want to get involved in. Waste of time.'

'No, no, no, I know when it's started.' She dabbed her eyes and mouth with a paper serviette from a tumblerful. 'Oh God, dear God, why must she be a puppet like that?'

'I told you. Lorna's upset because Clare's stopped out all morning.'

'I only wish *he* was here and not gone,' the distressed old lady wept, to Moorman's great sorrow and concern. 'How I wish . . . but you can't wish, can you? "Let's get the Hell out of this," he'd say when it started, when he was here. Back we'd go to our little safe haven at Wandsworth. Will you take me home if I ask you to?'

'Sure.'

'Oh, why did I come to this place again? I wasn't going to. I said . . .'

But the master chef was suddenly back in the room, a very dirty tea towel put over his shoulder. His resemblance to a Mexican was fantastic. He wore an expression of entreaty on his furious, mottled and newly-scratched countenance, and spoke to the company very nicely. 'Please come in and sit down now, Lorna says. It's on the table.' They followed him to the dining-room, where there was a big turkey, a dish of boiled potatoes steaming in a sheet of steam, but nothing at all besides, yet. The crackers were still strapped in their box. Lorna's mother tried to pick out one but simply picked up the whole box. 'Come on, who'll have a bom bom with me? You, dear?'

Moorman remembered his vivid pang of fear at the seating arrangements around that red table. Even if Lorna's daughter and the other girl rejoined the celebrations, he would have to lean a vast distance this way and that with hot dishes burning the tender skin between his thumb and forefinger; he fancied Mother was looking at him already and saying, 'Don't drop it.' The dining-room was very small and the table left very little space to pass behind the chairs. Moorman slid into one of the places next to the head of the table in obedience to Mother's pointed finger; she sat further down the table on the other side. Lorna's mother started at the other end, creeping, feeling and kneeling her way over several chairs, knocking her shins, until she arrived two places from Moorman. Then she again picked up the box of crackers and, for an instant, rattled it at him. Her face, like someone with chapped lips pinioned by a cruel flash cameraman, was exceedingly pale.

At the sideboard the master chef took up the carvers. The army fellow stood at the kitchen door ready to bring in more hot dishes as, from the kitchen, the sound came of sobbing and of saucepans being cast angrily about.

The master chef called out: 'Where's Clare got to?'

In the kitchen a distressed voice replied: 'Hell, I hope.'

'With Margaret.'

'Why, Bernard? Why'd they do that? Why doesn't someone pop and find them and bring them to dinner?' the master chef demanded in a hurt way.

Lorna ambled from the kitchen. 'That girl is,' she said with a new and clearer voice, 'the biggest and best diseased remnant of an afterbirth . . .'

Her mother, transfixed in the act of putting one of her boiled potatoes on a side plate: 'Oh! Oh! I can't—I can't stand that word. "Let's get the Hell out", that's what *he* used to say to me when it started; always used to say.' And finally the master chef put down the carvers and turned to the company.

'Where do you suppose they went off to?'

'I really haven't the faintest.'

Up jumped the army fellow, all smiles and reassurance. He offered to go and find them; they'd only be up the lane a few yards having a sulk; no offence to Lorn, women were like that; he'd be back in two ticks.

'No, Bernard, sit down, yours'll get cold,' Lorna said wearily, but he'd gone. With the eyes of the company on her, Lorna filled up her mouth to its limit, leaving a corner impolitely hanging open. 'I-got-no-stuffing,' she remarked to Moorman, there being no real reply to that. Then, with another of the day's endless cavalcade of rapid movements (not yet ended by a long way) she snatched off her sunglasses once again and turned the indigo eye on Moorman. 'Go on, go and have a good look. Get close. I don't mind who sees. I'm just a tool, hah, tool is right. I said it there, didn't I? Oh, the ignorant, bloody horrors of it, the buggering . . .'

'Oh, I wish he could be here. "Let's get the hell out of . . ." '

'Look, Lorn.'

She glared up and down the table as though she'd like to tip it up or come out of a layer cake and machine-gun it; and her expression of distaste at her mother ripened at once into scorn.

'Ah, shut up,' she snarled, whispered and spat. 'You got no idea what it's like you mixing old . . . . You don't care what happens to me, you mealy-mouthed old mare.'

'Look, *Lorn*.'

She paid no heed to the master chef's deepening voice and movement, glacier-like, from the sideboard towards her. 'I've been watching you. Heard you putting the mix in since you got here.' She went falsetto cockney: 'Waw waw waw, nice at Wandsworth Common, my little house.' Nobody gives a damn for your little house. Or your money. Or anything to do with you.'

'I've done nothing. Oh! Oh! Listen to her.' The old lady rocked to and fro in her seat, hardly making a sound.

'Come down here and ruin my Christmas, would you? *She*, ungrateful little devil, just walks out of the house,

I get clouted about in front of a score of customers and you creep about putting the mix in, don't you, you old bag. Don't you start limping and bleating around down here. Go back to bloody sodding Wandsworth Common if you want. *You* got money. I heard you telling everyone; you're not short of a fiver. Well, go on, I don't care. Get your coat.'

'Oh! Listen, listen to it! You horrible girl.'

'Lorn, shut it,' the master chef bellowed.

'Oh, listen to her. I don't believe it.'

'You admit it—bag. Old bag. You've never in your life cared a farthing about me. Just a mistake, wasn't I? The result of six gins and tonics, a gin and tonic baby? And you always held a grudge . . .'

'I've never held a grudge against . . . .'

'Oh, yes, you have. You held a grudge against me for the rest of my life because I was born.'

'Oh, I never. Oh, listen to it.'

'Grr. If I'd married the man I wanted, this wouldn't have happened. That was your fault, you horrible old woman. All your fault. That was thanks to you, you wicked deceitful old mare. Go on, limp off. Get a hire car back to Wandsworth Common. I'll help you carry your bags down.'

Mother was simply looking at her plate, what else was there? Moorman pressed a bit of cold turkey on to his palate with his tongue, then he began to chew it endlessly. As Lorna yelled and scolded on, the mouthful of papery fowl reminded Moorman of his illness. He'd spent eleven weeks in hospital while they kept an eye on him for polio, and in the end he'd moved into a side ward by himself and had a fine time; no cutting, no injections. He'd enjoyed watching the sun come up over the buildings. He'd seen an incredibly ill and old-looking man bump gaily out of a little black car and bounce-trolleyed inside by a couple of St John's Ambulance women volunteers. He'd had a swan made out of a printed furniture sale leaflet by a taxi-driver. He'd been puzzled by the ancient smell of a toy milkmaid; it must have been Edwardian. And Mother had hardly come to see him at all.

When he looked up from his plate, he saw that the master chef had his hands pressed down on Lorna's shoulders and was talking to her, enunciating every word carefully, even though Lorna was still finishing an angry speech at her old mother over his shoulder.

'The trouble with me is, I love you, I'll say it again; the trouble with me is, I love you.'

She lifted her set jaw to him.

'Come on, have your present now, eh, dear?' He showed her a little parcel and unwrapped it to reveal a very nice Colibri gas lighter. Its spare flints and the butane filler slipped from Lorna's knees to the floor. She might be going to hurl the lighter the length of the dining-room; twitching hands suggested this.

'Here they are,' interrupted a voice. 'Hello, hello. All's well. Look sharp, girls, so that I can pull the door to.' It was the army fellow, his brick-coloured pullover darkened and heavy with rain. He had an arm round Lorna's daughter, an arm round his fiancée, who carried quite a large leather shoulder bag, possibly made abroad. 'You've deigned to turn up now it's on the table, have you?' cried Lorna, in a voice even more infuriated and hoarse than she had hitherto employed, a highly dangerous tone, and Moorman saw the new direction. That poor fiancée. 'Go on, get out to the kitchen. There's some bread and cheese out there. Miserable over-done-up li'l tart.'

'Lorna!'

'Oh! Listen to the abuse, oh! oh!'

'Go on, don't expect to sit down with us, messing up all our Christmases. I don't know what Bernard thought he was doing, but you're not sitting down. Get your bread and cheese.'

'Piss off, you blowsy old worm,' replied the financée with an upsurge of good old-fashioned British pluck.

Lorna began to cry: 'Everyone's on at me. Morning to night. There's nothing to get up for. No comfort, no money, never a minute's peace. Just abuse, that's all, that's about it. Knocks across the face and cut lips and spat-out teeth. All of you.' She cawed abruptly at Mother: 'And you're no bloody help. You're a fine friend, I don't think. Yeah, you always was hated. Uncle Ted hated you, he avoided you, even in those days. Go on, walk out on us and see if I care, you and your drippy son. And *you* in the wig, get out of this room before I choke you and *you*, you old devil, go with her, in a hire car back to Wandsworth Common, because you got a fiver, haven't you?

'And as for you, you beast . . . you dirty animal, you abuse everything you put your fat paws on.' (This was properly speaking the beginning of Moorman's partnership with Leslie Langdon.) 'I hate and loathe you and want you out of the house, you stinking kitchen *porter*, you fat great baby, you dirty burglar . . .'

The taste of cold stuffing had been acute enough to take the top of his head off; Moorman's skull rocked with the taste as he watched the master chef leap excitedly to the small heap of parcels under the Christmas tree, select his gift from Lorna, the cabinet of shaving lotions, shop-wrapped, and throw it a long way away with a hollow laugh.

'You filthy, mauling . . . you stink of scent and sweat, you steal my takings . . . hit me around in front of . . .'

He crossed to Lorna, slapped her a blow across the teeth, a few more across the cheek, jabbed her arms with three fingers and, at the last attempt, actually put her senseless on the carpet, her head brushed by the red tablecloth. The army fellow was butted in the stomach when he started towards the master chef, his arms extended in a mollifying embrace, and he sat on a chair and put his head on his knees; a number of women screamed out; Moorman swallowed the stuffing and gripped the linings of his pockets; the master chef went out and slammed the door.

2

And Moorman's Christmas lunch consisted of just endless cold potatoes taken from the dish—they had chalky and hard little pieces hanging off them. (He believed that he over-ate to cheer himself up.)

Lorna, arranged along three of the dining-room chairs, snored in a handsome baritone. Her old mother, the daughter, the army fellow and his fiancée all left to drive back to Wandsworth Common and Mother sat down, her back to Moorman, watching a television that was pale blue with interference. Her one remark of the afternoon was, 'Here's the Queen now.' As six was chiming in the bar, Lorna got up from her rest to let them out. Her last words, before closing the studded door, leaving them to go to the car park through pitch-cold, had been: 'You both sure you don't want a mince-pie?'

The cold van, the icicle smell of fish and chips. Mother drove home through lanes ghostly with side-puddles and illuminated rabbits flashing over. Later, sitting up in bed with a tumbler of gin and tonic, a thick Howard Spring book on the bedspread, Mother agreed at once to lend him the £900 and added to that the sort of brief, angry hug that Moorman remembered from his earliest infancy, on the better nights. He'd got his capital, signed a document in terror, and here he was, four months later, in April, the co-master, with Leslie Langdon, of the amusement arcade at the end of Springbourne Pier, Isle of Wight.

The pier was the third largest in the United Kingdom (as Leslie always expressed it), three-quarters of a mile long. In later life Moorman remembered it best in a hazy morning, lying heavily out to sea, just as in a series of lifeless prints he remembered school, *The Gosport Herald*, R.A.F. Upwood, and the room behind the shop: Mother's nimble fingers hurrying bread and butter slices from a used to an unused side plate and he, upstairs, trying to understand the poems of Gerard Manley Hopkins.

The pier was in the industrial style but still far from unattractive. It had pale, scrubbed plants, and pale turquoise railing-work in ornate curls and fantails. On the way to the end stood a row of three pagoda-shaped shelters, which housed rows of old holidaymakers, arranged stiffly, like a jaunting cart's occupants. Their knees were protected by plastic macs. They watched the fishermen smear the planks with a big flounder, or claws and parts of a crab that had clung to a line and ridden right out of the water to be ground pitilessly under a plimsoll. Up and down the pier ran a diesel tram; all day, meeting the passenger ferries from Lymington. On a still night, Moorman could hear it from his room in the Tredegar Guest House at the top of the town, ba-bang, ba-bang, then a slide up to the platform at the pierhead. The tram driver was John Close, an old man with white and gold hair brushed back flat. His little dog, Tony, always sat beside him on the driver's seat, and on Springbourne Esplanade, utterly out of character, he kept an immaculate green A.C. sports car, and drove home in it, the little dog sitting beside him. He had a girl friend called Mrs Salter, an acquaintance of Mrs di Valvona, Moorman's landlady.

But Leslie said the pier also had its wicked side. When the tide went out, it did so extravagantly, leaving water only along the northern perimeter of the pierhead; the rest, black mud and broken wood stumps. Moorman could never understand how the prawn-gatherers dared venture about down there. And when the Lymington ferries came in at low tide, propellers boiled up the black water, and dead fish and old french letters appeared on the ugly swell. On the dock there was a public convenience which sent a number of little waterfalls down under the pier. These attracted grey mullet which from above looked like puppet turds as they twisted and played in the disturbed water. The thought of grey mullet was one of the new things that made Moorman grip the linings of his trouser pockets. He'd seen one of the fishermen pull up a grey mullet that struggled so fiercely, it had fallen back into the water, leaving its lips on the hook. He now knew that the mullet was a soft-mouthed fish.

This morning at about five to twelve, Moorman felt his accustomed craving for a bar of chocolate, and walked out on to the pierhead through the Pavilion's row of Edwardian glass doors. The Pavilion was his. And Leslie Langdon's. It was a very large, domed building, painted sun-blistered red and grey, and had once been a pierrot theatre.

Moorman stopped; his cavalry twill trousers felt like hot iron, yet the stiff yachting breeze caught his hair and blew it about ridiculously; he tried to keep his head averted, but it was no use; he walked over the concrete to Uncles' Rock Shop (Uncles was the proprietor's name) as if he had a stiff neck; and he was sweating all around the waistband of his trousers.

Moorman's first pleasurable thought after agreeing to take over the Pavilion with Leslie Langdon, was that, at last, at last, he'd have enough clothes; he could now dress the part of a company director in summer: pastel-coloured Daks, a fawn shirt, a tropical jacket. But so far they had been in business almost three weeks and he had not managed even a new shirt for himself (Mona Lisa di Valvona, his landlady's daughter had given him a tie for his birthday, it was true. But what company director would wear a tartan tie containing a silver thread, a black man's tie?) The days got hotter and hotter: still he had to concentrate on wearing one pair of heavy cavalry twill trousers. The suit that had been almost new when he spent Christmas Day at the Woolpack, now had no buttons on the jacket; and, on the day he had signed the agreement about the Pavilion's lease, a biro had burst in one trouser pocket. No amount of dry cleaning had quite erased the blue deposit on the lining. Whenever he wore the trousers, Moorman could not avoid putting pale blue smudges all over his lips and in the clefts of his nose; he couldn't prevent himself from gripping the linings of the pocket and then putting his head in his hands. The twill trousers had shallow patch pockets. Late at night, with John Close's tram banging up the pier, below the Tredegar Guest House, Moorman always turned the trousers upside down to fold them in their creases, and from the patch pockets, tiny pellets of silver paper from chocolate he'd eaten during the day, tumbled on to the linoleum.

Still trying to keep his head turned from the yachting breeze, Moorman saw the Pavilion's dome dizzying up into the sky, and for a moment imagined himself at the beginning of a television documentary of which he was the subject: 'One man and his theatre'. Sharply then, he pined to work in television; in cool offices, at steel and leather desks, tropical suits and dark blue shirts, a junior padding over a fitted carpet to bring in milk shakes from outside. He wondered if he would ever stop cringing at the thought that, during his entire three years on *The Gosport Herald*, he'd always had to make tea. They'd called him Schnoor. 'Tea Schnoor'. Sometimes he had to make two or three pots of tea if the Editor and chief reporter were in an expensive mood and played Stop the Bus in the newsroom. As Moorman stood, his head twisting in vain from the wind, a crowd of boys and girls barged past him. He looked away from them and straight into the roaring wind, which again stood his hair right on end. He hurried across the pier-head concrete, feeling in one patch pocket for his comb, intending to palm it like a concealed weapon. He arrived at the serving window of Uncles' Rock Shop, received a Mars bar and, as the flaxen-haired, dirty-faced old whore Uncles employed rummaged for his change, he had a desperate try at combing his hair in the reflection of the adjoining shop window. Then he was startled to see, behind the display of tubes of coloured sand, emulsion-painted seashell ashtrays, booklets that sent a string of postcards tumbling to the feet, Uncles himself was standing watching him. He smiled with a quiet satisfaction and smoked a pipe.

On the way back to the Pavilion, Moorman met the crowd of boys and girls again. They were laughing and skylarking on the railings around The Triangle, a trough of water in the pier concrete, where John Close dropped a casual lobster net in between tram journeys to the Esplanade. Each of the party would be about fourteen. The girls wore regulation navy school macs with butcher-striped skirts the length of running shorts, covered with dinner stains, and anachronistic, white, pointed-toe shoes that reminded him of Mona Lisa di Valvona. And they carried big white handbags and wore cardboard stetsons with fringed brims and slogans. Uncles sold those. He sold almost everything. The boys engaged their feet in the fantails of the railings and leaned backwards, their faces upside down, looking amused at Moorman. They straightened up and yelled and grinned contemptuously. Each one had a pale face with a point of oily hair right between the eyes, visible blackheads. The shirts they wore were so cheap that the wind threw the collars around like paper. Could they possibly be friends of Meatball's?

One of the little girls shouted after Moorman, 'Oo, I like him.'

Another one took it up: 'Ex-cuse me. Can you tell new Stork from butter?'

He gripped the Mars bar to the lining of one patch pocket and ran through the Pavilion's glass doors, up the steps at the side of the old pierrot stage, into what Leslie Langdon called The Amplifier Room. He was trembling and breathing hard, as if he had just avoided a dangerous fight. He unwrapped the Mars bar and found it white with age and sun-exposure; he ate it in two mouthfuls, feeling disgusting.

Each day, he found himself waiting for the evening, when the yachting breeze died down, and the yellow patches at his armpits didn't show. He consoled himself with the thought that the season hadn't really begun yet. Leslie was always using this term, 'the season'. It scarcely seemed to apply to the hot, quiet days at the end of the Pier now, although (if he did but know it) the Springbourne boarding-houses were already full and making a fortune. No, he imagined the season would erupt on them sometime around Whitsun and would jangle with expended coins, and people would arrive on the ferries blowing squeakers, and there would be an entirely new quality in the days, somehow. This, anyway, was not the season, so he mustn't feel too badly about being bored to death, about taking next to no money in the Pavilion.

Waiting for the evening, Moorman decided to look again at the slot machines he and Leslie Langdon controlled. He did so by putting his eyes to two peepholes in the wall of the Amplifier Room. He could still taste the fatty, creamy texture of the Mars bar. The peepholes, though, had an interesting history. They were left over from the Pavilion's previous occupation as a skating-rink. Mr Vernon, the previous lessee, had drilled the holes through which he could reassure himself that all the skaters went round in the same direction. Indeed, Mr Vernon (now in the workhouse, as Leslie put it) had been artist enough to have a huge mural painted on the outer wall, Skaters of all the World, and when you looked closely at the Scotsman, real eyes glittered in his face, a device which Moorman found invaluable in the fight against Meatball.

His midday feelings—boredom, fatness, insecurity, being publicly insulted by fourteen-year-olds—recalled to Moorman's mind Mother. What would she be doing now? Telling Miss Toye that where there was muck there was money? Speaking out against the Catholics, the Strict Baptists, the Four Square Gospellers? Reading a historical romance by Margaret Campbell Barnes? Resting, her feet up, in the room behind the shop so that the frying girls would not get slack. Mother, on that Christmas night, had scarcely asked who Leslie Langdon was, or why he should want someone like Moorman to be his business partner, and was he quite sure that Leslie wasn't a nancy-boy? She'd just written out the cheque for £900. Later, of course, she had left the shop to come down to Springbourne to see the Pavilion and meet Leslie. That was a day or so before they opened; a thundery, sinister morning, and she, Leslie and Moorman had had luncheon meat salads in the Albany Restaurant on the Esplanade. Her mouth, he remembered, had clamped into a traced line at Leslie's manner of speech, his silvery peals of mirth. When he half bowed and kissed her hand, seeing her on to the boat, her expression had been of the purest disbelief. When the ferry pulled away, she didn't bother to stay on deck, as everyone else did, waving goodbye. She went straight downstairs and Moorman, turning away to look at the great Pavilion dome, had this awful sensation that he might never see her again.

He picked up a letter from her that had been among the distressing mess of papers on the Amplifier Room's roll-top desk—spindly and curly writing much older than Mother herself was. She always used Canadian Brand writing paper, with the elk head on the cover, from Woolworth's. She finished a letter with a lot of crosses for kisses; but Moorman, from earliest infancy, had never regarded these as any form of exchangeable currency.

He had asked her for another £300. Mother said she was very sorry to hear that he was 'a bit pushed' but then she herself was; she had just installed her chicken barbecueing machine and had employed another girl, Maureen; besides which there were the repayments on her Swedish oil fishfryers—those odourless fryers whose odourlessness was still mixed up with Moorman's few clothes. When she had got Whitsun over and done with, Mother said, she would see if she could spare him a bit. And he must put his back into it and not live on just cups of tea and pies, if he didn't want to end up like his father; and she was quite sure he wouldn't mind: Miss Toye was sleeping in his room until she could find a new place of her own.

Miss Toye! Moorman pinned most of his childhood misery, his great shame at all Mother's living accommodation almost as much on this old lady as on the odour of fish and chips. She was a strange, wild, old junk and vegetable dealer, and pulled a blind poodle about on a lead. Her hair frizzed out in all directions and she was hawk-nosed like a Red Indian. Her legs were so unbearably fat that they curled over the rims of her shoes. She had filthy dirty fingernails. How had Mother grown so attached to this malodorous (yet finely spoken) individual? In Mother's opinion, Miss Toye had once been a lady's companion and, after that, looked after a succession of old gentlemen—she might even have snuffed out one or two of them. Mother showed her great regard for Miss Toye by giving her endless fish suppers, cups of tea and chocolate biscuits, with chocolate toffees for the poodle: Miss Toye in return made available to Mother interminable pieces of rubbish at special prices, such as wooden tree tubs, secondhand nose irrigators. She had once, very sweetly, offered Moorman a couple of alpaca suits belonging to an old gentleman who had died. She had come to stay at the flat just after the Woolpack Christmas. Because she was in Moorman's room, he was compelled to occupy the divan in Mother's. Mother still preferred to use what she called the Edgar Allan rather than walk downstairs to the lavatory at the back of the shop. Every morning, he'd never forget, this wild little figure in its nightdress came in, sat down on his feet and talked to Mother in this dreadful, unnatural lady's maid voice. The other queer thing about her was that, wherever she went, she appeared to be followed by Hungarian refugees, carrying paint pots and stepladders.

Mother's letter ended, 'Well, dear, must go now and do up my bank . . .' Moorman sighed deeply and had just sat at the desk to put his head in his hands, when a ringing bell disturbed him. Or, rather, a ringing bell frightened him to death. It announced the arrival of a passenger ferry from Lymington, and these were going to make his fortune and Leslie's, when the season really began; and, to begin with, they were going to provide Moorman with the first made-to-measure suit of his life. A beautiful black suit with slanting ticket jackets and trousers that were naturally tapered, not taken in by a disapproving old tailor smelling of cork tips.

The roll-top desk was pushed against the window looking out on to the pier dock, where the ferries arrived. Without looking down, Moorman groped among a lot of papers—lease details wholesaler's bills, a hire purchase agreement in respect of a rifle-range, Leslie's empty Gold Flake packets, and picked up a hand microphone. The lead blew free of the documents, showing itself joined to a small Trix amplification unit at the side of the desk. Moorman pressed the button on the microphone, made sure that the red light appeared at the side of the desk; he blew slightly and spoke to the docking ferry.

'Before leaving the pier,' his voice bellowed all over

the end of the pier, 'why not stop awhile in the Fun Pavilion . . .'

Simultaneously, from Uncles' Rock Shop, a vile voice took the air in such a patter that it seemed to have no definite beginning . . . 'Come along now, ladies and gentlemen, welcome to the Garden Isle, now across here at the shop, we'll serve yew straight away, toffee apples fresh-made, bars and boxes of chocolates, boiled sweets and toffees, postcards, views, novelties, some of them saucy, coloured sands from Alum Bay. Keyrings, jokes, mementoes. All holiday guides. Your local newspaper. Travel details—we are agents for the West Isle Omnibus Co. Ltd. Now, all you lucky ladies and gentlemen bound for the Little Totem Holiday Camp, please report to your Happy Button courier right across here at the shop. And why not look at our range of the latest souvenirs. No obligation to buy. Or a tasty toffee apple. Comics, home periodicals. Milk in cartons. Baby's bottles filled. Rock in all flavours, peppermint, greengage, or pineapple. Full details of your holiday entertainment from the official borough guide. Just across here at the shop. Let us begin a perfect holiday. Just across here at the shop,' said Uncles.

He and Moorman were only permitted by the pier authorities to talk to the ferries as they approached the pier, never when the crowds were disembarking. It was, therefore, a race, a duel, for Moorman, an unequal struggle.

'You know, I know what I'm talking about, and you've got a *very* good mike voice, Gordon,' Leslie insisted. Moorman, seriously, resumed: 'Yes, tea, coffee, minerals and light refreshments,' (he found 'light refreshments' a little tricky to say), 'are obtainable . . . are still being served in the tea bar on the Fun Pavilion's ground . . .

ah . . . ground floor. There is no queueing and no waiting . . .'

The ferry bumped against the dock, rebounded and shifted along a few feet to its allotted berth; a fetching composition of black and yellow. The captain himself supervised the arrival, looking carefully down from the side of the bridge. Half a dozen men in tight black jerseys threw slopping wet ropes to and from the pier concrete and the deck. The whole ferry tilted over with the weight of people about to get off. They pressed to the mouths of ancient green gangplanks, fifty years old at least, in Leslie's opinion. Moorman stopped his announcement. Uncles stopped his but fractionally too late, so that 'toffee apples' lingered on the airways as the first day-trippers poured down and came on in Zulu formation to the ticket barrier. Uncles knew how to do it. Moorman thought disconsolately that he would only have a chancc against Uncles if he, too, had been a fairground barker once after the war. Down on the Esplanade there stood an immensely rich amusement arcade, S'Lots of Fun. Its owner, a Welshman, had a white Cadillac, said to have been paid for with a lorryload of pennies. He had a daughter at finishing school. And he, after the war, had been, guess what . . .

Moorman gave it a few seconds; he kept his eyes closed tight for a few seconds, taking for granted that there would be a thick crowd at Uncles' Rock Shop wanting to allow the right time to elapse before seeing what custom the Pavilion had been granted. His eyes still shut he rose from the desk, turned and put his face to the peepholes on the wall. He opened his eyes. He saw that a crowd of boys in, dark grey Pakamacs had come in and were walking towards Leslie at the change-desk. No one else. Moorman raked the rows of machines with his eyes

—he liked to think of himself raking with his eyes; in fact, he was slightly myopic—he saw Leslie's bald head at the change desk, where no doubt he was applying his fanatical tidiness to the piles of pennies; he saw dear old Nell Sumption drying something up behind the tea bar and dear old Fred Wellspring reading, probably, *The Daily Sketch* on the rifle-range counter. He realized that his announcement had omitted to mention the presence in the Pavilion of the rifle range, its Remington 22 rifles, its valuable prizes.

Ignoring a note in Leslie's writing 'Ring Mona Lisa—PRONTO ! ! !' Moorman, with his characteristic, despairing, half-burrowing away gesture, picked up an old green book and began to look idly through it; a hardback war story left behind by Mr Vernon. It was entitled *A Bell for Adano*, and more or less fell open by itself at page 108. There were a number of stains and a couple of stuck, hard tomato pips here, from a sandwich Moorman had once eaten while re-reading the page. This he had done almost as many times as *The History of Mr Polly*. Almost every day he turned to page 108 when, the taste of chocolate in his mouth, he wasn't hungry exactly; he simply fancied some nice food. Two American army officers were described sitting down to a lunch including something called eggplant, which sounded most appetizing; and on mornings like this, how Moorman wished *he* could have been an officer in the American army. They dressed so beautifully; fawn shirts and blending ties, green suits, gold facings, chrome wrist watches, and identity bracelets, bottles of deep blue lotion, silver-backed hairbrushes, silver things to clip their dollar bills together, round, dark, leather stud boxes, snowy white T-shirts.

Mona Lisa, as it turned out, telephoned Moorman.

The phone buzzed and he felt excited for a moment; there *was* tonight. And at exactly the same moment, Fred Wellspring looked round the Amplifier Room door, tapping as he did so.

'Hello, darling,' Mona Lisa's small voice—small? In the background, Moorman fancied he could hear the scurry of little Italian shoes and a kitchen voice baying instructions. 'Darling. You there?'

'Yes,' Moorman said in the heavy bantering tone that always so impressed her. 'Ye-es.' He raised, or at least, imagined he raised an eyebrow at Fred Wellspring, and that old gentleman mouthed the word 'Copper' at him.

'Hello, darling,' Mona Lisa said tenaciously. 'Are you busy just now?'

'Yes, I am.' He felt a surge of well-being. He felt, for the moment, in character, a businessman. Two demands on his time were being made simultaneously.

'We're just about to have our dinner.' Her Glaswegian voice was intensified over the telephone. 'I was just ringing up tae . . .'

'That's a bit early, isn't it?'

'For dinner? Yes, darling, it is, but ma Mummy's cousins are over from Ventnor to see us.'

'Oh,' Moorman said elaborately, and then, 'Aha.'

Mona Lisa's accustomed slow manner of speaking was beginning to make him anxious about keeping old Fred Wellspring waiting. In his mind's eye were two pictures: one of the comfortable life Fred Wellspring led, with his attractive auburn-haired wife, the other of Mona Lisa di Valvona, standing in the coin box in the hall of the Tredegar Guest House, one of her mighty legs crooked slightly. She'd have on, no doubt, a gold charm bracelet, with, among other things, a model birdcage, a vintage car, and a Ruffino bottle attached to it in miniature. She'd be in her hooped floral skirt under the transparent pink overall. Nevertheless, Moorman felt his cavalry twill trousers, the unyielding trousers, constrict against the side of the desk. Mona Lisa di Valvona had the most enormous breasts he'd seen seriously worn in real life.

'I was just wanting to see how you were.'

He said he was all right.

'Are you happy, darling?'

He said yes.

'Ah, well, that's the main thing. Have I been in your thoughts?'

'Yes.'

'So've you, darling.'

'Mmn, I . . .'

'And I see you later on outside the inquiry office, do I?'

Moorman really felt anxious now about keeping Fred waiting, and he spoke dynamically to Mona Lisa di Valvona. 'Something's just come up. Must go now. Usual place? All right?'

It was at about this time of day that he began, in a way, to look forward to laying hands on Mona Lisa. He enjoyed pulling out her breasts and bouncing them around; it was really the most exciting experience he'd ever had.

' "Copper", Fred?' said Moorman.

'That Copper doings was playing up, Mr Langdon asked me to tell you. No, the Copper *Mine*,' amended Fred Wellspring. It's the machine that's got all the moving arms. A tray of pence is carried up in the air, kind of style. You know, it's got "Very Fair" and "Good" and "Very Good". That one.' He sneezed, like a furious rending of newspapers. 'Whoops, it's been a very *dusty* day.'

It seemed to Moorman that he had spent so much of his life in company with unattractive old people. A lack of grandparents had left him unaware of bad breath or incontinence in the old, but through Mother he was accustomed to noise and old tailored suits and copious gin-drinking in them; now there was Fred Wellspring and Nell Sumption. 'Our staff' (Leslie). Leslie had conjured them from somewhere, just as he had conjured the machines from Totland Bay Pier when it was running down in the hands of creditors, and most other pieces of the Pavilion's equipment, and the little change desk itself, and a great deal of credit. Surely Fred Wellspring was the perfect old man. He inhabited a world of big breakfasts, hot water bottles with cosies, clocks ticking away the late afternoon. How Moorman wished he was Fred. He was, for a start, so neatly dressed; his tie knotted so beautifully; he could please himself. He had nothing to worry about.

'Mr Langdon has got the key to the Copper Mine,' Fred said, 'he don't like to force it. "Can you come down a minute?" he says.'

Fred Wellspring was in charge of the rifle-range, the acquiring of which had involved them in a hire purchase agreement that only Leslie understood. Fred spread out his *Daily Sketch* on the counter. Occasionally, when he discovered a picture of some girl in a bathing-suit, or a very stout woman, he would make his moustache writhe with amusement; he shook his head and murmured to himself, 'She wasn't born, she was launched.' Or he might hold out an index finger to Leslie and say, 'You may think that's dirt, Mr Leslie, but it s'not,' which always sent Leslie off into peals of laughter. During the long intervals between customers at the rifle-range, Fred flicked a long-handled feather duster in a ruminative way over the prizes offered, the glass fruit bowls and sticks of novelty rock. He was, in effect, (thought Moorman, remembering the Hornblower books) the Pavilion's prizemaster, Fred was, because just supposing there was somebody who performed the impossible feat of guiding a tray of pennies to the top of the Copper Mine, or (as might happen) a customer succeeded in scoring several tens of million on any of the electric pin tables, then the prize would be handed over by Fred Wellspring. He took his work very seriously. Under the rifle-range counter he kept an ice cream wafer tin containing literally hundreds of squares of cardboard, each of which could be folded and bent into a small white box; and beside the tin he had a bottle of Sharp's mint toffees. The winner's claim verified, Fred Wellspring would manufacture a box—this excited the winner very much; would it be a small bit of jewellery?—then into the box he slipped one toffee (one toffee!) and handed it over with his courteous, old-maidish smile.

Fred Wellspring lived at the top of the town, in a cottage built on the side of a larger house. His front door contained a diamond-shaped pane of glass. He did the *Sketch* crossword with a Parker Duofold. He used a metal comb. Mrs Wellspring was still very nice-looking, and they kept an alsatian noted for its gentle ways. Their daughter, Sally, was the only edging of tragedy to their lives because, when she was seventeen, she had accidentally brushed the front of an electric fire with her chiffon party dress, and would now have to wear trousers for evermore. This had been for the best really, though, as she was a beaky girl with close-cropped hair; trousers suited her. She was also a devout Catholic, on the best of terms with the same circle of nuns that haunted the Tredegar Guest House; and her father looked so much more like an employer than either Moorman or Leslie Langdon. Moorman spent some of the hot, hazy days (before the season began) in thoughts of ruin, bankruptcy, disgrace—having once misreported them all for *The Gosport Herald,* he had a clear idea of the sequence of ruin—but he also felt they would never overtake him, not quite, so long as Fred Wellspring was to be seen, reading at the rifle-range or pulling pennies out of the machine collection boxes into a tin. Gratefully, he followed Fred Wellspring out of the Amplifier Room, among the machines.

Although they had been in occupation for three weeks, counting the time it took to install the machines, Moorman still found it hard to take in the Pavilion's interior at a glance. He sometimes felt elated, because there were so many more machines than he had thought. Or occasionally he would stand at the top step to the Amplifier Room and look right up inside the dome until he felt frightened, up to the tiny red glimmer of stained glass at the top; he would be thrilled to think that in a sense it was *his* dome, a kind of consolation prize for no nice suit or silver-backed hairbrushes. It was a very high dome. During the war, a company of the Royal Naval Signals (Leslie said) had been bedded out in the Pavilion, and had stolen incredible amounts of cigarettes, which they had hidden on the cross flats at the top of the dome. A friend of John Close, the tram-driver, had actually climbed up to see, but had found nothing, Leslie said, and had been sick.

The trouble with the interior was that it was gloomy. Day-trippers leaving the ferry could see nothing much through the row of doors as they hurried past to get on the tram. On the Esplanade, S'Lots of Fun contained all the latest machines. Even without the incredible display of lights, the peacock with its illuminated tail spreading and withdrawing on the front of the arcade, the entrance would have been irresistible. Electric machines punching circles and rocket tails gave a sensation of metal rainbow-coloured rain. There was also the noise of frying and the call of Bingo. The Pavilion's machines (although all credit to Leslie for buying them up so reasonably) were not, on the whole, electric. A row of pin tables dated from the 1930s. The others were Edwardian, in wooden cabinets; machines that did not pay out money but provided novelties. Almost every one of them had a card inside the glass, carefully lettered in scrolly pork butcher's writing: For Amusement Only.

There were four rows of machines on the Pavilion floor, two back to back in each row. Those who came in immediately saw four aisles ahead of them. There were other machines around the wall, two Automatic Palmists and about ten named The Allwyne de luxe, nailed to pieces of battening on the wood work. Additional light came from a string of coloured bulbs over Fred Wellspring's head. Even so, it was a job to see the targets. The tea bar, lit by one fluorescent tube, ran in a continuous line with the rifle-range counter; and behind was a little room containing a sink, an old gas cooker and an asset, the Jackson tea and coffee urn that Leslie had been able to pick up cheaply.

It was—was it?— threepenny-piece shaped inside the Pavilion. Right next to the Amplifier Room was the stage where the pierrots had once danced. Behind it there was a narrow passage terminating at the Amplifier Room at one end, and leading to a hardboard-screened private lavatory at the other, with a willow-patterned pedestal that someone appeared to have tried to mend with brown sticky paper. The hardboard screen had a name on it in chalk—Sergeant Swindells. Many times, waiting for the season to begin, waiting for the evening, Moorman had wondered about Sergeant Swindells. Was he one of the Royal Naval Signals? Had he become, after demobilization, a pierrot? Moorman had picked up other bits of Pavilion history during the waiting. In the Amplifier Room was a ledge with a fragment of looking-glass on it. Behind that, one day, he had discovered an old newspaper cutting from 1951, saying that Arthur English, the comedian, had been fined for telling jokes in the Pavilion on a Sunday; constables had taken notes.

3

Leslie sat up very straight in the change desk. He'd been busy arranging pennies in sixpences and shillingsworths.

He put to his lips a Gold Flake smoked so thoroughly that he really looked as if he was blowing a kiss with thumb and forefinger. Moorman thought his partner would be equally well able to manage with a lobster claw instead of a hand. So many of his gestures seemed to involve his thumb and forefinger only: smoking cigarettes to minute ends, picking crumbs from his plate and eating them ('very tasty,' he invariably said), sprinkling Saxin into his tea, picking fluff from around his fly, imitating a Jew counting money during discussions about money, which Moorman as a rule avoided.

Moorman went to look at the Copper Mine. Leslie Langdon could not be dissuaded from the view that he was very mechanically minded; it was an appalling delusion, based entirely on an incident in the car-park of the Club Marimba, Whittlesey, where they had been introduced just before Moorman left the R.A.F. Leslie at the time owned a yellow Vauxhall Cresta, and had found himself locked out of it. Moorman, fuddled by six or seven Double Diamonds and inflated by Leslie's immediate and powerful good opinion of him, had pushed a Royal Sovereign pencil, R.A.F. property, through the quarterlight to pull up the button and unlock the car. At the Pavilion they could not afford to employ a machine mechanic. Leslie said: 'Well, you'll be good at taking care of that side of it, now won't you?' As machines broke down, Fred Wellspring neatly printed 'Out of Service' cards for them.

Moorman had at least an interest in most of the Pavilion's machines, a powerful sense of history where they were concerned. The Copper Mine for example was a very interesting piece of work. In common with (Leslie said) about a third of the machines it had been made in the thirties; the steel cabinet was shaped like the older type of American skyscraper, and its front and sides were decorated with scratched thunderflash motifs. It worked in this way: the player was confronted with what appeared to be the cross-section of a mine. From the well of the cabinet, a tray of pennies began to ascend between two metal poles, each of which was studded with a number of small bars, like ribs in a skeleton; and as the tray came up, these arms jigged wildly, knocking more and more of the pennies from the tray. The higher up the bars, the greater the compliment paid to the player—Good—Very Good—the top one said Outstanding Skill—but there were never any pennies left. Now, Moorman saw, the tray had been arrested in its ascent. A customer (another customer) waited patiently beside it, wiping his nose, bending it back to right and left with the rhythmic, forbearing wipe. Moorman nodded briefly and took hold of the cabinet at arm's length. One day soon Leslie was going to discover his enduring fear of machinery, the fact that he hadn't the remotest idea even how to separate the correct key from the long chain to open a machine. Only Fred Wellspring did, when he emptied them. Moorman gave the cabinet a jerk and the tray began to move again and all the pennies were quickly dislodged.

'I just put one penny in,' the customer said.

'I see.'

A warm feeling stole over Moorman. He was about to make a company director's gesture. He put a hand in one patch pocket, there was a bad moment when his fingers became entangled with a ball of handkerchief, an old packet of mint Spangles, but at last he was able to catch hold of a penny, which he handed to the customer.

'Well done, that man,' Leslie's voice called out; and something else, which Moorman guessed was his partner's version of 'C'est bon.' (Instead of 'à propos' of something, Leslie Langdon said 'après vous' of something.)

Moorman wanted to go back to the Amplifier Room where he could put his head in his hands or dream of someone he'd much prefer to be: Hank B. Marvin, Cliff Richard's guitarist, Fred Wellspring. But he knew that Leslie would be hurt if he didn't exchange a few words at the change desk. Leslie wouldn't show it but he'd be hurt.

On the way across Moorman saw an extremely tall and badly co-ordinated girl wearing white ankle-socks rise from behind Leslie in the change desk where, apparently, she had been sitting on an upturned soft drinks crate. Taking pains not to meet Moorman, she hurried past the rifle-range and tea bar, out to the pier-head.

Leslie nodded to him; a nod and a bow.

'Leslie! Has that awful girl been hanging round you again?'

'Who, Gordon? Alicia?'

'I don't know her name. Her with the fat, red legs. Has she been hanging round you again?'

'Oh . . . you don't miss a trick, do you. . . ? Well, the point is, she's lonely, you see. She just wants someone to sit and discuss Elvin the Pelvin with. I don't mind.' The caressing quality in his voice was uncomfortably evident. 'She *means* well, I think.'

For a moment, Moorman felt himself transfixed by love and compassion for Alicia; Alicia, unnaturally tall with an idiot's expression, all by herself through the warm seaside evenings, the Esplanade lights picked up by the quiet high tide, luckier people kissing and crooning and rolling about on the powder sand below the sea wall: Alicia (he thought) eating endless toffee apples and Cadbury's Sliced Nut because there was nothing else to do, her father and mother, scorch-fronted, singing in the Wellington Tavern, the King Lud, or the Bodega. All she really wanted was a shoulder, a clean white shirt on a shoulder to lay her freshly washed hair on. Perhaps she had quite pretty hair. Moorman checked himself. Alicia wasn't so very much worse off than he himself was; in fact, she undoubtedly had a home to go to that might be in the Potteries, but didn't smell of Swedish oil, and no mad, wild old woman ever came and sat on *her* feet, so she could just piss off.

'Machine ticketyboo?' Leslie asked.

'Quite.'

'That's the lad,' Leslie said on a note of celebration. 'Going out tonight? Ho ho ho ho ho,' Leslie made this noise of disbelief at the back of his palate, looking roguish as he slid off the stool behind the desk. 'Must go and shake hands with the wife's best friend. The Future of Britain Lies in Your Hands. Oops! Can you mind the desk for a brief while?'

Looking after the change desk was hateful; the sour copper dirt on his fingers that Moorman would inevitably wipe all over his face at some later stage. Leslie kept the change desk all day and his hands remained beautiful. Often he sat there filing his nails, the little comb case with the pocket for the nail file on the counter in front of him.

'I want to drop a line to Upward and Rich as well.'

They changed places. Rather Leslie than Moorman to explain why the bill for three dozen bread rolls, six boxes of Munchmallows and quantities of tea and coffee, had not been settled yet. Moorman sat on Leslie's warm stool and his feet sank into the folds of the official bank navy blue copper bags below the counter.

'Here, is Alicia the one who wrote on that piece of paper "My mouth is full of blood?"' Moorman asked, popping his eyes and inflating his cheeks, as if he was about to be sick. (This was why the partnership must fail. They could never ever be serious. Moorman got the laughs. Leslie admired. Despite his own good head for figures and his innumerable contacts in the entertainment industry.)

'No, no, no, that was, let me see, Brenda.'

Leslie was always cheering up some giant of an unhappy girl.

'That's right. She had white socks as well.'

'And dancing pumps.'

'That's right.'

'Oh, dear.' Leslie said, shaking his head. 'Poor old Bottery. . .'

'What! ?'

He spluttered: 'I mean, Brenda from the butteries, I mean potteries. Always had her dancing pumps on, poor Bren! She was a bit lonely as well, bless her. Never had much of a good time.'

More pity jabbed at Moorman.

'Mind you: I suppose she invited it. When you think about it, I suppose she did, rather. Her teeth always had nasty bits of egg custard hanging off them. I mean, no young man's exactly going to be . . .'

'Egged on. . .'

'By that. No.' He pealed with laughter. 'Ooh, Ivan, you are terrible, as Catherine the Great once said.'

Moorman found himself peering anxiously around the Pavilion in case they were being watched, with amused expressions. He could see only a red-haired customer in the distance.

'Oh, ye-es. "My mouth is full of blood." That's right. Poor old Bren had to go to the dentist when she was here on holiday; that's not much fun for anyone. And she came down here straight afterwards. I mean, she couldn't talk, so she marches up to the counter, I was standing behind the rifle-range, Fred will bear me out, and she put this note down. "My mouth is full of blood." No, the one you just saw's named Alicia, Alicia Flood. Or is it Alicia Niblet? One of the two.

'Ho, hum,' (Leslie always seem to pronounce literally expletives he remembered from comics long ago: Tut, tut, even, Swoon!). 'Well, I think I'll just amble off to the Amplifier Room a minute, shall I? By the way, I could make your announcement to the multitudes if you like . . .'

Moorman gripped a shillingsworth of pennies, and they spread sideways into the next pile. Indeed, he found it tricky not to cry out in alarm at Leslie's suggestion that he should talk to the ferry. Uncles, in the Rock Shop, scored too many notable victories as it was. How could Moorman possibly explain to Leslie, without making his face fall, that if a ferryload of day trippers heard his voice as the boat came round to dock, that would be it; they'd put the word all round—Ben and Ruby, Sid and Tessie, Chas, Ivy, Louie. Hoi, 'Old on. Don't go in that funfair, not that 'un, any one but that. They got a N.A.N.C. . . .

'Better not? Quite right.' Leslie said cheerfully. 'Back in five minutes or two shakes of a kipper's flipper.'

'Watch out big Alicia doesn't press you against a pillar.'

'Careful not to spend too many pennies. No . . . I mustn't . . . I'm being flippant. This is a place of business.' Perhaps he wasn't hurt.

Lying awake at night, in the Tredegar Guest House, remembering various things, Moorman would sometimes try to evaluate his good qualities. The only definite one, it seemed, was that he hated to see people's faces fall. Mother had once employed in her fish shop a waitress named Kathleen. He recalled that she had been a conventional, if not a rather superior type of waitress—black dress with floaty bits on the sleeve, black flat-heeled shoes. Mother had said, however, that she smelled. Had said so to her face. Moorman was a witness. He'd never forget the sight of Kathleen's face, God; he gripped the linings of his pockets . . .

This partnership with Leslie: It was based on an appalling kind of grinning guilt. He spent half his time taking Leslie absolutely for granted, leaving him to deal with such monies as could be banked, with the bills and wages, with opening the Pavilion and closing it in the evening. Then he did everything he could to control his horror at most of the things Leslie said. To keep his eyes off the tight little trousers Leslie wore, with his buttocks showing like a pair of collar studs; to try not to stare when Leslie shampooed his receding hair and appeared with little pieces sticking out at all angles. So many people despised Moorman on sight. A few exceptions were fat women, women in spectacles with flyaway plastic rims and Leslie Langdon. Leslie believed that he had received a literary education and was the wittiest of individuals. The circumstances of their meeting . . . Moorman went with a vanload of leading aircraftsmen from R.A.F. Upwood to the Club Marimba, which Leslie Langdon then managed. Moorman had just happened to go with them; they weren't his friends. That night had a vivid taste. Moorman missed his R.A.F. meat tea and bought from the NAAFI a shilling box of Smarties to eat silently at the back of the van he got a lift in, sucking each bean until the chocolate burst out of the tongue-shattered shells, and his mouth was full of the dye from the red ones. That was also the first night he wore the suit, now in ruins. The trousers began to go almost directly he crossed his legs, sitting in the night club. A kind soul among the leading aircraftsmen had known Leslie and had introduced Moorman to him, believing Moorman was peripherally queer and Leslie, decidedly so. And Leslie began to admire him for his education.

The lavatory behind the pierrot stage flushed. Moorman was surprised by three people crowding round the desk at once, wanting sixpenceworths of coppers. He had to run out and tell a small boy, dressed in the white and navy blazer of one of the smart private schools, not to bang on the glass of The Prizefighters—another extraordinary machine: boxing figures dressed in knitted leotards, and the background of an audience, varnished dark like an old master. The schoolboy stared disbelievingly at Moorman, who noticed with a pang, the matching pen, pencil and ballpoint set in his breast pocket, the beautifully tailored grey flannels. 'Just give a shout if you get any trouble,' he said. 'Right,' the boy said, faintly mocking. 'Sir.'

Moorman peered aggressively into his face, just to make sure it wasn't Meatball in some diabolically clever disguise. Then the ferry bell rang. He called to old Fred to keep his eye on the change desk if he wouldn't mind, and he ran across to the Amplifier Room, where his partner, his nose almost on the paper, was writing a letter with his own hand, to the wholesalers. The ferry was cutting round in its circle to the dock, leaning over with the weight of day trippers. Moorman grabbed the hand microphone and had begun his announcement before realizing that the red light was still off. Leslie stopped writing as if the scratch of his ballpoint would cause feedback. Uncles' voice came on. His information came in the most horribly natural way. Moorman said his few embarrassed words about the Fun Palace and the tea bar. Uncles hung on to his words, extemporizing, pausing so that the ferry bumped the dock just as he concluded: 'Giant size novelty rock. Husband-beater. Wife-tamer.'

Moorman and Leslie stood at the door of the Amplifier Room, watching the crowd that beset Uncles Rock Shop, then hurried to the tram, past the Pavilion. Then (oh, no!) Leslie took his arm and they walked across to the tea bar, where old Nell Sumption straightened up abruptly, as if she'd been wiping her legs and ears on the only clean tea towel.

'Going to have a roll?' Leslie was roguish.

'I'll cut you a nice fresh one, pet,' old Nell said, and

at once ducked down behind the counter, doubtless to work open a roll with her bare hands. Moorman, peering over the counter, watched the flakes of red cheese being shaken in. He hoped the good old lady wouldn't bark her knuckles on the bread's sharp underside. He could still taste the Mars bar but was cravingly hungry, for something nice.

'Not very encouraging, is it?'

'Takes time to get going.'

'. . . pick up, but still . . .'

It developed into a discussion about money to which Moorman made himself deaf. Leslie disclosed that the Pavilion's average turnover in almost three weeks, opening at ten and closing at six, had been £27, mainly in pennies. Even though he and Moorman drew only £10 a week each, the wage bill for Fred and Nell, was £21. 18s. 'And then there's tax. That jolly soon catches up with one.' Thanks to Leslie's contacts they were getting the loudspeaker equipment for six pounds a month and paying off the balance on the rifle-range at £7. 14s. a month. For the final year of Mr Vernon's lease on the Pavilion, they had paid £500 and a further £300 for all the machines and £100 for marginal alterations like the pieces of battening that supported the Allwyne de Luxes, and £75 to have the machines brought from Totland Bay Pier, and set up in the Pavilion. They had put in £900 each. They were living on capital. They would need capital to take up the option on the lease if the coming season, when it came, was a good one. 'We're spending it hand over fist,' Leslie said. Moorman was alarmed to see him look really worried for an instant, not saying it would all be fine when the season really began. 'Look at those bloody signs for a start.' He was rarely profane. The signs had been done by the same man who painted the Skaters of the World wall frieze for Mr Vernon. They were aimed at discouraging day trippers from holding picnics on the glass tops of the pin tables and hockey machines; aimed at reducing a dreadful tide of peel and greaseproof paper. Moorman thought his own writing style and Leslie's prim manner of speech were both much evident in these signs: ONLY FOOD PURCHASED HERE MAY BE CONSUMED ON THESE PREMISES. They cost almost five pounds each, the price of a beautiful cool pair of Daks.

'Well, we must just wait, or wait on, as they say Down Under.' Moorman was relieved to hear Leslie back in this vein. Nell gave them their cheese rolls, Moorman took a large bite from his and discovered a small grey match stump, which he held in his hand and dropped a minute later, in case he should have made Nell's face fall.

'Leslie. You haven't seen that bloody little. . . ?'

'Our friend?'

'Yes . . . bloody little terror, Meatball. You haven't seen him about today?'

'Not to my knowledge. Nell? Has that little boy been in? No see?'

'I'll have his little balls off soon,' Moorman said darkly, but so that Nell couldn't hear. He took a step back from the tea bar and rested his forehead on his arms, so that he was staring down at the floor, at his scuffled boots and the livid, shiny marks where the laces wore away the suède. Leslie's dainty slip-ons were turned outwards. Moorman wondered if he should say he thought Mother might send them something, a little something to get them over Whitsun. He couldn't help seeing Whitsun as the beginning of the season, a solid, tight, penny-scrabbling mass of day trippers, exhausting old Nell's flinty rolls, Fred Wellspring's bottle of toffees; one ferryload might be enough to get him his new black suit.

'No,' Leslie said, 'I *lie*. He's here.'

'Meatball! Here!'

'Quick, see his little gym shoe just turning the far corner on the inside, by the What the Butler Saw.'

'That's it, after him,' Old Nell cried hoarsely.

Running on tiptoe through the gloomy rows of slot machines, the Pavilion's great dome circling above his head, with the pin light of stained glass; up the central aisle where the same red-haired customer was still playing The Uninvited, watching the skulls; skirling, sharp turn past the set of four Mutoscope peep shows, over the marks the roller skates had made on the boards, here where the beginners' bars had once been. He didn't often run. When he did, he felt like a timid cyclist. He imagined his face being rubbed along road gravel at 70 m.p.h.

Moorman began to stalk Meatball, an uncomfortable knocking in his chest.

Meatball was at work. He came into view, crouched under a hockey machine in the furthermost inner curve of the Pavilion. There it was; Meatball's tautened little boy's back, the knobs of his spine disappearing down the ragged underpants rim displayed above his khaki shorts, and the red and black Secondary Modern belt which he dared to wear on these expeditions.

The hockey machine was like a glassed-over coffin on four legs. Handles at each end operated a hunched iron goalkeeping figure which turned around and hit ball bearings at their opponent. With all his natural engineering brilliance, Meatball knew exactly where to force a little panel on the machine's underside, to get at the tray into which the inserted pennies fell. His spine heaved and bobbed industriously. He was, nevertheless, far from being a mercenary child; he enjoyed the simpler pleasures of defacing machines, disconnecting pin tables, knocking the Allwyne de Luxe on the side just for a free play, or etching words, 'Ebbo' or perhaps 'Cock Fun' on polished wood.

Moorman dared not kick him as he bent under the hockey machine. Supposing he happened to get kicked in the spine? He lived, Meatball did, in one of the grim, subterranean boarding houses at the remotest end of the Esplanade, and had, without a doubt, a tough Dad on the charabancs; he himself was already rather free with promises of legal action. His funnel-shaped mouth seemed made to protest his innocence. And in a year or two, his freckled, hollow cheeks, his nose with the bogeys trailing out, his Golliberry enamel brooch, would have become a superior strength, and would search Moorman out and beat him up: so Moorman dragged Meatball by the belt out from under the hockey machine and along the floor for some yards.

The boy got up shrieking and threw his fists at Moorman, then sprawled back on the ground to roll about. 'Swine. Rotten sod. You got my kidneys then, you did. I suppose you know that you've drawn blood.'

Moorman took him by the ear past the old pierrot stage, past the wall with Skaters of the World painted on it, past the steps of the Amplifier Room, to the doors on to the pierhead. The bright sunshine took him by surprise; the stiff yachting breeze rushed in and stood his hair on end. He pushed Meatball outside and groped in a patch pocket for his comb. The end of the pier was deserted. On the concrete in front of Uncles Rock Shop, several gulls were unstringing a flounder's warty corpse.

Meatball screwed his face up and rolled on the concrete for the benefit of any passers-by. John Close was just coming along to drop his lobster net into the Triangle. Moorman made an attempt to raise his voice and thus clarify the situation but he was no good at raising his voice effectively.

'If I see you around here again, I'll get the police.'

'Gar. Monkey Brand. It's all a swindle,' Meatball shouted back. 'I'm going to get my bloody Dad.'

'You clear off. Scrubby little villain.'

Even Meatball, though, was casual. That yellow T-shirt with Hopalong Cassidy in red, the khaki shorts, the black gym shoes; all were more natural than heavy cavalry twill trousers in summer; at least nothing was suffocating Meatball's legs. One day he'd be able to get a tremendous job as a mechanic; he'd go out with a girl who wasn't fat or in flyaway spectacle frames; he might even join a careless party on the beach; he'd be able to wear flared trousers and high-collar shirts and look perfectly natural. Meanwhile Moorman and a big girl would be somewhere else. Looking down from the top of the sea wall at the party on the beach. Sweltering in their clothes at the bottom of the hill. Eventually joining hands. He thought, 'Oh God, the Blue Lagoon swimming pool and Mona Lisa's life-saving lesson this evening,' and turned back inside the gloomy and dusty Pavilion.

4

He came through the pier gates, to the Esplanade, with a powerful erection. On balance, Mona Lisa di Valvona was more exciting than daunting. Those huge, red-starred breasts. On the Esplanade's broad pavement he was immediately surrounded by taxi and Mystery Tour charabanc drivers, hoping either for a fare or the opportunity to give him a leaflet; for a dreadful moment Moorman imagined himself beset by Meatball's Dad and some of his friends.

But there were always scores of these peaked-capped men at the gates of the pier, allowing the tide of fresh holidaymakers to break and snag around them. The taxi-men wore shiny charcoal suits, the Island Bus Company men white jackets with green facings, the Holiday Camp couriers ensembles of pastel and buff, so attractive that Moorman would gladly have changed places with any of them.

After a fortnight he recognized individuals in the crowd. (Leslie told him who they were.) And he was on nodding terms with a couple of taxi-men, having on a few occasions tried to make himself feel better by taking Mona Lisa home to the Tredegar Guest House by cab. There was, for example, a Mr Prior, who kept his old Triumph Mayflower so clean, and always seemed to be pinching his fingers into a 2d packet of K.P. nuts; and there was George Lay ('Lay by name and lay by nature,' Leslie said), who had sidewhiskers and an ancient Wolseley with yellow rear windows. Moorman had sometimes spotted George Lay late at night at the deserted end of the Esplanade, close to Bridewell Gardens, sitting in the Wolseley with a red-nosed woman beside him. They had newspapers spread over their laps. The notion of what they were doing there demolished Moorman's erection as he went to cross the road. A grey Mini van, driven by a girl, flashed past.

He had not meant to begin taking out Mona Lisa di Valvona, whose two great talents were swimming and the piano. Mrs di Valvona, on one of his first evenings in Springbourne, had kindly treated them both to the Scala cinema: Light Up The Sky, starring Tommy Steele. At the time, he'd believed that all sorts of expensive presents would be put his way if Mrs di Valvona really took to him; as well as all those great big lunches and dinners. He'd even imagined getting money from her. So, mad with heat in the Scala cinema, he had taken hold of Mona Lisa's gold-ring weighted, short, pointed fingers and, as she put her head on his shoulder, had received a mouthful of crisp bouffant hairdo.

On most evenings after work Mona Lisa walked down to meet him. They went for a walk, ending in bodily contact that was loud with her stiff petticoats and the machinery of her charm bracelet.

For the past few evenings, the promise of a look at those gigantic markers of hers had compelled Moorman to accompany her to the Blue Lagoon Swimming Pool, where Mona Lisa was in the final stages of an important life-saving test. He, typically, had never learned to swim and was ashamed of himself in bathing trunks. At the Blue Lagoon he either cowered around the pool's foot-slapped perimeter, his arms across his breast like a housewife, or he coughed and groped for the floor at the shallow end, convinced that beautiful, scornful girls were exchanging glances above his head. He owned no trunks but had permanent loan of a pair, a sort of flowered underpants which Mrs di Valvona had been kind enough to pull down for him from her airing-cupboard (that prospect of elephantine knickers!). He hadn't his own towel either. Mona Lisa always brought him a clean one. He felt trapped by this arrangement.

Moorman went over the zebra crossing, through the taxi rank in the centre of the Esplanade road, to the bright and busy front of buildings that swept round into the steep main street, St John's Road. On the corner, S'Lots of Fun buzzed, puffed, click-spark-bang-punched and up above the entrance the peacock's tail in lights spread out and withdrew again. Next door was the café where he, Mother and Leslie had eaten their luncheon-meat salads, next door to that was a chemist and camera shop (he'd never owned a camera) which, as Moorman came through the pier gates, he always took to be Greek-owned as it was called ACCOUSINS; he then realized that the signboard actually said A. C. Cousins. And next door to this was a most elaborate steel-fronted café and soda fountain, the property of Mrs di Valvona's estranged sister, Mrs Sangiorgio. A battery of machines that dispensed Sangiorgio's Gold Medal soft ice cream ('It's Good. It's Sangiorgio's') stood inside the doors.

Moorman swore to himself, as the erection died away,

that he would have a salad at Sangiorgio's, with no salad cream or bread and butter; he *would* try to lose weight. But directly he was on that side of the road, smelling the gravies from the open scoops of guest houses above the row of shops, the onions and crispy curled fat, he knew what he wanted to eat: egg, chips, baked beans, a banana split, a cup of orange dark tea, the very thin and pliant bread and butter peculiar to the seaside, with a gloss of marge over it. He looked swiftly round the strolling evening crowd to make quite sure he could see no one who would report him to Mrs di Valvona, and then hurried into Sangiorgio's. He had about half an hour before his meeting with Mona Lisa in front of the borough council's holidaymakers' inquiry office.

Unfortunately one of the only spare seats in the café was a stool facing a mirror. Moorman could see perfectly the little plantation of blackheads in the clefts of his nose and on his chin; the bristles on his upper lip which his old electric razor could never hope to cope with. Then another customer wanted the empty stool next to his, so that he had to try to eat with the great heavy jacket across his knees. Each time he opened his mouth he noted what dull teeth he had, and remembered the recurring shoot of pain at night that began in his right ear and tapered into his jaw. He dared not go to the dentist. The hot tea made him sweat profusely. A crowd of boys and girls skylarking round the ice cream machines reminded him that he could never ever be casual, and, once again, he felt so wretchedly fat that he got down from the stool, and hurried out of Sangiorgio's, his mouth still half full of banana, ice cream, bread and butter, tomato sauce. Life tasted like that, didn't it?

He crossed the road again. This reminded him of the girl who had driven by in the Mini van; stupid, affected little bitch. John Close's tram was banging to the town end of the pier, sliding to a stop. His A.C. car was parked with the hood down outside W. H. Smith's. Moorman thought he would walk through the municipal gardens to the west of the pier and approach the inquiry office from behind; it stood on the corner facing S'Lots of Fun and the illuminated peacock. He turned round and was astonished to see the Mini van again. This time he got a very good view of the girl at the wheel. She wore an open-necked gingham shirt and a watch with a black band.

For about fifteen minutes Moorman walked about the Western Gardens, putting himself carefully out of the way of bands of casual teenagers. For a moment he rested his brow against the side of a disused landmine that was now painted red and used as a collecting box for the Missions to Seamen. Then he walked to the other entrance to the Gardens, past the flowerbed planted to depict the coat of arms of the Borough of Springbourne. He could see Mona Lisa waiting for him outside the inquiry office, doing her best to ignore a couple of tiny children who were playing close to her winklepicker shoes. These were pink and lustrous with small black bows at the toe, and her flared yellow and black striped dress had a fawn Dannimac put over it, rather as if for the protection of a highly prized wicket. She affected not to see Moorman until he could easily have shattered her jaw with his elbow he was so close, then she said, 'Hello, darling.' She had very beautiful dark eyes.

Holding hands they began to walk up St John's Road, through holidaymakers with sunflaked chests and arms, individuals who seemed not to realize that the jewellers, the clothes and china shops they were ogling were all closed. The home-made rock shop was packed with customers. Behind them as they ascended the street, John Close's tram reached the end of the pier and slid to a stop. Before either volunteered a remark they were half-way up the hill; Mona Lisa was breathing heavily but trying to make it ladylike. (They had not yet burped in one another's company. Her exits to the Ladies were always 'to the little room' and at first she would always draw back from his kisses to avoid smudging her pains-taking make-up.)

'How was your day, darling?' She at least believed he was a tycoon.

'The usual.'

'I had a horrid day. At least, a horrid morning.'

'Look in that shop,' Moorman said.

'What for? Where?'

She also believed he was a marvellous eccentric, a historian, poet, writer, antiquarian, and wit, yet at heart a little boy, since he displayed boyish enthusiasm for all these things. Her gold-weighted hands often struggled through his hair, which he allowed, although it put his teeth on edge. And she admired Moorman the most when he spoke to her in a sort of heavy-bantering manner, with a gentle irony, accompanied by a mocking (he believed), cynical, untamed facial expression (he trusted). In the interests of this illusion, Moorman said: 'That's a wonderful old shop, you know. The old fellow who keeps it remembers Queen Victoria driving past.'

'Oh . . . aye, I see it. We bought wee Angelo's collar and lead and wee name plate in there.'

That disposed of that bit of boyish enthusiasm. Moorman surprised himself by grinning.

'What made you have a horrible morning?'

'Och, ma Mummy was ill again. She couldn't stop being sick and going to the toilet. She thinks she's going to die, darling. She always seems to take to her bed when we're specially busy; we had to do a lunch for forty-two child care officers, and she goes and gets sick.'

'Dear . . .'

'Remember I told you we had that time when she was in St Mary's and very nearly did die? And my Uncle Grimaldi got Bing Crosby to sing a wee song for her, and she screamed and yelled because they were bathing her when it was played? That was the same trouble—her tummy. But I think she uses it. I think she uses it, darling.'

He couldn't help it. He saw Mrs di Valvona not sitting on the W.C. but outlined in an opaque fashion through the glass of the middle landing toilet, a flash of purple cocktail dress and gold, then the whole arrangement leaping up to deliver monkey yells into the bowl . . . . He gripped the lining of one pocket. The erection was demolished at once.

Mona Lisa seemed, herself, rather distressed. She pressed the two rolled towels she carried to her cheek, quite disregarding her make-up. 'Then we had more trouble with Aldo Felice.'

'Is that the tall one?'

'No, you're thinking of Aldo Dinardo.'

Moorman realized he knew Aldo Felice. This lodger at the Tredegar Guest House was the living image of Anthony Quinn. He owned a large collection of enviable woollens, cardigans, plum-coloured jackets, narrow trousers.

'He's a bother, a devil. Ma Mummy feels responsible for him,' Mona Lisa said. 'Well, she feels responsible for all of them whilst they're here.'

'What did he do?' At last Moorman was feeling cooler and could pay her some attention, with later on in mind.

'Och, got the sack. Again! He was helping the chef at the Totland Royal and the silly boy threw a wild party in one of the bedrooms and they found out.'

'He's always been very pleasant to me.'

'Aye, well, he would be.' It pleased Moorman to hear her say this. Didn't it imply that however barbarous and daggers-drawn the Tredegar Guest House Italians were among themselves, *he* instantly commanded their civility and their respect—the tall and distinguished Englishman with the literary education? Moorman, for the first time that day, smiled, and felt happy.

What was more, the erection came back.

Then it shivered small again.

They were passing the St John's Road office of the *Springbourne Borough News and Advertiser*. Moorman remembered some of the mistakes he had made on the staff of *The Gosport Herald:* how, for example, he had once transcribed the name of the local prospective Liberal candidate, D. R. A. Spreckley as Dr A. Spreckley. But, oh, up it swelled again, because among the photographs taped to a board in the window was a picture of the Springbourne Carnival Queen in a two-piece bathing suit. He and Mona Lisa were now about to turn the corner into Union Square at the top of the hill; his erection fell away, and died *again* as a pair of nuns suddenly appeared.

Here on a gracious curve similar to that occupied by S'Lots of Fun at the bottom of the hill, there stood the long-established drapery store where Mrs di Valvona and Mona Lisa did most of their shopping; a large place reminding him of the Port Burdock Bazaar in *The History of Mr Polly*, with the name printed in curly gold leaf. And in summer they hung out big canvas blinds, stamped with the long-dead Southsea name of the manufacturers.

The blinds smelled of old cricket equipment and had winged pieces at the sides of the window, so that, coming round the corner, the two nuns inadvertently blundered and crashed through an area of canvas. Then they walked, one on each side of Mona Lisa: a tall nun and a rosy one, who said, 'Hello, Lisa, dear. Tell Mummy we may see her later on.'

She gripped his arm and pulled a face.

'I haven't seen the tall one before.'

'That's Sister Hoolican. She's new.'

'Hooligan!'

'Sssh, no, Hooli-can. She's just come back. She used to be my biology teacher at the Presentation Convent. She's hoarable. She gave me a slap once for doing a picture of a fish wrong.'

Moorman felt gloomy at the thought of sitting around with the nuns later in Mrs di Valvona's best room. He'd forgotten his resolution to take Mona Lisa into Bridewell Gardens tonight, instead of the furthermost Esplanade shelter. The erection came back briefly at the thought of lying on top of her, but it vanished again; he could taste Cinzano and feel the cigarette smoke in his eyes and his trousers heated all over again. He always received an enormous tumblerful of Cinzano.

An hour and a half later, they walked down St John's Road again: the town falling away in front of them; the pier lights going away at an angle, with the disappearing tail light of an all-night fisherman's bicycle: John Close's tram banging its way down.

Moorman went ahead of Mona Lisa. It was his custom from time to time to stride on in the manner of a young Churchill who could scarcely wait to butt and dazzle his way through life—walk on as if he had become slightly bored with her or slightly annoyed. Her shoes clickered behind him. Sometimes her fingers caught his hand but then he pulled it free. He pretended to gaze up into the universe, or to be appalled by something in a tailor's window. He felt, in fact, quite horrible. He had chlorine up his nose, his hair was stiff and absurdly curled out; he felt mocked and stale and defeated.

'Darling . . . darling . . . don't sulk. Please. I'm sorry.'

Moorman let her catch up and affected to smile. 'What is it?' he said. 'I'm not sulking.'

'Something was the matter just then, darling.'

'No, it wasn't.'

She made 'darling' sound like a warm milk shake.

'Darling, are you getting bored with coming to the pool? You know I've got to do these classes. We do see each other, don't we? I'm never long. I'm no long at all.' Unhappiness broadened her accent. 'Don't walk ahead like that: don't leave me.'

Really, he supposed, she was rather sweet. They were about to go to Bridewell Park. It seemed a good time to make an effort. He put an arm round Mona Lisa's shoulders and touched one of her considerable cheeks with his lips. She smelled nice. 'It's all right,' he said. 'It's just that I've got a lot on at the moment.' He was positive that would mollify her. 'I get a bit anti-social at times because of the good old business, that's all.'

'Does it get awful boring, darling?'

Quite wrong. She mustn't get the idea he sat around. 'No, it's just the sense of getting nowhere fast,' he said, affecting despair.

'Darling, never mind. Ma Mummy says it will all pick up for Whitsun. Our bookings are down as well.'

She really was very thick. She had to be to attempt a comparison between the Pavilion and her mother's high, redbrick, immigrant-packed private hotel. But he let it pass. He preferred to believe that everything would pick up for Whitsun, whenever Whitsun was. By the time they reached the foot of St John's Road, the conversation was easy and happy. Mona Lisa, with the afternoon off, had been to see *The Inn of the Sixth Happiness* with Ingrid Bergman and Robert Donat. 'Honest, darling, I *howled.* Me and Ella both had our petticoats up to dry our eyes. Och, it was lovely but so sad; the children and the wee Chinky fellow was so sweet.' He let her go on, touching the proposed holiday of her mother and herself in Parma (whence, via East Kilbride, their family sprang) and the beautiful portable radio and religious dolls she had received on her last visit to her grandparents. They went past the pier gates, past John Close's parked A.C., past the line of bus and coach stops, the Crazy Golf and repertory theatre and putting greens ('Casualties from the Royal George are buried beneath that'—Leslie Langdon) and so to the point where the Esplanade road parted to encircle the Boating Lake. They next approached a large Wolseley car. Moorman shut, yet strained his ears, for the sound of rustling newspapers.

They continued on the seawall side of the Boating Lake which, reflecting the diminishing street lamps, glittered and winked yet was absolutely still. The pedestrian shelters were of the same pagoda design as those on the pier; they walked past the last one. Ahead of them the Esplanade petered out into simply a walk along a seawall, Bridewell Park rising at a sharp angle above it.

Moorman remembered his great strength: that of getting a laugh. He wished to be thought incorrigible as he manoeuvred her into the park, so he said, 'What do those nuns wear under their habits?'

'Och, you . . . I don't know. We had a girl at school who used to work for Mr Long, the dental surgeon. She said that under their headdresses they wear close-fitted caps. Of course they had to take them off to go to the dentist's.'

'Didn't you have a special one who taught you lacrosse?'

'No, we played netball. I tried to get out of it.' She giggled.

'I believe they all wear striped football socks.'

Mona Lisa giggled. They had reached the very end of the Esplanade. To their left a row of stone pillars discouraged cyclists from using the seawall: ahead was the gateway to Bridewell Park, a small board giving details of the Ornamental Zoo it contained, admission free.

'Let's walk through here.'

'Through Bridewell Park, darling?'

'It's such a beautiful night. "The moon was a ghostly galleon swimming (he was unsure of the exact quotation but Mona Lisa certainly would not know it)—'er . . . swimming through the trees." '

'Isn't it, "The moon was a ghostly galleon tossed upon cloudy seas"?' she inquired. 'That's the poem with "Bess the landlord's daughter/The landlord's black-eyed daughter" plaiting a love-knot, and she gets her breast shattered by a redcoat's musket, I believe.'

He took a deep breath. He tried not to betray the destruction of his latest erection, its entire destruction by this combination of superior knowledge on Mona Lisa's part *and* a breast shattered by a musket. He couldn't help adding mentally the picture of Mrs di Valvona jumping off the pan to be sick in it.

'You aren't scared of the dark?'

'Not with you darling.'

Had he got it back? No.

'Just,' Moorman said playfully, 'for a wee while.'

She bumped his arm with her elbow. It jolted.

The park rose away from the seawall in the same almost perpendicular way of St John's Road. Old town guides described Springbourne nestling in lush woodlands, and this was a fact. Here there was a plantation of tall, straight and regular trees, as bare as tall pencils. They ascended a small path. So far the closest Moorman had been to lying her down was two days previously when, on her white ornamental bedspread at home, she'd shown him photographs of a camera shop in Rimini, shaped like a camera. They mustn't climb too high or she might begin to falter. Through the pencil trunks to their right he could make out the shapes and posts of the Ornamental Zoo buildings. He stopped and steadied Mona Lisa, kissing her cheek again. Adopting (he trusted) the careless ease of a white hunter, familiar with the territory, he threw his enormous jacket down on the grass. Mona Lisa put a hand down to feel that it was dry and then immediately sat herself down. Good: he joined her. She drew the light mackintosh closer around her shoulders and held one of his hands against her face in a very nice, soft way. Was it back? Yes. Below them, perhaps a quarter of a mile to their right, the pier stretched out. John Close's tram went down it, with distant bangs.

Moorman sighed. Not loud enough. He repeated the sigh.

'Darling . . .'

'What?'

'You're not still cross about going to the pool, are you?'

'No, certainly not.'

He sighed again. And again, even deeper.

'You *sigh* so much.'

He shrugged. This he meant her to interpret as the revelation of a big man suddenly as a small boy.

'Are you very unhappy, darling?'

'Deeply,' replied Moorman, and turned over and rolled on top of her, not actually contriving to part those big legs, much, much bucked by her absolute readiness to go back on to the grass, and also, fairly provoked by the rings and fingers at the back of his neck, and by her breath, smelling pleasantly of Gleem.

'Darling . . . you do understand about the life-saving exam?' Mona Lisa said, pushing up against him. She probably didn't realize that this was the case. 'You do understand about it?'

'I understand. I understand you.' He made his voice husky. 'Read you like a . . .' He clamped his mouth on hers and added 'book' which appeared to please Mona Lisa a great deal. A little pointed tongue began to knock at his teeth. Admitting it, he began to explore the base of one of her impressive breasts—cautiously at first as if he expected minute men to open fire from the summit. Well, here he was on top of her.

Oh, it was gone! He had begun to worry. The point was, whatever to do now? He intended to undress Mona Lisa di Valvona but hadn't yet decided whether to go any further than that. Oh, he had every right to feel confident. In his wallet was a packet of Durex, kindly re-hired by Leslie Langdon ('you dirty, lucky devil') with a printed message to the effect that they were perfectly all right until August 1971. He had practised the wearing of one. But he was well aware, thanks to Mother's frequent speeches against the Catholics, that Mona Lisa was not permitted to assist him, not like this.

And even if she did agree, did he run away among the pencil trees to put it on? And could he be sure that he would gain admittance? Oh, it was back, but gone again. He'd attempted this sort of thing only once in his life; seriously, that is. It was with a Leading Aircraftswoman from Hebburn-on-Tyne, and had been a total disaster. 'Oh, doan't, it's killun' us, man,' she had remarked terminally.

But his trousers felt so cool. He suddenly remembered a scene from Grace Metalious's *Peyton Place* which Leslie had lent him, about Rodney Harrison in the woods with that girl Betty; it was in this kind of setting. Accurate quotations about small pairs of pants swam in his mind, together with the light baby powder and faint perspiration smell of the large girl under him. He put his hands under the light mackintosh and began to loose the zip of her dress. She sighed and gave a little laugh that was exciting, absolutely out of character. Moorman began to move without thinking. Then abruptly, because of the loosening effect of the Blue Lagoon's chlorinated water, all the contents of his nose slid out, over Mona Lisa's upturned face.

Ten minutes later it was more chilly. They had been just sitting on the big sports jacket. Mona Lisa was back on the subject of the tall nun they had met at the top of St John's Road; it had turned out she had slapped the young Mona Lisa for drawing a fish with a balloon saying Ha—Ha—Ha issuing from its mouth. Moorman couldn't help but see her clearly in the brown and gold clothes of the Presentation Convent, the spots and growing collection of piano and swimming certificates. He wondered why she had waited so very long to take lifesaving. That business with his nose: it seemed to have halted matters, not irreparably. Moorman doubted if she quite realized what had happened. He intended to try again in a minute. Mona Lisa's conversation tacked sharply away to an Isle of Wight Music Festival of two years previously; then to the present difficult state of relations between her mother and her aunt, Mrs Sangiorgio. She also said, 'Ma Mummy thinks the world of you, darling. She raves about you.'

Good. Moorman felt his genitals tighten. He began to get his lips all pursed and to clear all the short thoughts out of his mind before attempting once again to mount Mona Lisa, undress her and see what else might be done. A reel of short thoughts first. Mother. She was thirty miles away but he still felt her eye on him. He still felt her eye on him but was fairly certain he'd receive another cheque from her shortly. School. There were a lot of Swedish boys there. How they had seemed to despise him, especially one named Mats Buring. *The Gosport Herald*. Dr A. Spreckley instead of D. R. A. Spreckley. The R.A.F. The Woolpack on Christmas Day last. Leslie Langdon. He might be eating pilchards, of which he was exceptionally fond, or reading a military history textbook, or doing a metal or crossword puzzle. When he thought about his partner and they were both off duty, Moorman felt just a pang of shame, a clip of false pretences, a nudge of embarrassment. Mona Lisa had met Leslie once and she said she couldn't bear him. Moorman always pretended that he did far more work than Leslie and was exceptionally tolerant of him, seeing qualities in him that no one else could, 'grinning guilt' again.

He escaped from this thought by putting his nose into Mona Lisa's ear and easing her, once more, backwards. He slipped one leg between both of hers. One of her legs came up and touched his side, which made him feel lively. Their tongues were soon pushing at one another. On this occasion the zip came right down. He could hear John Close's tram begin another journey far away and for the first time, a tropical bird from the zoo nearby made a noise. One of her hands came awkwardly round and rested on the heavy material at his front. He half sat her up and the dress slipped off her shoulders. Her eyes were shut tight. He knew he couldn't make attempts to unhook her brassière without possibly damaging a valuable train of thought. What he could do, though, was pull one heavily brocaded cup out a little and then downwards, so that a generous object, tipped in that grand, old, burst-fig style, jumped up and rapped his nose as if to say, 'Hoi. Here I am.'

The following movement he had rehearsed with some little care. His eyes, he hoped, bored into hers for a moment. Then he threw back his head and laughed: was it exultingly? 'I must have you.' He marvelled a little at the fluency with which he spoke. Mona Lisa nodded her head briskly. 'Please be careful.' Another bird gave tongue. 'Wark!'

The following movements had also been rehearsed, mentally, with some little care. One hand he ran up a leg, up the crinkly petticoat folds, checked for an instant by the appalling suspender, like an unlooked-for gin trap, and by the cold, new flesh, generously applied to areas above that. With her assistance he caught hold of the rim of her knickers. Now, what else: petticoat, stockings, brassière (how he hated that word) Moorman kept his eyes tight shut, enumerating these objects as Mona Lisa helped him relieve her of them. His eyes remained closed. Now the second piece of major artillery was taut against his cheek. Her fingers with the gold rings began brushing ineffectually against the hard front of his cavalry twill trousers, penetrating just inside the waistband so that he hauled his stomach in; his eyes remained tight closed.

'What was that?'

'A parrot,' he replied tersely.

Kneeling above her, his eyes clamped shut, he got his trousers and underpants off in a movement. Then came the awkward moment when he remembered his chukka boots, but luckily the laces were half-undone—his laces were always coming undone—the boots slipped off. A small detail he had forgotten, or rather chose to ignore, was the little precautionary packet of devices in a pocket somewhere impossibly underneath her, in a pocket, cut off now for . . . months. He thought he'd just, he thought . . . he couldn't understand why that girl from Hebburn had complained, 'It's killun' us, man.' That certainly was no tribute. He simply wanted . . . no, he was quite confident in her largeness and yield . . . his mouth was dry . . . he was astonished to feel himself rebound. Absolutely. Smartly.

'Darling . . .'

'Oh, my angel,' Moorman gasped.

'You forgot my roll-on,' she told him.

It was no good: he had to stand up, she had to stand up. There in Bridewell Park, the moon a ghostly whatever it was among the poles of the trees, the parrot making a noise in the Zoo, John Close's tram far away, beginning another journey, Mona Lisa hauled and rolled and pressed herself free of some great, black, appendix-waving object.

Then she lay straight down again and opened her arms.

He preserved his erection by swiftly putting himself in mind of the filthiest thing he possibly could: an exposed behind with its knickers caught just below the cheeks, flaunted in the face of an old age pensioner (why was this?). Immediately he was engulfed in what seemed to resemble strongly the bubble-blowing fluid he had occasionally been allowed to buy in a tub from Woolworth's, but the little soapy cylinder was always grabbed away by Mother long before it was finished.

'Oh, feel me,' Mona Lisa said. And: 'Och, darling, that's byeotiful.'

Moorman couldn't help wondering who the first tenant had been. He rolled from side to side, the rings on her fingers striving to form an impossible octave on his buttocks. And to his great concern, became aware that for all the pushing, the side-foraging, he wasn't contributing appreciably to the approach of whatever earthquake politeness demanded. His heart sank. He felt himself receding. His concentration began to wander away; to Mother's shops and the chickens barbecueing on the grill; to Leslie's collection of old roller-skating magazines, discovered after Mr Vernon's exit to the workhouse, to Lorna's slack rear quarters on Christmas Day, the blows that had been exchanged, the cold fish smell in the van.

'Och, darling, darling.'

'I'm there,' he assured her.

'Come closer.' This he interpreted as a very bad sign.

He pushed and pulled and pushed and pulled and pushed and pulled. Through his mind, like a refrain, ran, 'I pushed and pulled and kicked and knocked.' Well, he mustn't take her home in too crumpled a state. And he had seen, inspected, graded, passed . . .

'Darling.'

. . . Candled, tested, stamped . . .

She took a hand. 'Hold on.' With a great galleon action

she rolled both of them over so that now, underneath, his eyes and mouth were full of her newly washed hair. He was unbearably hot. He was caught by the lips on the big folded areas under her chin. All this was more and more of an imposition. He noted that Mona Lisa's hands were tightening underneath him. What? They rolled over again, and then again, and for a third time, down the slope. She ground her reeking face down on him (whaaat?) and shouted out. He felt as though dank, warm cables were about to throttle him. He was able to break his mouth clear and take a breath just as Mona Lisa gave a concluding yell. He looked up at the sky through the poles and then into the inquiring eyes of a small wallaby, standing a few feet away.

Mona Lisa's action had taken them up close to a fine mesh perimeter which neither of them had noticed. A wallaby happened to be taking a night stroll. John Close's tram began its journey to the end of the pier across the still water. Having watched with interest as Mona Lisa concluded her addresses, the wallaby hopped away.

5

His room was full of sunshine, he was too hot, his legs and feet twisted about inside the narrow bed in time to 'Forty Miles of Bad Road', as played on the twangy guitar by Duane Eddy.

At twenty-one, the apogee of his horrible mistakes period on *The Gosport Herald,* Moorman had sought admission to a noted Waterlooville group, the Phil Harmonics and, he believed, practically succeeded. They used to practise in a Methodist schoolroom, a vase on the book case containing pale green and greeny-pink rhododendrons. Moorman, with an encrusted and unsteady snare drum bought with birthday money and a number of stolen half crowns, was asked to give an exhibition of his agility on the instrument; and afterwards went into the corridor, which was hung with young children's drawings on stiff grey paper, as the four other musicians discussed his performance. The leader, a fat and curly-headed boy, was named Phil Gutteridge: the group took their name from him. His deep voice boomed out, 'We don't want 'im in.'

As well as being too hot, Moorman had an enormous hangnail on the outside of one thumb, which the bedclothes kept jerking back. He was starting to think about half-naked women but trying to fight off the visions by picturing Baden-Powell's own illustrations of stags in the rutting season, Baden-Powell's expression 'dirty acts'. All across the town below his bedroom, dropping away down to the Esplanade, he could hear water squirting in successful business premises, empty beer bottles being re-crated, even a little cannon report out to sea, beginning a yacht race; but it still couldn't get him out of bed. He ground his head into the pillow, which returned his smelly breath to him.

Last night they had also been, via the Blue Lagoon, to Bridewell Park. But this time, Mona Lisa gripped his arm tight. Luckily she had taken care not to roll up to the edge of the wallaby's promenade area; she had just rolled the other way. God, it all resembled some dreadful ballet of rolling, roll-on rolled off, roll in the parched grass until Mona Lisa, calling on one or two saints and Holy Mother of Mercy, was accommodated, and put a tear-wet face on Moorman's like a ton of bricks. She walked him firmly along past the Wolseley, to Bridewell Park.

Moorman had to get up this minute. The bed was foul, hot, small, his toe was in a hole and wriggling it larger. Suddenly he heard a commotion outside his door, a growl of conversation in Italian, a descent of pointed-toe shoes; someone rapped smartly on the glass of the middle landing W.C., and demanded, 'Eh, Pasquale—you writing bloody Old Testament, huh?' More footsteps went down the main staircase, further below. Now the voice of Mrs di Valvona herself was audible, jumping between Scots and Italian. Moorman heard the poodle bark, its claws tapping on linoleum. 'How dare you say ma wee Angelo's got cruel eyes. Holy Mother o' God, I'll strangle you, so I will.' He believed he heard the sound of a slap.

He *had* to get up. John Close's tram banged to the town end of the pier. There can be no misery greater than lying, thinking about your hateful face and clothes and job, while, everywhere else, on the hillside of a holiday resort, everyone else is getting busy, to earn or spend a lot of money. Moorman gripped the hangnail skin in his teeth and, using the streak of fearful pain that accompanied its tearing-off, he kicked away the hot bedclothes. Careful to avoid his reflection in the oval mirror above the sink, he went across to the eave window, where the lime-green paintwork had great scored marks, as if a child had scrawled with a blunt pencil on paint blisters. He looked out. The Tredegar Guest House was one of a very tall set of buildings at the very summit of Springbourne; the town dropped away under his window. He looked through trees and hotel turrets and lawn levels, where happy people were already sorting out deck chairs, down to the Canoe Lake's kidney shape with the white rim. The Esplanade was miles below: tops of parked cars and buses, blocks of green canvas beach huts, breakwaters lining the way out to sea.

To see the pier, Moorman had to lean right out of the window, into the stiff yachting breeze. It was black, literally black with day trippers. These would be from the 9.30 ferry. John Close's tram banged up, past them. There was a fringe of white Pedalos around the pier and, further away, a hazy sea, a horizon of white yachts speeding for some particular event. The cannon fired again. There was a little tower at the end of the pier used for beginning yacht races. A section of the yachts detached themselves from the rest, led by a red wings.

His eyes lingered on those beautiful sails; he wished he were out there; he leaned on the warm sill, picking wax out of his eye: waxy tears?

And, still avoiding his reflection, washed his face, hands and hair, flattening it down on his head while still wringing wet. He hadn't had a bath for something like a week. The glass door banging and general crowd activity on every level of the hotel made him nervous. He didn't even like going to the lavatory here. The door shook every few seconds.

From a tube so battered that the grey metal showed through, he crushed, kneaded and wiped off a minute coil of Gibbs SR for his teeth. After that he sat down on the bed, depressed by the shabby pyjama trousers, to try to shave with his ancient razor plugged in at the ancient point behind the bedside table. Sparks flew from the connection. He tried to take his mind off shaving in this way, he felt as though he hadn't washed; cold sweat was under his arms; he got up to touch his face with his flannel, but, having neglected to wring it out, it was now horribly inflated with dry soap. Moorman put his palm against his mouth and breathed out to see if his breath still smelled. It seemed to, very much. He combed his partially-dry hair and found it sticking out all over the place at the back like Leslie Langdon's: guilt transfixed him at the thought of Leslie opening the Pavilion by himself: he put his head under the cold tap and flattened down his hair all over again . . . as he often did, he cursed Leslie Langdon in expressions like 'bleeding weak tea' and 'fancy little dear'. Through the water in his ears he could just hear another scuffle outside the door. What was the time? For a minute, almost sobbing and screaming, Moorman hunted for his watch. He found it lying face down on the bedside table, which was a basketwork tray mounted on three antelope horns of different sizes. Had Miss Toye any dealings with Mrs di Valvona? Moorman experienced a flash of intense hatred for both Miss Toye and Mrs di Valvona. Simultaneously, on a distant radio, a voice intoned, 'It's Five to Ten.'

He paused. Footsteps came up the stairs, past all three landings. Mona Lisa's voice called to him in the formal manner she adopted around the hotel; formality touched by reproach. 'My Mummy says, will you want any breakfast?' Moorman in reply, used his voice for the first time that day and found it mixed up with his tongue in a halting conspiracy. 'No, I won't, thank you.' His failure to eat breakfast was just one sign of his incorrigibly Bohemian ways, he hoped they thought here. No breakfast in a house where there was a breakfast gong! Actually he would have loved a big breakfast. Mona Lisa was tapping on his door again. She hissed, 'Darling . . .' Then, when the toilet door on the middle landing thundered open again by someone, her voice resumed its full dress tone. 'My Mummy says it's way past ten. You'll be late.' From below, the deeper, exasperated voice of Mrs di Valvona called: 'Mona! Mother o' Jesus, Moona! That girl . . . I'll strangle her. Get down here to see to . . . this minute!' The stairs rustled with a nylon housecoat; were slapped by flat-heeled mules.

Moorman did his best to pull the bedclothes over his lower sheet, which bore disgraceful chocolate stains and, in one place, the mark of a late-night banana. He high-stepped, like a performing horse, out of his pyjama trousers. He drew back the flowered, plastic curtain that screened his clothes from view; his wardrobe. Every morning this fandango, this attempted composition of a new outfit from the remnants he owned. As usual he tried the suit trousers on. They were stiff with decay. He gripped the lining of one pocket and withdrew his fingers covered in old biro dust. The cavalry twill trousers closed, like heated funnels around his legs. He put on yesterday's (and the day before's) poplin shirt. All of his other three lay in horrible scrubby snowballs. Some night, after the tumbler of Cinzano, the nuns and the argument in Mrs di Valvona's best room, he *must* wash the shirts and try to drip-dry them. This one had no collar stiffener and a (tomato?) mark on the front. He was certain his breath was bad. He searched for a grey Polo to combat this. Finally he looked at himself. The shirt was rumpled and snagged at the waist. Then a white madness came: Moorman danced and said 'bloody buggers'. He heaved off the cavalry twill trousers and tried on those from the Woolpack suit again. He fought these off for a second time: his legs went inside the hot fawn pipes. It was as if forces beyond his control were pushing him around. One chukka boot caught an interior seam with a rending sound. He grabbed up the big jacket and reached the door. He looked back at the room, the lime-green chest-of-drawers, the bedside table with the *History of Mr Polly* lying on it, and the box from the Waterman's pen that he kept as a prestige thing, although the pen itself was lost. For the first time he saw the fairy ring: the numerous slugs of silver paper, the pieces of sweet wrappings that had dropped out of his patch pockets, unseen in the wildness of the dance.

The final descent to the front door was a broad, Paisley-carpeted staircase, which had the close smell of old gravies. Moorman, descending, used his ghost's tread. Mrs di Valvona's voice could be heard from the kitchens, and, he fancied, the sound of Mona Lisa grizzling.

In stealing out like this Moorman wasn't being deliberately rude or exclusive. Simply, he wanted to delay the moment when anyone saw him.

The dining-room door was half open. He caught sight of a long table with Italians sitting back from it, as if in the open air, their sleeves pushed back. His mouth ran at the scent of the coffee.

He had a premonition that there would be a letter for him. There was; quite a big packet stuck in the rack, which reminded Moorman of the boarding house at his school, and the privileged boarders, whose parents turned up to visit them with perhaps a cage of budgerigars or several cases of apples, if they were from Kent.

The Tredegar Guest House front door closed softly behind him, he eased the big knob back afterwards, then left the outer door from the small conservatory standing ajar, and tiptoed down the steps, down the long front garden, into Pell Lane. He was at the crossroads, where Dover Street dipped away to run down to the Esplanade opposite the repertory theatre, before he stopped to open Mother's letter. A green piece of paper fell to the pavement and a man passing by with a pair of yellow labradors, handed it back. Clearly, even in the other man's hand, this was a cheque for £250 signed by Mother (Mrs, in brackets).

'Dearest Gordon,

'The trouble with you is that you get mixed up with people on a lower level and they hang around you "on the make". You must know that place is as useful as an udder on a bull. I wouldn't care if in actual fact you bought yourself out, but don't know if that's poss. Enclose a small cheque, the most I'll be able to manage this year! ! You know you've got a job here if you like.

'Can't stop for too long as this is our busy day. Must do up my bank in a minute. Some of the girls have got a day "off". Hope all's well, love from Mum.

'PS Thought you might want the enclosed photo, which I found whilst turning up some old views of the Abbot's Kitchen, Glastonbury, to show to Miss Toye who asked to be remembered. You might like it. I don't want it.'

Moorman looked at a tiny snapshot of his father in R.A.F. uniform with the cap through one epaulette. He was standing in a backyard with a fluffy animal around his shoes. He had a widow's peak of hair. His expression was—absent.

'As you know, dear, he led me a bit of a dance. He ran away after we'd been to see some friends near Shoreham, a Mr and Mrs McIsaac, you don't know either of them. We stopped the Austin at a place that gave sweets off points and your father never came back out of the shop. He was like you, and couldn't stop eating sweets. He was a religious maniac and used to preach to the gypsies in Epping Forest. He ground his teeth. I never had any regrets. A lot of that kind of thing went on during the war. xxxxxxxx (millions).'

First of all Moorman took the cheque to the National Provincial Bank opposite the drapery bazaar at the top of St John's Road, where the nuns had fought the sun-blinds. Breathing heavily he moved through the crowds. Trampling across the sandals of perfectly inoffensive small boys, breaking through groups of foreign students: Swedes, Italians, French with shoulder-bags and striped jerseys. He cannoned into the side of a fat lady who'd stopped abruptly to point something out.

It was going to be a hot, beautiful day. He tried to keep under the shop blinds on the hill. At the foot of it, the hazy sea rose up like a wall, with the mainland in a line at the top. A liner passed the end of the pier, fringed by white sails. He saw Fred Wellspring's daughter in her slacks, and the alsatian on the other side of the road.

Moorman had about six pounds with the National Provincial Bank. He felt grotesque, indelicate, an intruder in the cool bank—the marble-topping, pretty girls in summer dresses, holding cardigans round their shoulders with one hand and important documents and messages with the other.

Moorman's enduring fear of money never allowed him to overdraw his account. He paid in the cheque from Mother. He bought a cheque from a young man of his own age in a grey tropical suit and made it out to Moorman and Langdon Enterprises Ltd, for £220, and received six five pound notes over the counter. After this he walked down the hill further to Barclay's Bank, where the Pavilion made a show of banking. He paid in the cheque for £220. He was breathless with guilt, this was overlaid by a sensation of irreparable lateness.

Further up the hill again, he looked in the window of Harold Bricknell and Woodnut, Tailor and Outfitter. The display, however, wasn't a fair indication. Moorman had noticed that seaside outfitters tended to give prominence to Jantzen swimming costumes and towelling shirts. Looking closer, his heart leapt, and he saw another display window inside the portico of the shop. There, laid diagonally, was a pair of pencil-thin brown trousers with the Strads label on them. Two headless models were dressed in light-coloured jackets which, by implication, matched the trousers. Underneath the jackets were soft shirts with American-looking collars.

On the floor of the window near the trousers, a spill of ties, Munrospun ties in amber and heather mixture colours.

Moorman went inside. Everything looked splendid: the glass counter with expensive Byford knitwear modelled inside, the maple-coloured shirt drawers, a long rack covered by polythene with jackets of plum-dark shades indistinctly visible. The tailor seemed all alone and anxious to please. He was slim and courtly, dressed in a blazer and grey shirt and black silk tie.

'Morning,' Moorman began, out of breath, hot, unsure that it really was *him*, 'I'd like to a, ah, a suit.'

'Good, sir. I've got some very lovely ones,' the tailor replied. He guided Moorman, out of breath, hot, unsure that it was really *him*, down to the far end of the shop to the fitting mirrors where an unlooked-for skylight poured sunlight down.

He crooked one sleeve. What glory in a row of five buttons. In the smell of brand new cloth, warmed by the sun that penetrated the changing room curtain. In the smoothness of both lapels. The cold billow of the trousers. They were a little on the wide side but the tailor said they could be tapered—he said 'tapered' not 'taken in'—to what? Seventeen? 'Sixteen,' Moorman told him.

It was a Daks charcoal-grey suit with a label shaped like a red carnation. Outside on the glass lay two Tern shirts he had chosen; one grey like the tailor's own, the other blue. Moorman had also been shown a third shirt, a Rael Brook shirt it was true, but the tailor laid great stress on the coming fashionability of 'the Ivy League satin stripe'. Moorman thought he'd have that one as well. Buying three shirts at once. It smacked of the

Burlington Arcade and *The Importance of Being Earnest*. He'd never even bought two shirts. He had occasionally bought one, or been bought one, which he had hated as soon as he put a finger smudge on it, trying to make the collar look right. The 15½ collar shirt from the previous Christmas came back to mind, so did the one of the Christmas before: both from Mother, handed over in a St Michael bag.

The tailor made a chink in the curtain and asked how it was.

'Absolutely lovely,' Moorman replied. He pulled the curtain right back, quickly zipping his fly; and the tailor said, 'Yes, it is an unusually good fit, it will go perfectly with either one of the shirts, and perhaps a wine-coloured or muted yellow tie.'

Moorman felt passionately happy. As usual, in this uncommon frame of mind, confidence bubbled out of him. 'It just shows, doesn't it, that it pays to get something really good? How to get a marvellous fit, mm? I suppose at somewhere like Shirt King's I'd have all sorts of trouble . . . I mean, I've been told, given to understand that I was a funny shape and now, well, this fits so beautifully.'

'A funny shape?' the tailor said. 'I wish every suit I sold a gentleman was as good a fit as this, really.'

Moorman asked the price. The tailor had to part two sides of the carnation label to find out: £21. The Woolpack suit was £12. 17s. 6d. Moorman looked at the cavalry twill trousers lying on the fitting-room floor like thick rubber wellingtons, and at the big jacket, hung without a loop, on the peg. He had the wild, lovely thought, of putting the jacket in an Esplanade litter basket.

'Would you put the other things in a bag?'

'You'll wear it now? Certainly.'

'Yes.'

'Cer-tain-ly. And you'll want—excuse me for a brief moment.' He darted away and back. 'I don't know if this would interest you at all.' He had a pleasing light tenor which the flat vowels of the South Coast rather suited. Between thumb and forefinger he held a tie, a slim, very long tie. In overall effect it was red. Dark red. But there were darts in it of pale red and shady mauve leaves that reflected the light, seeming to revolve and swallow and then disgorge the pale reds. Pinned to the tie was a stiff bit of card with a price written in ink, the sign of a really expensive article.

'Christian Dior,' the tailor said.

'Only bought half a dozen. *Could* only buy that amount because of their being in such short supply. Only six on the whole Isle of Wight. This is the last of them, and for my money, the nicest of all. Try it against the shirt. There. So. My, now that's . . .'

It was perfect.

'I'm afraid it's thirty-eight and six. Handmade silk, do you see.'

Thirty-eight and six! Mother's idea of a fair price for almost anything, shoes, trousers—pullovers for a lot less, shirts for a lot less. Most of her shopping on his behalf had always been done in a shop called insultingly 'Men and Boys' Outfitter'.

Moorman nodded and repeated: 'Lovely.'

Beaming, the tailor let the curtain fall.

Moorman took off the grey suit and put it carefully back on its hanger. Out came the tricky, ball-headed pins from the grey shirt, the new, crisp grey that slid on his back and touched his wrists. It had double cuffs, secured by links, little tiny twists of blue cord. The length of the shirt concealed the shabby pouch of his Y-fronts. Moorman pulled his socks up as far as they would go and took down the suit trousers, seeing with purest delight that instead of buttons outside the waistband, they had small horizontal zips. He pulled the trousers up, the delicate black linings against his skin, the full, empty pockets. At his throat, the Christian Dior tie assumed a perfect shape. He put on the jacket. The tie vanished into it, the collar, the knot, the lapels of the suit forming a composition of incredible beauty, but now there was a stab of unhappiness. These always intruded. Wouldn't the trousers have to be tapered? Moorman, striking male model poses in the full-length mirror, realized that this wasn't really necessary; the trousers looked tapered as they were. The beautiful cut was responsible, he supposed. For the first time in his life he wore beautifully cut trousers. Even his chukka boots failed to spoil it. They added, he thought, a touch of eccentricity, a touch of the sports car. He had forgotten the time. He struck more male model poses, half-closing his eyes to make himself more glamorous. He heard another customer in the shop: the tailor's voice, then a la-de-dah woman.

'Ah, I want some jeans. Men's jeans.'

No, a girl's. He found girls rather exciting who specified men's jeans. A slight erection in the cool interior of the trousers. The tailor replied something and drawers were opened.

'Mmmm. Mmm. Uh huh. 'Spect they are tailored but as I'm sure you realize, Mr Woodnut, I'll immediately rush off and sit in a bath to get them tighter.' (Laughter) 'Okay if I try the pale blue *and* the black?'

'Yes, of course you may. Use the one on the right.'

Moorman stood, in his warm suit, watching himself

from all angles in the mirrors, frozen. Only a hardboard panel divided his and the girl's cubicle. He heard the brisk 'zapp' of slacks being loosened from each side, then a high step, a deep breath, another high step, and the coarser sound of a zip fly rumbling upwards on its tracks. Moorman was faced with the dilemma of being in one ground floor W.C. when Mona Lisa arrived and sat down in the adjoining one. Should he stay until she had gone or risk leaving at once, with the possibility of a confrontation outside? He remembered that this was a fitting-room. He remembered he was wearing a new suit. He had just been fitted. There was no chain to pull, no paperback Western story to ram down the front of the trousers like an ice hockey goalkeeper's box: so he walked out, and so did the girl next door, at precisely the same moment.

At the counter, the tailor beamed at them both. He was busy with white string, paper, and a small penknife at the end of a chain. He caught up, concertina fashion, the parcel he had made of Moorman's coat and trousers. He swivelled and patted it, and cut away the ends of string.

The girl went and pirouetted in front of a mirror on a stand. She put her hands on her hips and then pointed one toe like a ballerina, then swept right backwards and turned round on her other stockinged foot. She whirled right round again, a full circle and laughed. 'Perfectly fabulous,' she said. Moorman had seen her driving a Mini van when he went to cross the Esplanade two nights before. He particularly remembered deciding that she was an arrogant little bitch. And Fred Wellspring was of the opinion that Mini vans cornered dangerously.

'I'll take these then,' the girl said. She spun round and saw, at the door of the fitting-room, Moorman in his new suit. Although he was nowhere near her, she stepped to one side and said, 'Sorry.'

'Sorry,' Moorman replied, passing her with yards to spare. He took up a position by the glass counter, searching the folds of his wallet for the wad of £5 notes, that blue mystery. The girl, all in one swift movement, dashed back into her fitting-room, reappeared with a pair of dark blue trousers over her arm, made as if to run directly out of the shop. Moorman toyed with the idea of putting out an arm, his palm flat on the wall, Bogart style, as he said, 'Not so fast, sister,' only there wasn't a wall opposite, just the Cellophane-covered rack of coats and cardigans. As she ran past him, the girl called out, 'These are fine, Mr Woodnut. I've left the others folded up on the chair. Don't bother to wrap the oldies up; and can you please put them on Billy's account? Bye.'

A moment later, when he was trying to hide his eyes from the sun, Moorman saw the Mini van race past him towards the Esplanade. She leaned forward and waved. He turned round and saw Mr Woodnut the tailor in the doorway, returning the greeting. Zoom, zoom: off she went, Moorman thought, to have a cold drink of beer out of a cabinet, not straight out of the cupboard, and no doubt Billy would be standing around, horridly casual and superior, unless he was out in a yacht, a speedboat, or a private aeroplane.

Moorman walked down St John's Road. The liner was still out there, a soft shape, black-banded red funnels. Moorman kept himself under the sunblinds, in case of a yachting breeze, but walked lightly and proudly to the curve into the Esplanade. In bright sunshine the bulbs of the peacock's tail above S'Lots of Fun were almost invisible. The suit thrilled him so much that he gave not a thought to chocolate, even though he could smell from Sangiorgio's the soft aromas of Cadbury's Flake thrust into their ice cream; and also the fried bread from their late breakfast service. It thrilled him so much that he was going to take a taxi to the end of the pier: a taxi, a taxi, the thought ran through his head like a refrain.

The first one of the crowd to touch his peaked cap was not, thank God, George Lay, but a little chap whose head-dress was very much tilted to one side—a style that always put Moorman in mind of the 1930s. Taking this taxi was a truly wicked extravagance because first they both had to walk across to the rank and then drive round in a circle about fifty yards to a small roundabout before they could approach the gates of the pier. Furthermore, with the half-a-crown for the taxi, there was a shilling pier toll. The man at the gate grabbed the money. With a single wrist-snapping action he drew a bolt free, and the barrier swung away to admit the taxi.

It was lovely. The warm day came through the windows. Restrained by the 10 m.p.h. speed limit for vehicles, the taxi just sighed over the white planks. John Close's tram passed them but clangorously, with no real dignity as, in its outward journey, it went backwards. John Close and his little dog, their two faces, went ahead. Then Moorman was surprised to find the taxi overtaking old Fred Wellspring on a moped, a quiet fizz issuing from it, and Fred's knees pumping high. Surely he was never so late as this? Then Moorman understood. There was a basket between the handlebars of the moped, containing a jar of liquorice all sorts. The day before a deputation of angry Londoners had come and complained about the age of the liquorice comfits inside the two crane machines, all of which were now a pale bird's-egg green with disuse: God knows how long they had been there, with the odd gilt ring and packet of five tipped Weights. Fred had obviously been to buy new models. There was something ineffably comforting about this.

People were walking from the end of the pier, the remnants of the eleven o'clock ferry's discharge. The taxi drove gently through these individuals. 'Gor,' remarked the driver loudly but agreeably, 'Loog at 'em. Sheep.'

'The herd instinct,' Moorman said.

'I beg department?'

'The *herd* instinct.'

Friendly relations proceeded on this basis. Moorman kept straightening his trousers to protect the creases, and shifting his position to avoid crumpling the back of the jacket. When they reached the end of the planks, the taxi driver was saying: 'The girl oi originally married died, but oi done it again. Married a real little cracker. Pfwaw! You want to see her.

'Here, you remember that evening last week when it pelted with rain. Remember? I was home at five and twenty to six, I was, had a bath and got in bed in time to see Day by Day on Southern I.T.V. She gives me me dinner in bed. Can you beat that, eh? I says, can you beat that? Pfwaw.'

He handed over a printed card with the name and address of his garage on it, and they said goodbye cordially. This morning, even the yachting breeze was merciful. It blew behind Moorman as he walked into the big, dusty place and screwed his eyes up to take in the overcrowded gloom. From the room at the back of the tea bar a snort of steam happened: Old Nell learning to handle the Jackson tea and coffee urn or 'Jack's cooker' as she preferred to call it.

Moorman paused on the Amplifier Room steps to look down at his trousers, the peak shapes of their perfect creases. He felt glorious. He noted that a pair of little girls were in the Pavilion, playing the pin tables; nice, clean, hair-parted little girls, he concluded. The morning was slightly spoiled when he discovered Uncles sitting next to Leslie at the roll-top desk, all their elbows among the bills.

'Oh, hel-lo, Gordon, Mm, I like the suit.' But Leslie's heart wasn't in the salutation, not at all, it was perfectly plain.

There was no question at all of any hostility between Uncles and the Pavilion's tenants. Leslie, in conversation, referred to 'Ned Uncles' and frequently received lifts in the Rock Shop man's Standard Vanguard. Indeed, Uncles sometimes obliged them with Softytop Ice Cream tins for the emptying of machines. When Moorman bought those interminable Mars or Bounty bars, Uncles gave him a perfectly agreeable look through the window. Leslie had always been of the opinion that it was only right and just for Uncles to operate a public address system if they did: he wasn't aware of Uncle's great superiority of diction and Moorman naturally would not admit it. He was across the way: his grey hair was never touched by the yachting breeze, he wore a lovat suit that never looked spoiled, he was neat and smoked a pipe with a metal stem: there he was making a fortune with a quiet kind of confidence and gloomy relish that Moorman naturally found very upsetting.

'Morning,' he said. 'How are you?'

Leslie said, 'Now what do you think? What *do* you think? Ooh, it's put me all of a twitch just thinking about it.' He spoke to Uncles again. 'I think that pier master's a bit of a deceitful devil, you know; going behind our back like that.'

'I didn't think it was very nice, no,' agreed Uncles. He

looked genuinely put out about something.

'"Not very nice". I should think it's not.'

In a new suit, and Moorman felt terrified. He felt hot in those cool black linings.

'What's up?'

'Oh, by the way,' Leslie said distractedly, 'Mona Lisa called and said please ring her back.'

'You can appeal—well, sort of appeal.' Uncles took a pocket diary out. 'You have to write to a Mr Petty, the Divisional Administrative Officer's assistant.'

'What's up, Leslie?'

'I think it's bloody disgusting.'

'*What* is?'

Leslie told him.

6

The third loudspeaker system, giving details of bus and Island train times and cinema and theatre attractions in the town, came into operation almost immediately at the end of the pier. After the deplorable incident outside the Rock Shop involving Moorman, Uncles, and the representative of Softytop Ice Cream ('None Nicer' Brand) Ltd, it continued successfully as the only public address. Permission for the other two was revoked by a special meeting of the Borough Pier and Entertainments Committee and a notice to that effect issued.

The third loudspeaker also announced particulars of music festivals, regattas, Gala Nights at the town hall, rifle shoots, The Isle of Wight Marathon Road Race, the hill climb at Ventnor Cascade.

For three days it spoke in competition with Moorman's voice and Uncles'. It was handsomely the winner from the very beginning. It also revealed the cash advantage of special runabout holiday coach tickets, launch trips into Southampton Water and ladies' football events at the borough recreation ground. The official volume was much in excess of that produced by Uncles' equipment: it was also permitted to continue announcing as the ferries unloaded. The pattern now was as follows: the ferries cut round to the dock with three voices babbling. It arrived at the dock; two voices ceased, the third told them things to their advantage. The Rock Shop suffered little in fact, because they still crowded round its windows, and the Pavilion remained about as deserted as before. The new voice, the voice that won, belonged to a man named Taffy. At the end of that season he was discovered dead in bed.

As for Moorman, he was surprised to find time at the end of the pier suddenly animated: five or six days filled with strangers, his lonely bars of chocolate neglected.

The same Monday that Taffy began the official announcements, a man in a brown thornproof suit, knitted yellow waistcoat and powder-blue socks, entered the Pavilion and engaged Leslie in conversation. Moorman, strolling dejectedly past the mutoscope peep shows, a routine anti-Meatball sweep, suddenly heard his partner cry out: 'You're *him*. No, not Lobby Lud. Wait a minute. The other one. You're the Man.'

The Man was a *Daily Mirror* reporter. At that time, several dangerous convicts were at large and the *Daily Mirror*, wishing to test the awareness of the man in the street, had put their own man on the run with a cash prize for whoever recognized him. Leslie had the *Daily Mirror* delivered to his caravan and remembered the man from his photograph. He therefore received a cheque for £50, with which he at once paid Upwaad and Rich the wholesalers.

And, that afternoon, two celebrities came into the Pavilion, pursued by children with autograph books. They were Pharos and Miss Radar, a mind-reading act currently on the variety bill at the repertory theatre on the Esplanade. Pharos had a chin beard and plump little face. Every time a child asked for his autograph, he replied, 'By all means.' Miss Radar had a pink feathery frock on, and black stockings. She seemed not to be taking much in. On stage, Leslie said, she wore a radar scanner, which appeared to move round and round by itself. Both of them received free teas at the tea bar, old Nell Sumption blushing and bobbing to wait on them, but they didn't give any sign of having enjoyed their tea (Moorman was furious to see old Nell's face fall). They looked at several of the machines but didn't sample any. They left, and caused a sensation on the tram station, leaving behind tea slopped in their saucers and fizzled out ends of Passing Cloud cigarettes. Leslie told Moorman that he was slightly acquainted with Miss Radar yet she had looked right through him. 'Soppy cat! But they're pro's, real pro's. I never have understood how they made that scanner thing go round.'

The big girl Alicia had now gone home. Her spectacles flashed longingly across the pierhead from one of the evening ferry queues. Leslie now took pity on Maureen. The difference with her was that she brought her mother to the Pavilion; a lady with a black beret jammed right on her head, rather after the style of Miss Toye. However hot the day, she had a waisted red coat buttoned up to the neck. Whenever Moorman walked haughtily past, she devoured him with her eyes as if unable to comprehend why there and then he didn't get off with Maureen—the same size as Alicia, the same white socks and spectacles.

Still on the same day, Moorman lost his standing with Leslie as a gifted mechanic. He'd always realized this was bound to happen but it nevertheless made him depressed.

He remembered it, though Leslie (trust Leslie) never mentioned it again, never suggested that Moorman was any the less brilliant.

At about four-thirty old Fred Wellspring announced that it had been represented to him that 'See Him Sweat' was stuck.

This was perhaps the oddest machine in the Pavilion. Leslie believed it to have been made of shell casing by Polish prisoners of war.

The scene behind the glass was a castle keep. The insertion of the penny caused a drawbrige to be lowered, revealing a room where a cut-out model of Hitler, surrounded by guards with swords and night sticks, sat on a pot: there was even a cut-out paper turd fixed underneath him with a thread. For a second his head turned this way and that, then the drawbridge snapped closed once more. Moorman had sometimes considered writing out a card to warn parents that this was unsuitable for children or pensioners . . .

Now, Fred Wellspring reported, the drawbridge refused to open. A child had reported the fault, Leslie got Moorman to pull 'See Him Sweat' slightly out of the line of machines and together they found the key and managed to open it. An amazing creation of push-rods, wires and associated mysteries was thereby revealed; this was one of the few electric machines in the Pavilion. Clever, those prisoners of war. And it was still switched on. Moorman didn't think of this and stuck a finger into the outer complexes of the mechanism, hoping this would be sufficient. A powerful electric shock caught him. Leslie happened to be standing close to him, close enough to invite comment, so close, looking so attentively at what Moorman was doing that his chin actually rested on his partner's bare arm: the shock was communicated to him, his chin became fixed to Moorman's arm, and both of them remained joined to 'See Him Sweat', screaming and yelling until Fred Wellspring came to rescue them.

Fred printed 'Out of Service—Sorry' on the back of one of Leslie's Gold Flake packets and taped it to the glass of 'See Him Sweat': it remained there until the machine was moved into storage, the day Moorman lay on the Esplanade pavement and the machine stood all over Springbourne, being played.

Two days later the affair of Uncles, himself, and the representative of Softytop Ice Cream ('None Nicer' Brand) Ltd took place.

It was typical of Moorman and Leslie that they just accepted the appalling burble of sound their loudspeaker produced in competition with Taffy's official voice. Uncles, however, campaigned: a land campaign. He bought himself a small trolley of the kind used to pick up soiled crockery in cafeterias and loaded it with novelty rock, toffee apples, cartons of Spangles, Barrett's sweet shrimps, and humbug lollies. This he caused to be wheeled along the queues that formed up on Saturday and Sunday evenings, down the pier planks, for the homeward ferries. The operator was a dwarf of a fellow whom Leslie called Johnnie the *Star* man, because of some former newspaper-selling concession. The trolley was a marvellous idea in fact, because he had a nice style of patter; and queues, especially disconsolate ones, can always be induced to eat sweets.

Uncles was convinced that he was on the way to ruin, even so. His cordiality even towards Leslie diminished. He seemed to think the advent of the third loudspeaker system was fundamentally their fault. He ceased giving them empty ice cream tins for the machine-emptying.

Now, old Fred Wellspring was a surprising man. He had, he told Moorman, served in the Royal Marines when they had to wear blue uniforms and white topees for most of the time. Leslie once said: 'He got chased through the streets of Alexandria, didn't you, Mr Fred, by chaps with knives?' Fred Wellspring wrinkled up his nose, made his moustache writhe, and said: 'Yers, we did. Coo, I don't know, the cats used to have a field day in Alexandria.'

As well as being a joy and a comfort, a fine-spray sneezer, a man to judge the occasional rifle range customer and hand over single toffees in boxes, Fred Wellspring was charged with the twice-weekly emptying ceremonies. This simply involved unlocking each machine and emptying a tin of pennies into a larger tin or bank bag. Now Fred was faced with a container problem. The bank bags were too few, and Uncles was making a point of throwing away ice cream tins, dropping them into the Triangle instead of passing them on to the Pavilion. So Fred Wellspring used to climb down the iron ladder, right into the Triangle, almost to the dangerous water, to pull the tins out. He actually collected far more tins than the takings could ever hope to fill. He had an old chap's joy for hoarding: it was exactly the same with the quires of old *Daily Sketches* under the rifle range counter.

What none of them knew (except Uncles) was that the tins remained the property of the supplier, Softytop Ice Cream ('None Nicer' Brand) Ltd, and that the company was very funny about this sort of thing, being a family concern that abhorred waste as much as old Fred Wellspring did.

Moorman was back in the cavalry twill trousers (he couldn't wear his suit *all* the time). Leslie was engaging the outstandingly plain, sad girl and her mother in conversation, it was quiet between ferries (no real sign yet of the season, Moorman thought) and large gulls screamed and circled the dome. A chiming van drew up outside. Steel tips made an unnatural noise inside the Pavilion. Moorman had just been struck by the awful thought that Mona Lisa di Valvona was a Catholic, for which religion Mother kept up a lasting frenzy. The stranger peered exaggeratedly round the Amplifier Room door and came right to the point.

'Are you using our four-pound tins for your own purposes?'

Moorman, with unutterable loathing, saw that his visitor's hair was pasted flat with cream that clearly had not been revised for some time, possibly some years. He had a long neck and sharply manipulated his Adam's apple.

'Yes,' he replied, 'we take them out of the water to put coppers into.'

'Are you a customer of ah'rs?'

'Um, no.'

'Then I submit,' the other man said nastily, taking a dirty envelope from an inside pocket, selecting a biro from the battery of pens and pen torches that shared his breast pocket with a six-pointed paper handkerchief, 'then I must point out that you've no *right* and I put it to you that they are returnable tins. In fact, this is a condition upon our supplying of them.'

Informed of these facts, Leslie stammered: 'Oh no . . . your people mustn't blame us.' Moorman felt suddenly angry. Leslie's face had fallen. Originally he came into the Amplifier Room and said, 'Aye, aye, my covey, what's the row?' having been reading *Oliver Twist* in the change desk.

'I'm only interested in fax,' the man replied. He appeared to enjoy the horrible atmosphere he had caused. Moorman felt irritated, yes, but also a little stimulated; he suspected he could defeat the ice cream representative in conversation.

'Look, go and see the man across the way about this,' he barked. 'Across the way' was one of Mother's expressions.

'Thacks not the point. *You* been misappropriating the four-pound tins. I mean, two wrongs don't make a right. I mean, be fair.' He kept on saying, 'Be fair.'

'But how were we to know?' Leslie wailed.

'Thacks not the point.'

'It *is* the point.'

'Look, friend, be fair . . .'

Moorman got up and said, 'This way. You stay here, Leslie. I'll see to it.'

'Shall I? All right.'

Moorman took the ice cream man's arm, not aggressively, but it was such a skinny arm and he snatched it away and narrowed his eyes. '—your hands off me,' he said in an amazed voice.

'I'm not touching your arm. Will you come?'

He went out of the Pavilion and the ice cream man followed: the stiff yachting breeze took Moorman's hair and stood it on end, he recoiled, and the ice cream man jumped violently. Uncles was standing outside his Rock Shop, staring across the pierhead concrete at one of the smaller docks, a side-dock where a brilliantly coloured Royal Navy pinnace had just tied up. As soon as he saw the ice cream man, Uncles took his pipe out of his mouth and remarked: ''Lo there, young Ted Long, and what's new in Elmfield circles?'

They were brothers-in-law.

On the sunny, windy pierhead, a short conversation took place. As it proceeded, Uncles began to shoot glances at Moorman, and a groove of exasperation appeared in his forehead. Moorman had to keep turning his head away from the yachting breeze, so that he heard only snatches of the discussion, such as, 'Oh, is that so? Did he?' and 'Ah, well, we'll see.' Uncles and his brother-in-law agreed that the unlawful jettisoning of the four-pound tins must have been Johnny the *Star* man's fault. They agreed this as if it had been a foregone conclusion and mutual pardons had already been granted, and really the whole matter was too absurdly trivial to have been brought to arbitration in the first place.

In an inward pirouette, the yachting breeze for the moment behind him, Moorman began: 'Look here . . .'

'Well then?'

Moorman for the first time noticed that Uncles had on a linen summer jacket from which the breast pocket was all but torn away. He also realized that there was a faint, not unpleasant, quite fresh smell, Pale Ale, summer beer, on the rock shop proprietor's breath.

Moorman saw Leslie's worried face looking out of the Amplifier Room window. He knew that this could be interpreted quite easily as an ugly situation. Fear swelled in his throat: so did the beginnings of ungovernable temper.

'Look, old boy,' Uncles said unbearably.

'I'm not your boy . . .'

'I said "look, old boy . . ." Silly little boy,' Uncles said. 'Look, silly little baby boy, why not admit . . .'

Moorman put his hands on Uncles' lapels and pushed him. He went quite a long way backwards. After that, Moorman kicked the brother-in-law's shins, so that he staggered back, grasping the shop's outside rack of saucy postcards for support.

'Bloody little toads . . . dirty little (he recalled Lorna's Christmas language) diseased remains of afterbirthses. "Be Fair. Be Fair." A little learning is a dangerous thing all right.' Moorman yelled. 'You just shut up, you farty little sods, *pair* of sods. You and your uneducated . . . you make me want to . . .' A good deal of the Pavilion and Bridewell Gardens, and a great many teas with banana splits, were absorbed into the expression Moorman used. 'You think I care what you say or bloody well do? Just leave me a-bloody-lone, you silly and inconsequential pair of little hang-balled objects.'

Results in this kind of situation are always unexpected.

Uncles, instead of trying to box Moorman's ears, as his former tone had implied he would, turned round and ran away. He simply ran away. He slammed the door of his rock shop, swinging round a cardboard mobile that said SORRY, CLOSED, CALL AGAIN FOR YOUR MINT CHOCS. MINTED BY LYONS. And the brother-in-law straightened himself up against the rack of postcards, sucking in air. 'I'll ev the Law on you,' he sobbed. (Strange how the ritual phrases *were* used.) 'You lay a finger on me, so much as one finger . . .'

'Piss off, shit head,' Moorman shouted.

He was thin, his clothes were thin, his shoes were coming apart at the back. And still he tried to boss people about and get nasty, did he? There was a little weed like that at school: Tozer. Bed-wetting Tozer. His top pocket was filled with pens and pen torches as well. For two years Tozer had sat against the wall in the Art Room, rubbing away the plaster with his finger in his tie. Over the years this produced an enormous hole. Moorman recalled creeping through the showers once to jump out and terrify Tozer as he sat by himself in a bath. Now, barking excitedly, Moorman chased the brother-in-law round the chiming van a few times, then the ice cream representative broke away and ran up to the railings of the Triangle. John Close, who was preparing to drop in his lobster net, stared in astonishment. Moorman went after him. But, amazingly, instead of dodging round again, Uncles' brother-in-law started to climb on to the railings and went a few rungs down the iron ladder, his mouth lolling open, a wicked high tide chopping green below him. Moorman leaned over and shouted: 'I'm coming down, too, I am. I'll rip your trouser snake off with a pitchfork.' (And he remembered the beautiful sequence of threats from *The History of Mr Polly*.) 'Grrr, I'll cut bits orf you, I'll kick you ugly. You'll cry, you will.' The man hanging there, gobbled with terror.

Then there suddenly was a great click.

Uncles spoke, at maximum volume, over his loudspeaker.

'Take your dirty hands off my brother-in-law,' his enormous voice ordered.

Moorman felt madly happy. When had he last felt like this? He waved at the white oval—Leslie's face looking through the Amplifier Room window—and he shook his fist down into the brother-in-law's face. He took no notice of his hair in the yachting breeze; into the Pavilion and up the steps; grabbed the microphone, clicked the On button, the red light, and replied.

'Keep your orders to yourself . . .'

'I'll . . .'

'Pinky . . .'

'You *saucy* . . .'

'I'll cut bits orf you,' *The History of Mr Polly*, his favourite book, sustained him, 'I'll get you with bo'lls. I'll kick you ugly.'

‘Saucy little villain . . .’

‘Go and piss down your leg and play with the steam,’ he extemporized.

‘You stupid little comb-hairing Teddy Boy.’

‘Balls.’

‘Glug. Glog.’

This conversation might have continued for some time had not the passenger ferry suddenly begun to slide into view, packed to the eyes with day trippers. Moorman ceased insulting Uncles and announced with more heat and joy than ever before. Uncles rather fumbled his address. And it happened that this ferry had brought from Portsmouth dockyards a good half of a Royal Navy ship's company, and all of them poured into the Pavilion. For an hour or more, nothing could be heard but pin table bells, hockey machines rumbling, the crisp sound of the airguns; blue sleeves were pushed out of the way to reveal red and grey tattoos; one of the sailors gave Fred Wellspring a bottle of Brickwood's Sunshine Ale; they all laughed a lot at the single toffees they received for prizes in the paper boxes.

The tea bar took £9. 12s. and old Nell Sumption was kissed a number of times.

Then it seemed to Moorman that horrible things began to jostle for their turn. That night in Bridewell Park, in trying once again to harness Mona Lisa di Valvona's tremendous natural energy, he was appalled to notice a dim little figure break away from the slim tree trunks, a voice yelled ‘yaaaaaaaah’ and then something hit the grass just short of her spread-out Dannimac and then it jumped up and flew around in a series of explosions—an out-of-season firework. Mona Lisa screamed and sobbed. How often had Meatball followed them and watched with interest as Mona Lisa performed her rolling trick? The little figure escaped down the slope, the parrots shrieked at the intrusion, he whacked the trees with a stick, shouted with laughter letting off a small cap gun as he went.

Two mornings after that, ducking through the hall at the Tredegar Guest House, Moorman's heart sank: there was a long buff envelope containing a summons for assault on a representative of Softytop Ice Cream ('None Nicer' Brand) Ltd. As he walked down Dover Street and along the Esplanade he was certain that girls laughed and pointed at him. At the end of the pier, Leslie was looking desolate. Old Fred Wellspring had left a note in the rifle range till, vouchsafing that he would not be able to come in to work again. His wife objected to his working on Saturdays, he was sorry to say, and there were pressing claims on his time from the Elim Church Men's Fellowship and the Springbourne and Totland Greenfingers Club. This was dreadful.

They had to devise a new scheme for the Pavilion. That is, Leslie volunteered to look after the change desk *and* rifle range, and carry out such machine-emptying as he could manage. He would also help old Nell with the urns as Fred Wellspring had done. 'I'm afraid this is going to mean an increased load on both our shoulders,' Leslie said glumly: Moorman found it difficult to see how his own life could be changed. They had been told that they might no longer use the loudspeaker system. The equipment had been returned. All he seemed to have to do was sit and read *A Bell for Adano,* and pray that he'd catch Meatball and kick his spine, regardless of consequences.

To prevent calling on Moorman to help in the change-desk, Leslie brought Mary Kenny, his electronic organist girl friend, to help out on three afternoons a week.

However, she refused quite sharply to entertain the notion that she might also put the single prize toffees into the boxes. She wore a flowered full skirt and sequinned black bodice. She was scared of damaging her nails on the piles of pennies, so she never made them into little piles as Leslie always did. She counted each amount and crooked one index finger to push them across to a customer. As well as a bad ear she had a squint. As she sat behind the desk, her fingers tapped incessantly on its hardboard rim, her foot pumped on an imaginary bass pedal among the bank bags, she hummed through the numbers she was to play later that evening in the Albany Lounge: 'In the Middle of an Island', 'The Railroad runs through the Middle of the House', 'Pretty little black-eyed Susie', 'My Song goes round the World', 'Railroad, Steamboat, River and Canal', 'I could have danced all night', and 'Magic Moments'.

Plainly she disliked Moorman. When she saw Leslie talking to a big unhappy girl, she gave *him* a really murderous look.

Also, Moorman was aware of a change in Mona Lisa di Valvona. Her manner no longer seemed exclusively of half-suppressed admiration for his wild ways and unpredictable, brilliant conversation above her head. No, not quite.

She'd taken to wearing mauve and lilac-coloured woolly jumpers with elaborate roll necks (in spite of the heat) and when Moorman was being irreverent, giving highly glamourized accounts of his life in the VI form, in journalism, in the R.A.F., Mona Lisa would drop her chin into the roll neck, her eyes looking reproachfully at him. On several occasions her reply was: 'You know what your trouble is, don't you? It's that you don't want any responsibilities.'

Later, just before the walk to Bridewell Park, Mona Lisa's dark eyes brimmed with tears. 'You never . . .' she wept, 'you never *say* anything.'

Moorman's heart was savaged by the sight of the tears. Unfortunately at the same moment he saw a waiter pass the open bar door, pushing a flame trolley. He had never in his life eaten anything 'cooked on the lamp'. He imagined it tasting of petrol and possibly lemon. Nor, as Mona Lisa cried, could Moorman stop his hands plunging into the cloth-lined basket of cheese clublets.

'Never say anything? Say what?' He really was mystified.

'Oh, you never, I mean . . . oh, nothing . . .'

'No, come on, out with it, or I won't sleep. Never say what?'

Mona Lisa took out a little handkerchief with 'Mona' embroidered on it (her bedroom door had a china plaque with 'Mona's Room' printed on that). She smudged her eye make-up and replaced the hankie in her sleeve.

'Och, it's the others,' she said.

'Others. What ones?'

'Och, ma Mummy keeps saying . . . the trouble is, you never say anything. You never tell me if,' she spoke in a quick tumble now, 'never tell me what you want me to do. If you want me to help you save or . . . or anything . . . we just go to the Zoo and you never say a word.'

'I do.'

'Ye don't.'

One thing was clear. Mona Lisa had a much inflated idea of his own pleasure when they rolled on the slope, her fingers reaching for out-of-the-question octaves on his behind, yelling. She was looking at him reproachfully because she thought he was deliberately trying to get her pregnant; she thought the bubble bath was a mutual work. Hah. Moorman felt himself getting into a bad mood. She sniffed. He thought darkly that it wouldn't be long before she would yell her satisfaction directly her bare mountain touched the Dannimac. Or how long before she'd come up to him on the public highway and pick him up and put him on like a tap fitment.

Mona Lisa made a concluding remark that evening in the Coachlight Bar of Hobson's Inn, where they were having a drink. It was: 'Ma Mummy says "two can live as cheaply as one".'

Down she sat on the black leather sofa, with a rustle and hiss of rearranged petticoats. Moorman chose the straight chair behind her. He looked weakly around Mrs di Valvona's best room—at the seated nun and at Mona Lisa's Uncle Grimaldi; above and around them weakly, at the small queue of madonnas and saints on the mantelpiece, the photograph on the radiogram of Mona Lisa in her Confirmation clothes, the colour photograph of the Pope set into its own little niche in the Regency striped wallpaper, the long photograph of Mrs di Valvona's wedding that, from a distance, suggested a still from some intellectual silent film.

With Mona Lisa on the sofa, Uncle Grimaldi balanced a plate of spaghetti on toast on the arm and ate, together with strands and noise. At his feet were a number of shoeboxes. He had troublesome feet, and had to buy three or four pairs of specially-made shoes at a time.

Mrs di Valvona, the victim of excitement and sorrow, shouldered round the room, her right hand pressed to her side, her curiously small, dry and pale lips clamped tight against the efforts of Uncle Grimaldi and the nun to reconcile her with her sister Mrs Sangiorgio. 'Sister, it's all very well for Jeannie to say I should make it up.

That's what Father Doupe says to me when he got his tea here the other Friday. "It's no a Christian quarrel," he says to me. I know that. I know that fine. But who started it in the first place? Eh?'

'Perhaps if you could . . .'

'Sister, as long as I live, I'll never forget that Boxing Day. Never. I was so *ull*, Sister, with ma stomach and all. I couldha' died for all that heartless bitch cared, och, I'm sorry to be speaking that way but it's *her*: her that's done this thing to me.' The sister talked in a low voice, and again Mrs di Valvona shut her lips firm. 'Nup! I'll no seek to mend it. Nup.'

It wasn't, Moorman thought, simply a case of being stout. . . .

'And ma poor Daddy's nearly eighty-seven, and all by himself in Dublin, 'side his bingo game, and Jeannie's "too busy" to go there right away, as she should . . .'

. . . Not simply a case of being the stoutest woman in town, far more so than her sister, Mrs di Valvona had once nearly died of her size: her arms were so fat that the bracelets seemed set into them like ornamental borders, her legs were so fat and her feet were so fat that her dainty Italian shoes were in peril of folding away, like inadequate scaffolding.

The bosom: a broad confusion of beads and hard, black, crinkly embroidery patterns. A cameo brooch pinned just below that pale, moist causeway between the . . . Moorman gripped the linings of his pockets, which were cool and beautiful because he was again wearing his new suit.

She had, seated on top of augmented chins, a babyish face and big eyes which she would cross violently in relating the dialogue of some adversary. Her sister, Moorman knew, was thinner and swarthier, altogether more taciturn. Mrs Sangiorgio had well-kept auburn hair, and Mrs di Valvona's was only a poor sowing of knots and twigs, because of the unfortunate happening at Chez Inez in Rowett Street. But even ruined hair could not prevent Mrs di Valvona's obsessive attendance at church doors for weddings. She put round her shoulders the £500, dangling heads-and-tails silver mink, snuggling the pelts around her neck, jamming on a lilac-petal hat so that the thin hair wouldn't show. She adored weddings. And the hands were exactly Mona Lisa's. One dainty plump wrist carried her dead husband's gold Omega: her fingers knocked with rings but were also slippery with the fat from the half chicken she carried on a plate, together with three or four buttered Mazza biscuits.

Mrs di Valvona took Uncle Grimaldi's plate and put it violently on top of the radiogram, causing her poodle to tap to its feet, growling, from its sleep behind the leather sofa. She addressed it in mad, high, wheedling, dreadful tones.

'Aaaaaaaaaaa, it's his Mammy's wee darlin' baby. What is he? His Mamma's wee chichy darling then.' Down the voice dropped again, to suffering. 'I told her on the phone just now, Sister, ma Daddy's got that *yuge* bingo game to look after and only a wee Irish chap to help him. She's nearest to 'm. Och, I feel so *ull.*' Up, up the voice went. 'Weee bebby—tha'swat he is, wee darling. Mummy give him lovely powder then, bless him, bless his dear wee eyes. Mona, I don't know how you could say he's got cruel wee eyes! Is his little tummy sore then?' Mrs di Valvona routed among a lot of pink knitting under a trolley and shook a tin of baby powder all over the poodle, which turned uppermost a livid, purple-patched abdomen. 'I sometimes think you say these things just to make me worse. I'll strangle her,' she remarked to Uncle Grimaldi.

'Was your sister-in-law well when she rang up?' the nun inquired.

'Aye, well enough. Mona! Before you went out with your young man, did you put the sugo on to cook?'

'Aye, Mummy, I did.'

'Are you sure you done it properly?'

'Aye, Mummy, I told you.'

A fine powder dust hung in the room.

'Will you come back here tomorrow, Gordon, for your dinner?' Moorman's heart leapt. 'I'll give you a wee bit of sugo on some bread. It's byeotiful. I'm no allowed to eat it but I know what good things go in. Go on. Stay.'

As he left the Tredegar Guest House in the morning, Moorman sometimes caught the aroma of the spaghetti sauce; it generally engaged the attention of both Mrs di Valvona and Mona Lisa, and therefore allowed him to get out unseen. Late at night, the stair carpet often seemed to exhale the tomato taste. It reminded Moorman of the smells that used to come out of restaurant gratings when almost everything one ate in a restaurant was something he didn't like. Later still at night he'd seen the remnants of the sugo, sticking round a black-coated pail on the gas cooker. The first time he'd ever put his tongue into Mona Lisa's mouth, he had been bending her backwards over a pan of cold-sticking sugo. And, above the stove, a fingermarked, typed notice asked the Virgin Mary to protect the kitchen from devils and schisms.

Uncle Grimaldi took a perfectly laundered handkerchief out and wiped his eyes and ears. He had tomato round his mouth. He contributed a few remarks, mainly inaudible, about Mrs di Valvona's feud with her sister, mainly, 'It's a very bad business.' Then Mrs di Valvona jumped up, causing the poodle to leap and snarl. 'Och, sorry . . . I was forgetting.' She crossed over the carpet to the lacquered cocktail cabinet and returned with an eight-ounce tumbler of Cinzano for Moorman: not that she was generous: she was mean, but regarded Cinzano as a cheap drink. Then she settled down again on the edge of her armchair. A vast lap. Little legs crooked so that—he gripped the linings—he could see what was either the rim of one knicker or evidence of a bandage beneath a surgical stocking . . .

7

Mrs di Valvona was absolutely right: two *could* live as cheaply as one. That was to say, they could if they occupied the top back bedroom at the Tredegar Guest House, which had coconut matting, a washstand, and an ancient chair commode; this, as a rule, was tenanted by Sardinian kitchen porters.

They could live as cheaply as one if all they had to eat was sugo on slices of bread, and tinned spaghetti, this in exchange for a nominal rent, and what Mrs di Valvona, pursing her lips, described as 'light duties'.

It really was the very least Moorman could do, bearing that enormous wedding in mind, followed by a reception in the senior dining-room of St Theresa's Presentation Convent, Mona Lisa's old school. Moorman saw all the presents, seventy electric blankets, cordoned off; and a nun leaping over the barrier to read the cards; she gathered up her skirts, revealing high boots.

Miraculously, Mrs di Valvona's old father rallied, rose from a bed of pain and came from Dublin to give away the bride. He was like a model of an ape in a biscuit-coloured suit, and he dribbled objectionable things about 'lots of little babies'. Mona Lisa and her eight bridesmaids and one matron of honour and three pages, wore lemon ballerina-length dresses with purple sashes, and carried posies of lily of the valley and maidenhair fern. The dresses had been made by the wife of the man who ran the Pedalos from the end of the pier.

Mrs di Valvona paid for the reception. There were as many spam sandwiches as anyone could eat, followed by custard trifle and 'Morning Coffee', a type of biscuit she specially liked, and the sherry and coffee flowed. Father Doupe in an address said that all the tiny babies would have to be brought up in the Catholic faith. Mother was incommunicado, save through legal representatives, and suing him for debt. In fact, a whole crowd of private detectives and trade debt collectors were to be seen looking through the stained-glass window during the Nuptial Mass, and at the merrymaking at the reception. Afterwards (in the familiar style of *The Gosport Herald*) the couple left for a honeymoon in Torquay, the bride travelling in a beige two-piece with ruffled blouse, a lilac matelot-style straw hat and white shoes and handbag. Her bouquet was placed on her father's grave. The week in Torquay had unfortunately to be broken to allow the bridegroom to appear in Springbourne Magistrates Court to answer a charge of assault against the person of a representative of Softytop Ice Cream ('None Nicer' Brand) Ltd, with a further one of misappropriating that company's four-pound tins, a further one of misappropriating one iron ladder, the property of the Borough of Springbourne Pier and Entertainments Committee; further, 'that in a certain public place he did, with the said fat-arsed young lady, wickedly, lewdly, against the Order of Nature . . .'

Speaking of which, he and Mona Lisa had, of course, transferred their game, their galleon-action, to a sagging double bed with sheets made of cavalry twill. Each night the springs set up a noise like a nest of baby mice being worried and tossed by a playful dog.

And every morning, early, the door burst open and in came Mrs di Valvona and Sister Michael Joseph (that was the nun's name—nothing to do with the publishers) to examine the sheets, as was done on the Continent, and to give Moorman his bountiful cup of steaming Cinzano.

Then it was his duty to give the Italian lodgers their coffee, trying not to let their compact appearance and handsome flared trousers worry him. There were rooms to sweep, too, plaster madonnas to dust ('Oh, I'm *so* sorry, Mamma Mia-in-Law, it came away in my hand') and in the middle of the day, after her salami and garlic sandwich, he had to take Mrs di Valvona herself upstairs for a much-magnified version of what took place between his little (hah!) wife and himself. His head in the pale, sweating valley, his leg, by mistake, in the bubble mixture. Great handsome bubbles floated out of her lips. And she, in her delight, clouted him on the side of the head with her late husband's gold Omega; so that in the end Moorman could break his married life down to the following components: sugo, bread, using a commode chair in the middle of a sub-tropical night as a distant tram banged to the end of the pier, bubblebaths six or seven times daily, neuralgia.

He had to sell his new suit to buy a carrycot.

The gold bars of his watch, old Ingersoll, showed five past twelve. His eyes ached from the bright light and his mouth was sour. Mr Grimaldi, having wet a corner of his pocket handkerchief, was busy twisting the linen to a point for attacking the wax in his ears. Mona Lisa had one arm resting on the back of the sofa but her head was turned away from him. Behind, the poodle was asleep but manifestly approaching the conclusion of a wet dream. Everything was lovely. It was true: there had been a certain lightening of the atmosphere since the nun's black folds had flicked off home, or wherever they went.

Despite her vast bulk, Mrs di Valvona's movements could be quick and birdlike. Expressions chased one another from the high mounting of her face. It might soften and simper when expensive clothes were being discussed, or members of the nobility and gentry, or else the time her dead Larry played 'O sole mio' under her bedroom window in Rimini on the piano accordion.

Then, often the matter of the quarrel with her sister darkened her countenance, and Mona Lisa whatever she said, would be threatened with strangulation or a slap. The bright room vibrated with her displeasure.

Moorman, for all his weariness, did his best to cloud his expression at the right instant, to show that he alone really understood, to nod sympathetically where this was called for. 'We'd always go to theirs on Boxing Day to see what presents Grampa Brivati had sent from Dublin for them, see Gordon?'

His chance to stretch himself at the end of a lull, to say he ought to go to bed, was lost.

'Moona! Remember ma byeotiful wild silk dress from Pettiford's of Springbourne? Eighteen guineas it was. But that Boxing Day I was so *ull*, Gordon, I can't tell you how I was. And Joe!' She turned full face on Uncle Grimaldi. He appeared not to blench. 'If that wasn't enough for anyone, ma wee dog wasna' well either, and

I believe I'd given our Mona a slap for something or other. I tell you, Joe, I could scarcely draw ma poor body up them stairs.'

'That was a lovely suit you'd on, Mummy,' Mona Lisa said, trying to keep things light.

'Aye, that's correct, byeotiful wild silk. All of twenty-six guineas it cost me from Pettiford's of Springbourne. I'd been so *ull* and still didna' want to spoil the Christmases of anyone else, see?' ('Christmas!' thought Moorman sharply.)

'Mona, do you remember all that cheating and deceit on the subject of the wireless that Grampa Brivati sent for you, expressly for you?'

'Aye, Mummy, don't think of it.'

'Don't *dare* take that tone o' voice with me, or I'll strangle you, so I will. Och, you lash me with that tongue o' yours. In front of everyone. You just be careful you don't lay me in ma grave, you ungrateful wee girl.' From behind Moorman saw that Mona Lisa had gone scarlet, and it made him bite hard on the rim of his Cinzano glass. To his horror he actually bit out a small piece.

'Mind, ah could tell she was in a mood,' Mrs di Valvona continued, 'she'd just bin taken to court for—hang on a tick—' Mrs di Valvona rummaged in her bag and produced a much-folded cutting from the local newspaper, and read out: 'she did knowingly sell for consumption food below the required standard, namely one sevenpenny individual mandarin trifle containing part of the wing of a moth.

'Did you hear that! Part of the wing of a moth! And her with her gold medal ice cream, hah! So you see, Gordon, as I told you, Joe, she was in a wicked mood to begin with when we went there.

'But it was me that needed the comfort,' Mrs di Valvona's voice grew piteous. 'Me with ma pain and ma wee dog no well and ma Larry no cold in his grave eighteen months. And next to no hair because that wee bugger at Chez Inez permed it all wrong. Ah had to keep ma hat on for six months nonstop. Och, when he took ma head out of the dryer, it was all stuck like a bird's nest round the edge . . .' Her face dissolved now into a sub-plot of hissing and malice: 'But don't you fear. Ah sued them buggers all right. I wouldna' let them palm *me* off with no ten poond wig.

'So she was in a wicked mood then, and there was this disagreement about the wireless what Grampa Brivati sent for our Mona, but she claims that it was for her Ella and no for Mona. But in spite of ma great agony, ah smoothed things over. Och, Joe, *Joe.* You know ma Daddy always preferred our Mona to that other spotty wee article. But the peace had to be kept. I says, "Don't you fear, I can afford to buy our Mona a dozen wirelesses, a hundred bloody wirelesses, without having tae stoop tae thieving."

'Suddenly, Mother o' Mercy, I gets this rush to the tummy.

'Och, I'd been so *ull*, Joe, you know what it's like. I tells her I've got to go somewhere. Heartless besom that she is, 'You don't have to pay here,' she says to me, and me half dead. Real nasty she says it. Och, oooh, and I'm just about to get up from the toilet when, God help me, I slips, I took a hold of the bath tap and it turned on and came away in ma hand: this *gigantuck* jet o' water playing all over the carpet: och, ah wept, all over her new Autumn Lime fitted carpet. It drench't ma wild silk suit that ah paid thirty quid for, and I hadna' even pulled the chain.'

Moorman stared at the light globe, still feeling a fine

shell of glass in his mouth.

'Do ah get any sympathy from her, eh? You know what it was like, Joe, ah've told you millions of times.'

'Yes, you did,' Uncle Grimaldi unexpectedly remarked.

'All ma knees was bruised from where I fell. Our Mona had to run in and pull me to ma feet, didn't you, Mona, yes, you did. I tell you, Gordon, if you could know the stabs, the *stabs* that ran through ma stomach. And the abuse. Oh, the *abuse*. The Names I gets called. I'll never forgive her those as long as I live, Holy Mother o' Moses.'

Uncle Grimaldi contributed another soft remark, which made her voice drop, made it level and menacing. 'Sorry, eh? Sorry. Is she just! Hmm, I'll believe that when I see it made plain. And a written apology for all the lying, heathen . . .' It died away. From the folds of her chair, Mrs di Valvona took a bottle of *Je Reviens*. She sniffed mightily; she painted her wrists and outer neck with it, tilting the bright bottle with unusual force.

This made the poodle step out again from behind the sofa. Mrs di Valvona, by some miracle of spontaneous engineering, got to her feet, she took the baby powder and sprinkled the poodle's raw stomach with it once more, uttering her strange little cries. The poodle rolled over and sat up, turning malicious eyes that matched its face on Moorman. It jumped up between Mona Lisa and Uncle Grimaldi on the leather sofa, and seized Uncle Grimaldi's arm. A candy-coloured thing shot out of the black fur to attack the heavy blue melton of his coat. There was no whisper of a difference in the man's ruminative expression as he made his arm frigid, and shook it discouragingly.

Mrs di Valvona was, once again, calmed.

'Och, Gordon, ah know what I wanted to tell you

about. Give me ma bag a moment, will you, off the radiogram, and I'll be much obliged.'

He met Mona Lisa's eye. 'User of me,' it said reproachfully. The eye make-up was beginning to vanish in streaks and bands. He picked up Mrs di Valvona's handbag, maroon patent leather with an imitation belt buckle clasp and a little gilt attachment for carrying a pair of gloves. The poodle leapt across the room. Its teeth whipped the edge of his hand. No blood, just a mark, which meant that the poodle received shrill congratulations for its skill as a guard. 'Chichy wouldna' let anyone get Mammy's handbag, then. Just give it here quick.' Moorman bit his tongue and sat down.

'He'll no let anyone go near his Mammy's bag, the wee darling bebby honey-lambkin dog,' screamed Mrs di Valvona. She fetched the bag herself and took from it two slips of blue paper.

'How would you like . . .' she began, enunciating each word, so that it came out with a touch of the toastmaster. Hoo wud yew laeke . . . 'How would you like to take our Mona to the Grand Buffy Dance at the Royal Springbourne Hotel and Brassiere next Friday, for the Springbourne, Totland and District Conservative and Unionist Association?' He'd just had an idea. Why not replace the Pavilion's machines with a self-service cafeteria?

'Ah hear it's to be a lovely do Friday. The M.P. leading the dancing and that, Joe. Some of ma boys here are going to help do the refreshments. Now then, Mona, you can come up the town with Mummy tomorrow and buy a nice new dress from Pettiford's, because it's to be formal. Gordon! Have you got a dicky bow? Och, well, a dark suit 'ud do well enough, I daresay. Here,' she handed the tickets to Moorman, 'you can settle up any time you please. When I get ma rent will do. Look on the back. Grand Raffle. You can win a Vespa.' She was simpering, and, abruptly, more cheerful.

'Och, I love *Je Reviens*. "I'll Return." Hey, did you look at Mr Grimaldi's shoes? Show'm, Joe. He has to get his shoes made up special because he's got awkward feet. Special fittings. Show'm, Joe.'

Mr Grimaldi removed the lid from the top shoe box, clapped it underneath like a professional shop assistant, and drew a black toecap shoe out of the tissue paper. Mona Lisa passed it on the flat of her hand to Moorman. 'Adventurer. Dallier' her eyes said, the eye make-up gone: pale eyes. It was a thick-soled shoe; disappointing to someone who had never even toyed with the idea of having his shoes made, whose dreams did not even include made-to-measure shoes. His idea of a bespoke shoe was something unnaturally thin, so dark a brown that it was almost black.

The shoe hissing back into its paper, Uncle Grimaldi got to his feet, and put on a black homburg hat, not previously visible. This called attention to his almost black ensemble, relieved only by a tiny expanse of white shirt and a black string tie secured by a longhorn steer's head silver clasp. In the following speech, his cigarette jumped up and down with the words.

'Getamy shoe-hes made up special.' He looked Moorman right in the eyes, and Moorman had to look away. 'Get hall things made up special. Twenty three pun-ten. Five pair at twenty three pun-ten, understand?'

'Oh, yes, very good. Mm. Nice.'

'Did you come on your motor bike, Joe?'

'Yes. Staying in the Great Eastern Hotel, Norwich, home of da Norwich Union Assurance and Norwich United, understand. Naturally, put pair of shoes outside my bedroom door for to be cleaned, understand?

'You know what they did?' The boxes belted together in Uncle Grimaldi's arms as he stood blocking out the light bowl. 'Clean him *brarn* wax. Wrong colour, see. Brarn wax. Know what I made them pay? Twenty three pun-ten. Well, ta ta, and if you can't be good, be careful.'

He spoke briefly into Mrs di Valvona's ear about coming to the conference table with Mrs Sangiorgio. She scowled again and said 'Nup'. He kissed Mona Lisa at the hairline and she followed him out, to put on her and her mother's electric blankets, or 'bed blankets' as they called them.

'Gordon. I've got a wee something to say. Ma wee speech for the night.'

He'd been getting up to go, weary-eyed but pleased that he could withdraw without having suggested it.

'Will you sit on the settee a minute?'

He joined her there. An entire section of the black leather had seemed to fall away as she put her bottom down. Tiny knees were visible from that monument. 'Mona'll no be a second. Och, ah get so cold. Ma blanket can stop on all night as it's got a thermostatical control *and* I like a hot water bottle on ma tummy. Sixteen guineas each these blankets are, but so *byeotiful*. Ma dear Larry used to say I ought to have an O Sole Mio. Have ye no heard of an O Sole Mio? That's a big pink blanket ye can just snuggle intae. You don't need any other bedclothes. Oooh, lovely to get into. I think I may treat myself and our Mona to one for the winter-time. But what I was meaning to say to you was: I know she's mad about you and you're mad about her; I mean, a mother can see as much wi' her own eyes. I don't know what your plans are, Gordon, nor would it become me to ask questions—intrudelike, at this stage of the proceedings.

'And the long and the short of it is . . .' Mrs di Valvona said, as Mona Lisa's petticoats could be heard ascending the main staircase, 'this is the thing: ma Mona won't think of accepting any engagement ring under £250.

'They got some byeoties in Frank Hobbs and Partners,' she concluded.

The next morning, Moorman opened the window and a cold, overcast day touched his face. The cavalry twill trousers had been made for exactly such a day. He walked to the end of the pier, feeling snug under the fierce skies. Of course, he remembered Mrs di Valvona's remarks of the previous night; but his moods took no account of circumstances, or scarcely ever. As he stepped off the planks, on to the pierhead concrete he noticed a dredger butting the dark water a few yards out to sea. He thought: how wonderfully reassuring that there are still men who devote themselves to dredging.

He was early. There wasn't a breath of wind. Mary Kenny didn't look after the change desk today. Not a breath of wind, so he could look in all directions. Hardly a soul coming off the ferries; Taffy's announcements re-echoing round a deserted pierhead, with tar-coloured seas all around.

Leslie wore close-fitting white trousers and a V-neck pullover with no shirt underneath.

The rolls at the tea bar were fresh, soft, white. Moorman began: 'It came to me last night that perhaps we could try something else.'

'*Oh.* "Came to you", did it. What?'

'Did you hear about the grocer who put his tool in the till . . .'

'Tool in the till,' Leslie spluttered. 'Oooh, that by itself is funny.'

'A customer said, "You look very flush, Mr Jones," and he said, "Yes, well you see, I've just come into some money." '

When Leslie had recovered and wiped his eyes, Moorman said: 'What about self-service?'

'Service before self, that's my motto.'

'What about a self-service cafeteria. They make mints.'

'So do Murray's.'

Could they ever be serious?

'I'm not joking, Leslie.'

'A self-service cafeteria? That would cost hundreds of pounds.'

'Wouldn't the Bank . . .'

'They wouldn't.'

'Couldn't we,' Moorman said lamely, 'well, sort of make it ourselves?'

'But, using what?'

'I thought perhaps it wouldn't be too difficult if we could just get hold of a few second-hand chests-of-drawers.'

'A few what?'

'Second-hand chests-of-drawers.'

Leslie gazed at him as if he had really surpassed himself for reckless devilry, and pulled out a Gold Flake packet to see how the idea looked in a drawing.

'You are a one,' he said.

When they were in Bridewell Park on the Wednesday, Mona Lisa was rather disagreeably sick. As they had just come from one of the final lifesaving classes at the Blue Lagoon, Moorman was prepared to attribute this event to a fry-up or winkles and whisky for her tea. But she came back up the slope complaining of a terrible pain in her side, shivering. She coughed and doubled up on the spread-out Dannimac. Moorman grew alarmed and helped her down, along the Esplanade, past the Canoe Lake. 'Och, darling, I can't go much further on. Och, knives.'

Ahead of them was the shape of the parked Wolseley. Surely taximen gave service at all hours. Mona Lisa leaned against the sea wall, groaning. Moorman scraped his foot along the kerb, then tapped on the nearside window, hurting his shin on the running-board in his confusion. There was a rustle of newspapers from within; the window came down with hot air and a coarse challenge. Moorman denied that he was a special policeman. The driver and his lady had several packets of cigarettes in there, tins of Mackeson, and a box of Cadbury's Milk Tray. They might have turned nasty had not Moorman succeeded in making them believe Mona Lisa to be in need of a vital injection. Finally, the taximan agreed to take them back to the Tredegar Guest House. Moorman sat with his arm round her. The back of the Wolseley was so spacious that he couldn't touch the driver's partition with his feet. Through the yellow windows, the street lights made him feel peculiar himself. He noted with interest that the ashtrays were packed tight with petrified orange peel and that, left behind on the leather upholstery, was a leaflet advertising the Caryl Jenner Mobile Theatre.

Moorman stood whistling, turning quickly away to look at himself in the hall mirror, on the edge of things during the scene by Mrs di Valvona, the burst main in Hell that preceded Mona Lisa's removal to St Mary's Hospital for a perfectly straightforward appendicitis operation.

How funny life could be. The taxi that called for her was driven by the man who had taken Moorman to the end of the pier in his new suit; the man who had been given his dinner in bed. The tail lights drew away. He couldn't help thinking that it was all his fault, and that Mrs di Valvona, behind her mask of tears, thought so too. She accompanied her daughter to the hospital. The Tredegar Guest House was left oddly quiet, oddly Moorman's.

He went into the kitchen, picked up an old roll with cress dropping from it, looked at the cold sugo pan, and the fish fryer. It occurred to him to wonder why he had not been asked to go to the hospital. He went to bed and lay awake worrying, not eating the Kit Kat he'd been hoarding. He couldn't stop thinking about Mona Lisa's dark head, beautiful in its way, on a strange pillow and in pain. He even cried a little.

The next evening, he found her ringed by Italian friends and acquaintances who were knitting or reading copies of *Oggi*; all the fatalism of Continental people in a waiting-room or occupying a new set of trenches.

Mrs di Valvona was not in the ward, but stretched on a bed in a room down the hall, which was glass-screened, rather like a Japanese tea house. She was prostrate with fear and worry. She had a big lump on her cheek, caused by a Glacier mint, that moved about as she sobbed. The room was really for the use of relatives of the dead and dying.

On Mona Lisa's locker, on the moving table at her feet, metal vases held absurd quantities of tulips and daffodils, already palsied by the heat of the ward. Moorman, after only a few seconds broke out in a sweat. He saw strange and terrible old women cry out from surrounding beds, and whacked the enclosed playpen sides; deathly-pale, a girl sat up with tubes issuing in all directions from her, fixed by squares of plaster. An obese girl walked by, trying to smile, her dressing-gown was around her shoulders.

'Och, poor girl, she fell down a bank. It turned malignant and she's had to have an arm removed. But it was too late to catch it.'

Mona Lisa had the bedclothes drawn up to her chin. He bent and brushed her lips with his. She did her best to make sad and beautiful remarks, but could not contain her deep interest in the condition of the other women, nor disguise the fact that her own complaint was extremely slight. She whispered 'thinking of me?' and Moorman said he was. He couldn't wait to get outside. He was only human. He went directly from the hospital to the Tredegar Guest House, bounding recklessly past Mrs di Valvona's best room door; he put on the Ivy League shirt, so excited that the pins would hardly come out, and his new suit and the Christian Dior tie. He kept telling himself that he was only human. Then he hurried down to stroll languidly about under the illuminated peacock of S'Lots of Fun; he drank a number of cups of coffee at Sangiorgio's: he was even able to engage a girl in conversation as they both made a show of examining the equipment in the camera shop window. She was red-headed and quite awesomely formal in her dress. Moorman had seen her attending to customers in John Cox and Co., the small grocer's shop five or six doors along the Esplanade from Sangiorgio's. He sometimes bought Mars bars there. The girl wore a rigid mauve cocktail dress and red shoes, which clacked on the concrete shop floor as she disdainfully fetched frozen waffles or broccoli from the deep freeze.

On this slight acquaintanceship, Moorman persuaded her to drink a gin and lime in the lounge bar of the King Lud; but failed to get a laugh from her in the accompanying conversation. She was not interested in literature or his standing as an eccentric company director. He was allowed to see her home, via the darkening Esplanade, past the parked Wolseley. He said: 'You know, you really must tell me to shut up about literature.' The proper reply was: 'Oh, no, I like to listen to you.' 'Shut up about literature,' she replied.

They tilted for a while in the furthermost pagoda shelter. The girl kissed him but at the same time seemed to be propelling him away. In an attempt to get more comfortable, Moorman rubbed his cheek along the paintwork of the seat. Finally the three or four old age pensioners who had been sitting on the other side, got up and went away, making remarks. He turned and looked at the girl, hoping his eyes would bore into hers. All he got was a sight of her face, spittly around the chin, caught in the street illuminations; her expression definitely bored. Then he walked her home, for miles. 'My Dad built the rose arch,' she said, 'I reckon we ought to call our family The Archers,' and with that, disappeared.

That Conservative and Unionist Buffet Dance altered his life. The Royal Springbourne Hotel, where it took place, was an ivy-coloured building with false battlements. Its proprietor could never forget that in Coronation Year he had had made enormous papier mâché Grenadier Guards, which had stood on the battlements for the Queen to see as she reviewed the Fleet off Spithead.

The hotel did look like a small castle. It had done honourable service in two wars as a rest home for the wounded. Long sepia prints of this epoch were still hung about the hotel. Moorman always found the old-fashioned nurses a little spooky-looking, Angel of

Deathly with those large headdresses of theirs. The proprietor of the Royal Springbourne was, however, a bright little button. He was old and gold-pencilled but had a young wife, Peachy, and a Cadillac. He advertised at the Scala Cinema: The Huntsman's Lodge, a bar jumbled and nodding with wild-cat heads and assegais on the walls (he meant Hunter's Lodge) and the Children's Den, a fountain where the young might drink colas under the supervision of a qualified nurse. Set in the ivy of the hotel walls were all manner of coloured tablets: R.A.C., A.A., Coach Parties by Appointment, Antediluvian Order of Buffaloes, Springbourne Rotary Club. It was here that most of the large Italian weddings took place; the entire ballroom hired and little old men, risen from beds of pain in Dublin, come to give away the bride.

Moorman walked along the Esplanade towards the conservatory side entrance of the hotel. He watched as, gradually, the coloured plaques in the ivy formed themselves into letters of congratulation and of recommendation, suggesting wonderful steak dinners, cooked on the lamp.

He'd just been to the hospital again. He felt a cruel devil. Mona Lisa had been able to shuffle down the ward and back, holding his arm, her hair in a stiff lacquer disarray. After putting on his suit, he walked to the Esplanade, not down Dover Street—that was too public—down a parallel cobbled lane, so steep and uneven that the Council provided a handrail for the final descent: this brought him out opposite the Crazy Golf Course, about fifty yards on the pier side of the hotel. He'd told Mrs di Valvona that he'd passed on the dance tickets to 'two employees'.

Would his lies ever catch up with him? Moorman

walked and looked down at his feet, pleased by the way his turn-ups flew out ahead of him. He'd worked on the John White toecap shoes with Meltonian until every bit of the white mould was removed. He'd washed his hair successfully that morning. There wasn't at the moment a breath of wind. The sun slipped away, soft pinks and golds behind the pagoda towers of the repertory theatre, corrupted by the green glass panes at the rear of the municipal bandstand adjoining. The Esplanade was quiet. People, he thought, were still sweating over their boarding-house dinners.

But then again he felt downcast. It was the line of cars that did it: silver-lined and polished cases along the Esplanade pavement. He passed three, no four—it was *five* new Ford Zephyrs, all lettered with advertisements for Bristol cigarettes. Sometimes, when Moorman felt especially miserable, he would console himself with the thought that at least he wasn't a salesman: he didn't have to wear a serge raincoat with a belt and make himself small in front of shop customers or eat the fried eggs George Orwell had mentioned in one book, 'with a yolk so pale, it's paler than a lemon'. He rather thought the Tredegar Guest House would be in that style. But now, Moorman thought, life seemed to have managed to present him with most of the discomforts of being a salesman but no car. No commission, either, of course. He thought: you could make a nice little secure warm world inside a car; a rug, a nodding-head dog, little kits in tins, boxes of fruit pastilles. Even the salesman had his own little clutter of privacy, folders, leaflets; a kind of private furnishing no matter what miserable little bedroom he happened to be occupying.

Moorman avoided the hotel's main entrance because the arriving sports cars would have made him feel inferior. He entered by way of a glassed-over passage, past several early drinkers in basketwork chairs, then into the hotel foyer, of which the principal feature was an enormous glass case containing the stuffed head and shoulders of a lion. He turned left, past a cabinet of Delft china animals containing cherry brandy, into a lounge of which the principal feature was an enormous, grubby, rigged and balconied Dutch man-o'-war on a stand.

Ahead of him, down one or two steps, was the ballroom. Moorman could see a table, a money tray and a handsome chap of about eighteen, obviously sharing a joke with some girls in gold shoes. And my God, a distant dinner jacket. Taking his wallet out, clumsily, prematurely, Moorman went back through the lounge to get himself a drink in the Huntsman's Lodge. There was a richness, a security, in the phrase 'Gordon had a drink in the Huntsman's Lodge'. Actually it was very dusty and crowded, soaked Babycham mats and a toasted sandwich machine. He had to stand sideways and breathing in, stand between a lot of mirthful red necks, and brilliant stiff collars, until the woman behind the bar had satisfied all her favourites; they simply nodded or flashed their cuffs from yards away and she knew what they wanted.

Moorman bobbed and moved and kept meeting her gaze with both his eyebrows raised. Finally she agreed to give him a lager so badly poured that he could taste nothing but warm foam. The others stood about, holding half-pint tankards against their thighs; all the conversations were about Mike, with occasional Daves.

When he couldn't bear this any more he went into the foyer again, trying to shoulder his way through people like some reckless, heedless individual, a man of mystery. Going into the lounge he suddenly felt an enormous blockage in his nose and, with a lightning flick-away movement, had removed it; but it was nothing like the disposable object he had thought. This was a grey, curling, slithery-tailed devil, a proper oyster, impossible to let fall. And now Moorman was up to the entrance to the dance. Educated voices offered him the chance to win a Vespa; a man in a dark suit and Royal Artillery tie introduced himself as David Lallow, County Agent. The slithering finger horror! The County Agent passed him lightly down into the ballroom to shake hands with the Member of Parliament. What would the M.P., who was additionally a Q.C., make of that plump, fogged bogey if it were relayed to him? The M.P. smiled from a distance, genteely ferret-faced. In that instant Moorman saw his pepper and salt suit, the gold watch chain, the tie discreetly loud. All the man of mystery, the company director, could do was plunge his hand in his pocket and lodge that dreadful thing in the new black linings. His last thought, before he was greeted by the Member, enfolded in the heat of the dance and the music of the Stan Douglas Swingtet, was that he'd ruined the suit; he thought he would ruin it sooner or later.

8

He was absolutely the wrong sort of young man for this dance.

The right sort were all around him: about twenty years old, with long wrists and a piece of sun-bleached fair hair falling over their eyes. Didn't he happen to be wearing a very nice suit? Yes, but not the right sort of suit—three-piece, loose-fitting but expensive, the work of the tailor who in his window only exhibited yachting caps and a case of old medallions.

There was also, if he had a partner, the right way to dance. A lazy, amused grace. An exaggerated quickstep from the public school social, suddenly breaking into a few jive movements, one arm held up in a ring-a-rosy style, the gold links shown, as the girl on the end of the arm did all the work.

Moorman *should* have worn: either a yacht club tie, a school Double Colours tie, or a knitted silk tie. And a watch and chain, as if he'd had a very profitable twenty-first birthday. Also, a rigid cutaway collar that left a red mist on the neck—but the red suggested cologne and the face on the Gillette packet, not pimples.

These young men were all over the place. They controlled not only the topmost Young Conservative girls but also the ones lower down, the white cardigans and triple rows of chunky brown beads, Mona Lisa-weight bouffants and charm bracelets. There wasn't a girl in the room whom any of these trainee Members of Parliament could fail to captivate.

Facing the ballroom door was a small hatch bar. After shaking the M.P.'s hand, not daring to look into his face, Moorman crossed and was able to buy his second fizzy lager. Everyone else seemed to be dancing. He was served by a youth with eyes that crowded nervously around the bridge of his nose, and who wore a white bum-freezer and butterfly wing collar. 'Lager and loime, sir?' he asked in a bass voice. Moorman grimaced—a boulevardier offered the ultimate drinking insult, and shook his head patiently; unfortunately no impressionable girl saw this. At least, Moorman thought, he wasn't this youth, one of whose spots was on its way up, saucily, right at the tip of the end of his nose. Even so, he couldn't help wondering if the youth might not have rather a pleasant secure life in the hotel, sleeping close to the hot pipes, with each afternoon passed in the cool and quiet.

The dance floor cleared. He could see down the ballroom as far as the end; he could see the band, and a member of it in flashing spectacles, drinking from a stemmed beer glass.

Thick pillars went down each side of the dance floor; long tables with checked tablecloths went off at right angles, looking as if they belonged in American community picnics. Every table was full. People who wanted to get to the inner chairs had to squeeze and stumble past compressed backs of chairs. As more people drifted away from the far end, Moorman could see, above the band, a hanging box on which illuminated letters said INTERLUDE.

He bet he knew exactly what the Stan Douglas Swingtet were like. Bald men wearing sateen-faced suits. The whole scene reminded him very much of dances he had attended during R.A.F. service—the draughty village halls of Huntingdonshire, the girls in flyaway rim spectacles and their hoity-toity attitude—too glib; one of them lost her glasses and said 'Huh, that's ten quid gone west'; unattractive and glib. Elsewhere on the hanging box, another word presently lit up WALTZ. This was the signal for a glass dome in the middle of the ceiling to begin sending out flecks of pale colour, greens and oranges, up the walls, across the harassed bum of the poor youth searching for Canada Dry, over brilliant white collar back elevations at the tables, and the floor rustled with a crowd.

It was impossible to see if there were spare girls, even just to look. In the village halls of Huntingdonshire, Moorman's experience had been that in any case girls generally declined to waltz in a gloomy atmosphere with a stranger; or, if they accepted, backed away all the time, their stomachs drawn in for fear of being rubbed. He just stood there in the darts of light and was able to identify most of the waltz tunes, having heard them sung in the Pavilion's change desk by Leslie's Mary Kenny. He half wished he were sitting up in bed with a bar of chocolate reading *The History of Mr Polly* again.

Moorman went into the Gents to look in the mirror. He found a perfectly maintained little room, the pipes shining almost unnaturally. Over the door, continuing the hunt idea, a notice said 'Bucks!'

He bent his knees in front of the square of looking-glass and tried to comb his hair so that a piece would drop over his eyes. It was far too wispy to do tricks like that, as well he knew. Again he pinched and moulded the knot of his Christian Dior tie: to interfere with it much more would probably ruin it. But he thought he looked quite presentable, through half-closed lids. His fingernails were clean with toothpaste still in the crevices. He smiled. He thought: as long as he could smile at his reflection, he'd never go quite mad, then he wasn't so sure about this.

Moorman spun round from the mirror, convinced that the room was full of trainee Members of Parliament, chortling at his expense. But it wasn't. Only one person was at the stalls, consulting a vibrant fountain.

He turned: he was an old, old man in snake-thin patent evening shoes (that was Moorman's idea of a bespoke shoe) and a dinner jacket and black bow tie with a white horizontal stripe. Was this the bandleader? For a long time he stood on the step, shaking his old, old man's old, old man. Moorman saw that he was in his eighties, perhaps even in his nineties; the sort of old man Moorman imagined in just his vest, old, old jaws working with a dead lechery at the experience. Moorman couldn't help thinking of this old man's cock. It was not, he was certain, that he, Moorman, had any queerness in him. At least he had that to his credit: none at all. His interest in words was to blame. He knew that in this old man's case 'prick' was a misnomer. It would be so small and white and without prickles, exactly like a baby's button. 'Button' he thought far more appropriate or, yes, 'knob'.

The old man came down from the step, looking over half-moon glasses at Moorman. His mouth was relaxed, like one of the grey mullet. At once he began to talk to Moorman; his voice, though edged with complaint wasn't querulous, it simply made observations with the freedom of someone who knows he is wonderful for his age. (That, Moorman thought, must endlessly be passport to wicked deeds, hands up nurses' outfits, and contact with small boys' buttons: they had to submit if the attacker was wonderful for his age.)

'One thing an old chap like me can't be disturbed in and that's a peathful pith,' the slack jaw remarked. 'One thing you can't beat'—he was only pretending to lisp (wonderful for his age!)—'is a peaful piff. You cannot.'

Then he said: 'I've just bin bought a double gin and lime. I should imagine that was responsible for making all my waterworks red 'ot, wouldn't you? It was red 'ot just now, anyway. Young man, allow me,' This octogenarian Young Conservative gripped his sleeve and immediately let go again; a strong smell of T.C.P. 'Young man, my staff car was once cut in two by a shell. The driver lay dead beside it, cut in two hisself. Two distinct harves. I took a photo of the two harves there, and then, no, beg pardon, four harves since the tin lizzy was also bisected.' He remembered his lisp. 'Bifected. By the self-same shell.

'I was taking official war photos, as I did later at the Zeebrugge Mole, where a good many sailors, a good many failors never et another breakfast.

'My trouble at the time being: I 'ad to submit to painful furgery for an intestinal complaint. Thif resulted, the doctors said, in several feet of my inteftines being removed. A cable. Entirely done away with. It's just the same as a coiled spring and this is why at the present time, strain, ftrain, must be avoided at all cos'. You see, my pulling and straining might break the narrer whatsname. That is why strain must be avoided and a peaful piff is the thing.

'Would you say I looks ninety? I'm wonderful for my age, hey? Pa'rn?'

The house lights were turned on in the ballroom. Moorman's heart leapt at the sight of two unattached girls at the little bar. On the board it said archaically JIVE. Moorman knew that the twist was no longer performed, but had no idea of its successor. He thought of the Stan Douglas Swingtet. Rocking and rolling until all their narrer whatsnames popped and unrolled. He clutched the inside of his pocket, remembering what was lodged there. Trainee Members of Parliament gave it all they had; strands of sunbleached fair hair flew about.

The two girls had their heads together but he caught their conversation easily enough.

'Oh, that's where you met your little Ray of sunshine.' Nasal.

'He was sitting around with Mike Spooner and that lot.' About the same.

'"Little Ray of Sunshine." I like that.'

'Well, his name's Ray.'

'Mm, quite sweet really.'

'Nice clothes.'

'Well, I don't go much cop on his shoes.'

'He's rather sweet; all hairy and cuddly.'

'Does he tell corny jokes?'

'Not as many as Dave.'

'Is he getting all keen?'

'Little Ray of Sunshine?'

'Mmm.'

'He's a bit inclined to be dramatic and possessive. "I must see you tonight." You know.'

'Oh, Gawd.'

'But he's trying to pass the exam of the Institute of Grocers.'

'Wha-at?'

'The Institute of Grocers.'

They were dressed in combinations of dark brown. The worst thing, apart from the hunched housewifely shoulders, were the legs, which were simply straight like the trees in Bridewell Park. At least, he thought, Mona Lisa's rippled with muscle: these were just occupied nylons. Now he was uncomfortable again at the thought of her dark head on the pillow; he felt close to tears inside his third warm lager.

'I think I'm going to chuck little Ray of Sunshine quite soon though.'

'Are you?'

'I've got my eye on another lovely chappie.'

Two men arrived at the counter on Moorman's other side. One of them laughed and nudged his companion with such force that Moorman himself felt it, and winced and froze, as if a fight were about to start. His heart sank down on an ottoman as one of them said, 'Sorry, friend,' and went on: 'Watch it, nightingale. Look who's over there. The old ground sheet,' referring to one of the hunchbacks in brown. These two girls, for all their mean mouths, had now been surrounded by a group of loutish fellows, some of them in tweed suits, one in leather elbow patches. There was a good deal of laughter from the girls, mostly at the expense of the elbow patches.

As for Moorman, he found himself dislodged from the bar by a satanic-looking youth (they were all younger than he was) wearing a dark suit and plum-coloured waistcoat with gilt buttons.

He'd noticed this Young Conservative already, and

wished he could change places with him. He was at the dance with a girl who looked almost exactly the same: slim, taciturn. Were they brother and sister employed at the same branch of the Trustee Savings Bank? More likely young lovers employed in the same branch of the Trustee Savings Bank. They drank together, halves of cider, and spoke so calmly, with the self-sufficiency of people who take bike-rides together.

Moorman looked down the bar again. One of his thumbnails had a black rim now. The board above the Swingtet again said INTERLUDE. He'd have one last look around and then get back to his chocolate. He walked down the line of bar customers, horribly conscious of the beautiful girls it contained, pretending to look gloomy, tough, and abstracted. Naturally he was amazed and a little frightened when a ferocious-looking Young Conservative stepped out of the line in his way, saying, 'Excuse me, would you mind dancing with this young lady?' He bolted. There was a kind of shared chortle behind him. Out in the tiny Gents again, Moorman examined his damp double cuffs. The County Agent relieved himself and walked out, giving no sign that he had once shaken Moorman's hand. Standing in front of the mirror he gripped the lining of his pocket and encountered what he took to be a rolled-up bus ticket: the bogey. The bogey was now a cylinder. He'd go. At least the Kit Kat wouldn't let him down. Moorman walked back into the dance by mistake, having meant to walk out through the lounge. The letters spelled TWIST. He didn't like to look at the dancers, because dancing girls made him miserably, hopelessly randy. He noticed a blonde girl sitting by herself at the end of one of the check tablecloths, left by herself just for an instant by some freak of good-mannered pairing-off. Or else someone was fetching her a Pimms No. 1. She looked at him. This meant she would guess he only owned this one suit and had scarcely taken it off since buying it. The bogey rolled off his finger. Moorman tensed, expecting a crash.

'Excuse me, would you like to do this one?'

'I'm not very good at these, I'm afraid.'

'Well,' she said, 'Nor am I.'

Moorman went into the thick of the dance after her, feeling sick and winded. The blonde girl faced him and smiled broadly. Before anything else, Moorman noticed that she had a round forehead, very unusually round and sweet, and what is best called a full, generous mouth. Or, uncharitably, a largish mouth. Teeth of a worrying quality: brilliant.

Her skin was perfect. A quick check could find not one single mole nor freckle nor peak of dead skin. Soft, pink. On one wrist, she had a fine strand of bracelet with a tiny gold padlock on it. Her lips and shoulders began to move like the dancing girls on Top of the Pops; he *couldn't* bear it.

'Let's just do a normal one,' Moorman said.

She actually laughed *(laughed)* at the wisdom of this. They began a cool and reasonable quickstep on the spot, without the hint of the possibility of a reverse turn, as all round them, bits of sunbleached fair hair flew and sweated. Her cool, light hands. She said she was afraid her name was Diana Kingsley-Pink. 'Pink by name . . .' she said, looking down at her dress. Around the hem and square neck there was a kind of purple embroidered band. It was quite exceptionally short. With the coolness of her hands, the recovery of a damp collar and double cuffs, a cool breeze now in his armpits, Moorman could say: 'I think that's the prettiest dress in the room.' He knew this was well delivered.

'Thank you, sir. My great aunt made it.'

It was a lah-de-dah voice, rather deep. But Moorman was certain it was a voice he could easily amuse, especially if he pretended to be educated but also a bit tough.

'It's very unusual.'

'My dress? It came from an old bale of silk.'

'A very old bale of silk?'

'That's right.'

They stood still for a few moments. WALTZ flashed on and they moved in exactly as before. 'Well, tell me about it,' Moorman said, preparing to bring in the howitzers of his literary side. 'I love all old things: old manners, old wine . . .' (What was next?) 'Do you remember that from *The Rivals?*' he asked. (Was it *The Rivals?*)

'I do know *The Rivals* but I've forgotten most of it. We have a big day out about once a year with my stepfather, with things like Tussauds and the London Planetarium, but Billy loves musicals, so it's generally something like *Oliver* we see. Have you seen it? Actually the silk belonged to an old lady who lives with us. She isn't really my great aunt although I call her Aunt Het. She's my stepfather Billy's old aunt. The bale was up in her room for years, on top of a wardrobe with a lot of old furs and hatpins.'

Moorman, full of light and splendour, nodded. Her *stepfather*.

'She's not a very clean or well-kept old lady. Mummy wanted to disinfect this before it was made up. Mummy once had to shake the pepperpot over her head to get Aunt Het to wash her hair. But she occasionally brings out these marvellous old things, wonderful old things that have been in her room for years—albums with gold clasps. And, you know, silks. She can't see a lot any more, but she's still wonderful at needlework and crocheting, and she made up the dress for my birthday.'

'You're lucky,' Moorman said.

'Why?'

'I'm fond of old people. I haven't got a grandmother.' This was said with exactly the right amount of manly restraint and boyish wistfulness, although it wasn't exactly true: Mother was fifty-eight and, throughout living memory, had behaved more in the style of a marauding and unpredictable grannie.

Diana Kingsley-Pink looked at him very nicely.

'She made a beautiful job of your dress.'

'Thank you again. Aunt Het's really *marvellous* at embroidery. I wish I was. I took some dressmaking, but I used to just burst into tears and took it home for Mummy to finish off.'

He seemed to have been dancing with her all his life. When QUICKSTEP came up again, she said: 'Would you mind if we went on dancing for a little while longer? I'm enjoying dancing with you very much, and there's someone I particularly want to avoid.'

'Who's that?' He made his voice dead cold and menacing.

'An erky devil called Jack Wilde who keeps on at me to go up to London with him afterwards, to a club called the Bandy Parrot or something. At first I said, "Oh, yeah, anywhere, I don't mind," but I've discovered what a twit he is, and I don't want to get involved.'

'Shall I see him off? Which is he?'

'Well, if you spot a fat object who keeps going "mph mph mph" with his lips as if he'd tasted something nasty . . .'

'Oh,' Moorman said, on a note of celebration, 'a fatty buster!' Her laugh made him feel recklessly far outside obesity himself.

'He's awful. *Awful.*'

'Shall I bop him one smack dab on the pimple?' This was one of Leslie's expressions, but Diana wasn't to know. When she laughed, her eyes creased at the sides and her mouth opened wide, with the carelessness of people certain that their breath smells of fresh herbs.

'His father's fat, just the same as he is. Have you heard of him, Trevor Wilde, the art dealer? He's trying to get made High Sheriff. About twice a year they have a busload of oldies from all the homes to their house to look at the paintings; these two porkers running about, switching on little lights over pictures, as if the poor oldies *cared*. They never get tea, just flipping pictures. I think it's a swizz.

'Jack Wilde is just too bad. He's turned up at our house a couple of times without being invited, to swim and play tennis, and all he does is go "MHAH MHAH MHAH" and show us his fat red legs. I think if you bopped him one smack dab on the pimple, he'd just pop like a balloon.'

The box said INTERLUDE. They were leaning by one of the pillars talking. What was most amazing was how Diana was picking up his expressions and using them with evident pleasure, 'bop him one' for example. Moorman's excitement was a little reduced by the mention of swimming and tennis, two pursuits far outside him. He asked what she did.

'Well, actually . . . not a lot. I'm taking a few courses at the Shire Hall—cookery and flower-arranging and that sort of thing.'

'That's . . .'

'Bad. Because I'm getting so fat.' She patted herself. 'It's because we keep getting tastes of all the flans and things we make.' Her frankness about weight made him wonder if she might not say. 'You're fat,' when they were acquainted better. Then he looked at her delightful expression, remembered how cool he felt and stopped worrying. 'I'll just have to eat nothing but bananas and milk,' she continued, 'I mean, eat bananas and drink only milk.'

She pretended to square up to him.

'Now come on: you must tell me about you. What do you do? What's your name?'

'Rasputin.'

'Oh, come on—I've seen you in the town once or twice when I've been shopping. You don't work in a shop, do you?'

The heat boiled back in his blush.

'I thought you might be working in a shop in your vacation,' Diana quickly amended, 'You looked a bit like a student, you see.'

That was perfect: Moorman could now describe himself as a company director because she'd think he was so young to be so important. He said he was spiritually a writer but had been compelled to spend a year or two in business in order to earn the money he needed to devote himself to writing. He described the Pavilion, cracking it up as a sort of undergraduate jape. Diana Kingsley-Pink said, 'Oh, so it was *you* making those announcements!' He said she must come down and see the Pavilion and she agreed that she would. Moorman rested his arm against the pillar so that it almost touched her shoulder. It did touch her shoulder at the smallest movement. She didn't recoil. He sensed a profitable new line and asked if she had a middle name. This would indicate to her the perfectionist side of his nature, the quest for detail only natural in a writer.

'Ye-es.' She pretended not to want to say.

'What is your middle name? Go on.'

'Margot.'

'Margo?'

'Actually, Mar-*got*. The German pronunciation you know. Mummy came to England when she was eighteen. She's English in every way but she was born in Duisberg, you know, Germany. She was a shabby little thing in those days and I'm terrified of taking after her. She married my father in the war, but she was really far too young. Her old Mother, who's a real old German *Hausfrau* still lives over there but visits us. She almost drives my stepfather mad! "No, Billy, you must do this, you must do that." And she keeps putting little things on his plate at meal times.'

Moorman allowed an artistic pause, then asked if he could fetch her a drink. To his horror she appeared to hesitate. 'Well, that's a bit difficult because I came with a rather sweet little partner.'

He tried to be brittle.

'Will he be getting restless?'

'Oh, no, nothing at all like that, Gordon. I 'spect he's found himself a nice little floozy. He just comes and takes me to places when I haven't a proper partner, you know, and sometimes buys me fish and chips afterwards if I'm starving. He's a dear little fellow.

'But I am in a sort of party: with David Appleby, this little fellow, and some others there. Look: why not come and sit with us for a little while?'

Moorman pretended to think this over carefully.

'Who else will be there?'

'Oh, just little David and I suppose that flipping Jack Wilde, oh, and a couple of vicar's daughters, but no one takes any notice of them. They're man mad and I imagine they've latched on to some dreadful robots or other; it's just a race to get married as far as they're concerned. Jo and Caroline Ince. Come and cheer us up.'

He almost fainted with pleasure when she grabbed his hand and made a bit of a game of dragging him to a table and introducing him, a reluctant man of mystery, to the Young Conservatives seated there.

Moorman did stiff little bows which he knew amused Diana. There were two very tall girls distinguished by the suspicion of a hereditary harelip, and by ancient-looking floaty dance frocks, but with haughtiness and piety to carry off these misfortunes, and tiny evening bags. There was a fat youth in a very good suit, whose mouth moved as if it had lately been compelled to suck a private part, that old, old man's button, for example. 'Gordon's going to sit with us,' Diana said, and the fatty buster said, 'Wonderful'; he might have been saying, 'Wonderful for his age,' so Moorman could smile superciliously at him. There was a boy in a brown suit who seemed to take an immediate liking to Moorman. This collection talked to the other people of the table without actually being with them; comments were occasionally shouted down, but Diana's party just consisted of the six of them.

The little boy, David Appleby, was interested to hear about Moorman's years in journalism, and asked questions about it: What were the training schemes? The starting salaries? Moorman gave highly romanced answers. He was aware that the vicar's daughters were exchanging glances about him. Only one of them spoke to him. 'What's become of Seth?'

Diana interrupted: 'That's David's brother. He's wearing a blue suit with white stripes.'

'One of my Dad's,' the little fellow added pleasantly.

'He's much too much of a skinflint to go to Burton's . . .' When Moorman affected to pull a face, David Appleby said: 'As a matter of fact, I very much like the suit you're wearing. Jolly nice. Is it a Daks?' And Diana leaned forward, took one of Moorman's lapel buttons between a thumb and forefinger, leaned back again and nodded: 'Mmm. Very smart. Did you get it in London?'

He nodded, hoping the lie wouldn't pounce on him later. He said in a bantering voice: 'What I've really got my eye on in Burton's is a nice Lurex-threaded black jacket with cloth-covered . . .'

Suddenly Diana cackled and said loudly, 'Whoops, I thought you said Durex.' The vicar's daughters heads snapped away to the party at the next table. Jack Wilde closely examined a document from his wallet. 'Whoops, Kingsley-Pink's off again,' Diana said in a plummy voice, less attractive than her normal one.

Jack Wilde stood up. His tie was arched extravagantly out. 'How about a swift slow foxtrot?' Diana said she wanted to sit still for a minute: he glowered, his lips went 'mph mph mph' and he removed one of the vicar's daughters instead, and Diana made a face behind his back. A trainee Member of Parliament approached for the second vicar's daughter; then David Appleby himself got up. 'I really must strain the grapes,' he said, 'if I may use such an expression. On my way back, what'll you take? Have a drink.'

'Wash your hands,' Diana said.

'Oh, yes. Oh, yes.'

'I'd like a Dubonnet with ice and a bit of lemon. Not a bitter lemon. A bit of lemon.'

'Gordon?' It thrilled him to be called by his first name.

'A small Teachers if they've got it.'

'My word,' the little chap said. 'Connoisseur of whisky.'

He was completely deceived.

At one point when they were by themselves, Diana said: 'At last, someone really original.' And she said: 'Well, anyone can tell you've been a journalist: you're an expert at making people talk, talk away as if they'd known you all their lives.' Later she said, 'Forgive me mentioning it, Gordon, but you are *clever*. All your little jokes and voices. It's ages since I enjoyed myself so much.'

David Appleby brought them their drinks and then vanished after a girl he adored. With the whisky inside him (two whiskies, three heated lagers), Moorman said could he see her home?

'Oh, *there's* Seth. Over there. One of the Ince girls has finally collared him, it looks like. Jo will be livid. They both want Seth, you see.

'He *is* funny. Do you know, he doesn't seem to have got any older in about twenty years. He still giggles and looks about sixteen years old. He's never properly grown up. I remember when I was a little girl he called to take out my cousin Irena, he was in his twenties *then* and had a funny little threewheel car.'

So Diana Kingsley-Pink was simply being rather garrulously polite to him: she was just being nice to him: she liked him very much as a friend.

'Now seeing me home's a bit difficult because we live fourteen miles away at Hemingford Priory. Out in the wildes—oops, sorry, Jack. Why, are you very bored with the dance? What time is it: five to ten or five to eleven? Oh, ten. I mean, do you like it much here?'

His heart unfixed. 'Not much.'

'Well, you see, I promised Mummy I wouldn't be too late home because Honey our dog is about to have puppies. Couldn't you come back for a coffee or something? Do you have to go on anywhere? The only thing is: I'll have to go now, once I've made certain that little David Appleby is okay for a lift to Gransden. Jack can take the Inces: he deserves them.

'I must go now. It would be just like Honey to have her babies at night, and she's so hysterical, there's bound to be a fuss. You really don't mind acting as a sort of midwife? Oooh, and you don't mind me driving, do you? We won't have any head-on-ers.'

9

'I had nine weeks away from school altogether, with glandular trouble that flared up after this other thing. And for the fortnight, I had to be in the children's ward. Oh, there was a bitch on that ward. "Eat your mince," she'd say, or, "Have a cigarette, go on." I *refused* to smoke. Anyway, in the end, I got a private room because of Billy being the ear, nose and throat specialist; and that was quite fun.'

'You were in hospital nine weeks?'

'Yes, how long were you?'

'Six months,' Moorman lied. It had also been about nine weeks. He was planning a self-portrait; the studious little boy who wasn't expected to live; the little boy the doctors called 'The Professor'; but Diana interrupted.

'Phew! Gosh! As long as you didn't have to have all your sinuses washed out. That's frightful, that is.'

Moorman's knees were drawn up to his chin: it was the first time he had ever been inside a Mini van. They reminded him of fox-hunting. Diana herself looked funny at the wheel. This seemed to be set flat, like a bus-wheel. She'd just taken a bend quickly. Away, far to his left Moorman could see a brilliant interlaced spangling, the night lights of a power station. 'You wouldn't believe it,' Diana said, 'David's elder brother Seth—you know, the one who hasn't aged a bit—works over there. He just has to sit and read and turn on a few switches now and again.

'Let's wave to him,' she said, and one hand came off the steering-wheel and she flapped it lifelessly. Moorman was aware that she was doing most of the talking. He felt, in a friendly, cosy, quite confident way, that he'd like to put a stop to this for a while. All the same, keeping at bay a thought of Mona Lisa's head on the pillow, he couldn't help snuggling against the door on his side, enjoying the sensation of being driven fast by a girl.

They went into a ghostly maze of trees. 'They've had some rain here,' Diana said. 'Oh, out of the way, little rabbit,' as a small animal hurried into the grass at the side.

Moorman could lean right against his door because, before they left the hotel car park, Diana had leaned across him to secure a little catch, the hem of her camel-hair coat brushing that excited cylinder his leg. But he was unable to enjoy himself for long without worrying. Wavering trees reminded him of the drive back from the Woolpack on Christmas night, and the smell of Mother's van. Quite illogically, he was also reminded of being smacked over the legs. On the way from Lorna's the trees were just like this except that, he distinctly recalled, one had the words Labour Camp chalked or whitewashed on the bark.

'By the way, did you know that chap in the hotel just now?'

'Which one?' Moorman said.

'A little foreigner, I think. He was giving you a very funny look as we walked out.'

'No, I didn't.'

'He looked a lot like that actor who was in *Attila the Hun*.'

'I didn't see him.'

'He gave me a funny look as well.'

Moorman wasn't really listening. He thought that another odd feature of these Mini vans was the little winking bulb on the arm from the steering column. Mother had to hang her arm out of the window. The bulb puffed green like the cheeks of the toad in *The Living Desert*. Puff-green, puff-green. After Diana's abrupt turn into the wood the indicator had failed to right itself, so her face was illuminated in blinking pale green. This appeared to accentuate her nose and (Moorman thought) a sort of cleft of weak skin between her eye and the bridge of her nose. In this light, her nose seemed a fair size and hooked. But she had kicked off her shoes in favour of some driving slippers and was showing a lot of leg. The spread of her legs on the pedals looked exciting. So did the way her blonde hair swung forward in profile with her nose.

They rounded another severe bend, Diana saying, 'The-ere we go.' Large moths flattened themselves against the glass. It was so noisy, and Moorman didn't have the kind of voice that was raised successfully. He was becoming desperate for something to say. Was it true that a Mini van cornered dangerously? She shook her head. Was this her mother's van? Diana said that she and her mother shared it; Billy had bought it for them.

'Anthony Quinn?'

He stared.

'That was who the little foreigner in the hotel looked like; the one staring at you. Oh, those moths make a noise. Splattt! ! !'

'I've just realized something.'

'Can you speak up? It's so noisy.'

'Well, I've never been inland on the island before. Only on the fringe of it. I've only just realized we're going inland.'

'Oh, yes, ducks,' Diana said, putting on a voice. 'Bit of class inland. Evening dress all day and grapes in the house when everybody's well.'

'Where do you live exactly?'

'It's called Hemingford Priory. The village *and* our house. Billy's house that is.' Diana began to talk very rapidly and fluently again. Moorman felt worried by her superiority in conversation; he felt he wasn't dazzling her but could think of nothing to say. He waited like a cat with a bell round its neck at the end of her sentences, waiting to say, 'Where the *hell* is this?' with a sort of perplexed, amusing masculinity as soon as she left a pause between statements, but she didn't.

'Mummy was keeping this little pub called the Eight Bells all by herself, and Billy used to keep coming in and finally he proposed. He sent me right off to Overstone School in Northants—you know, Overstone. He's been very good to us all really. He just gave us this van and a rocking-chair for my last birthday; and he's spent hours in his little workshop making hobby horses if the Gleaners are doing a little pantomime for the old folks. He loves making up little plays and doing all the words and music and trying to play all the parts by himself, and he . . .'

'Where the *hell* are we?' said Moorman, too late to stop himself. Her blonde hair swung round. 'What's the matter, are you bored?' she asked sharply.

'Oh no,' he gobbled against the noise of the Mini van, 'Oh, no, I'm not, really. I . . . I just couldn't place . . .'

'Well, so long as you're not bored; I mean, say so if you are bored,' Diana said crisply. 'I do go on rather a lot. Tell me to shut up.'

Moorman's head snapped to the front. He almost screamed. He felt his eyes screwing up and his heart wringing. The van was hurtling, rushing headlong down an extraordinarily steep hill, but it slowed down, ground down to a human speed and then grew much slower as they climbed up the other side.

'This is the Cinques. You know, French—CINQ etcetera. I haven't a clue why it should be called that. Billy's got a little book, or Aunt Het has, where it's all explained but I forget. And there's Neville's pub, the one Mummy used to keep, so we go in there just for old time's sake. He's got naked women stuck on the wall in the Gents. We live about three miles from here, on the other side of Whitefield Woods.'

'Is it a nice place, the village?'

'It's the village where . . .' her words were drowned by gear changing and she gave another of her cackles, which made him feel she was becoming just a little too uproarious at her own jokes, and was forgetting his brilliance, if she ever had thought him brilliant. How he wished he had a voice that could penetrate the roar of these little things. He could see very little but occasional glimpses of that unusually delicate forehead, which seemed quite out of place with a cackle like hers. But then she turned to him, smiling rather than laughing. 'All the children in Hemingford Priory have got ginger hair. Almost all. And *we* believe this can all be laid at the door of old Mr Noakes, who's generally sitting on the seat under the clock wiping his ears. Just think: he's all of their Daddy. Aaah, sweet.' Moorman wished she would say 'Aaaah, sweet,' as a reference to himself.

'Naughty old gent,' he said, with confidence, and she reacted well to that. His felt his lips getting ready a mention of the old, old snare drummer in the Gents at the Royal Springbourne Hotel. But he dared not; he dared not mention bodily functions to her, even though she seemed quite at home with them.

The Mini van stopped. Diana said: 'Here, don't think I'm awful and crude but I've simply got to nip in the bushes for a minute.' She hissed through her teeth and slammed the van door. He heard her feet on the grass verge and desperately listened to avoid hearing what must follow.

Moorman himself was, of course, madly anxious to pee. It had begun at the table at the dance, set off by excitement and the unexpected compliments. Then he'd forgotten all about it as one does. Now the pressure came playfully back, Hannibal and his elephants battering. He couldn't hold it up for another millionth of a second but he would. He remembered his first night in hospital, sitting up all night under the assault, too embarrassed to ask for what he had to ask for. Should he jump quickly out and pee in the road? She wouldn't mind. Moorman could hear an extra rustling in the night. But he couldn't now, not now, because she'd know he had wanted to go when she'd first stopped the van but had been too bashful to say so. The very whisper of the trees seemed to encourage Hannibal's elephants. He thought, involuntarily, of fountains. He hissed, as she had, and that made it worse still. He was alone in the middle of the night on a lonely road in a beautiful blonde girl's van and *this* had to butt at him. Mother's view was that if you held it, you couldn't go in the end. Moorman fumbled at his left sleeve until he found the little metal catch to unlock the door. There was the faint possibility of opening it swiftly and scattering, from where he sat, the most thrustful of the elephant battalions: no, no, no, no, one might drench the mat or one's toecap shoes, making them all white again, he was dreadfully frightened of putting a sour smell in the van; and here she was again sighing with relief. The van raced away again. Could the pressure be any greater? Much! She said: 'Mummy came over here from Duisberg originally to train as a nurse. When she wanted me to do a twinkle in my potty, she used to go Pss Pss Pss Pss and it always worked.' It certainly did. It brought them on, the elephants, quicker than fountains. Moorman almost bit his knees.

'It hasn't made you want to go, has it?'

'Oh, no.'

'That's good, it does most people. Oh, I do hope Honey hasn't had them yet.'

'Who?'

'Honey. Had the puppies. I do hope Billy'll be there because Mummy might get in a state. He might have been held up at the hospital, you see.'

'The hospital. Is he having some treatment there or . . . . is he ill or something?'

Diana cackled again. Moorman didn't like it. Then in an affectedly world-weary fashion she said: 'No-o, he's a sort of ear, nose and throat man, at the same time as being a V.C. and a sort of farmer, breeder, all sorts of things. I'd tell you, but you'll find out when you meet Billy.' That was the trouble. He would wither up in front of this superhuman doctor. The van slammed to a halt once more, headlights cutting away into the dark, insects dancing on to the windscreen and escaping. 'Hoi,' she yelled out, 'hi. Is that Miss Margaret? *Oi*. Over here!'

'Who is it?' He was petrified.

'Ssssh a mo.' She had twisted in her seat, for a moment revealing suspenders, underslip, dark frilled pants; suggesting a tall, slim schoolgirl not quite used to these engines. 'I thought I saw someone nip across the road; someone I know. I bet it was. It *was*. Oi! I say.'

'Who?' Moorman bleated.

'Miss Margaret! Over here!'

A face appeared close to hers.

'E-Lo.'

'El-o, my darling,' Diana said.

'El-o, my darling,' said the face. Moorman could see now that it was hideously ugly with a red gash for a mouth, like a wound, a square-face, a lantern jaw with cosmetics on: the voice, gravel. 'Well, well, well, well, you're out late. Oh, no, you're not at all really; it's not eleven o'clock yet, is it?'

'Ten to,' Diana said.

'Where've you been?'

'The Y.C. do at Totland, I mean Springbourne.'

'Oh, that.'

'Yar.' (He hated educated girls who did that for Yes.)

'What was it like? Nice?'

'Blooming awful,' Diana said; and he felt associated with it.

'Well, I'll tell you something; I can't stop because I've got Dennis's whatsisname here, and I want to go down the bridle path to give it him before he goes home.'

'Well, anyway, meet Gordon.'

The dreadful face inclined towards Moorman and gave a nod. 'Howdy-do.' That voice, now that he'd had time to accustom himself to it, sounded less like a monster's and more like an over ripe principal boy's. The face was made-up but no worse, really, than rugged.

'This is Miss Maxey, the famous Miss Maxey.'

'Of Renown,' said the face, and Diana cackled. Diana's cackle! Moorman was thinking how he must always curb the conversation, steering it like a dodgem around topics that amused Diana so violently. He'd forgotten what she looked like as well.

'Now I'll really have to cut orf if I'm to give Dennis his doings before he locks the church up so. Goodbye and tell Mum I'll be up Thursday for my game of cards. Cheer-ho.'

Miss Maxey moved in front of the headlights. She was, to outward appearances, a man. She was dressed in tartan, a coat that shone enough to be velvet, a white shirt, bow tie and wellington boots turned down. She nodded in the lights and smiled; and then walked away. Her arms were encumbered by something that looked like a dead Victorian baby, with the lace folds hanging—a vicar's surplice. Holding this carefully out, she leapt a ditch and was gone.

'Miss Maxey launders the vicar's things,' Diana explained.

'She's a . . . is she much of a character?'

He braced himself for a cackle but Diana simply answered: 'I'll say. Great character's not the word. I must tell you all about Miss Maxey and you can write a story about her.'

That was better. 'Oh, I'm . . .'

Diana cackled. 'Her father wanted a little boy and called her Jim until the day he died. *She* says anyway. The Dennison Swords, who live opposite, are always complaining about the tricks her pigs get up to in the field. She's tougher than any man. And she doesn't like cleaning and cooking very much; once when she spring-cleaned her room she discovered a little bird's skeleton under the bed. Oh, and she's always in our little pantomimes, the things that Billy organizes. Usually she takes the part of Ali Ha Ha, the robber chieftain, because she loves to put on an artificial nose and wave a cutlass about. In fact they sometimes have a disagreement because they both want to do it *all:* write the words and the music and sing and act and dance and read the commentary.

'Yes, I must remember to tell Mummy that it's Thursday that she can come and play cards. The two of them sit and get sloshed while Aunt Het sits there, taking it all *dead* serious, sipping her tonic wine.

'Miss Maxey likes to be called Miss Margaret. She thinks it's more "stately", she says.

'I must tell you again about this little buzzbox of a car of hers, made about a hundred years ago. She *mended* her own gearbox with a bit of wire. She runs about these woods at night like a hare. If she was threatened I think she'd just run the fellow through with her enormous bunch of keys or just shoo him off. She's got one brother, Johnny, who married a girl named Nadine Lois . . .' Diana cackled, 'but he emigrated to New Zealand or one of those places. All Miss Margaret ever hears from him is that he's earning a pound an hour washing cars or else he's got a bigger motorbike, and he can hardly read or write. He signs his name "Johnny" in a mixture of big and small letters.' She cackled.

'One of these days, Billy's just going to be going out of here, and there'll be a head-on,' Diana said, the van's winker puffing green. He felt as if he'd been listening to her for hours. He was still madly excited by her. He thought she was a bit too preoccupied with car driving terms. He'd said very little and had begun to feel car sick and thrown around.

They turned into a driveway. The lights revealed aristocratic red crumbled brickwork opposite a darkened station yard.

'Before Billy gave us our van I used to have to catch my train from there; it's Hemingford Priory Station,' Diana said, 'There's a pub there too, The Sultan. Isn't it a nice name?'

They went down a farm road: the moon came on suddenly so that Moorman saw poplar trees on either side and the silhouettes of farm buildings and unusual tubular metal gates. In front of them a blank wall seemed to jump up. Diana swung and squeaked the Mini van round the sharp corner and up on a grass verge, the front wheels against a white boulder. 'Billy is in,' she said. There was a big black car humped on to the verge just ahead. 'Can you get out all right that side, or will you have to squeeze out of mine—all right?'

Moorman hauled himself through the half-open door, steadied himself against the wall and smelled a beautiful grass-scented night. Sometimes, very rarely, he found it pleasant to shut his eyes and pretend to wake up suddenly: how on earth did he come to be standing here, at the T-junction of a farm road, with insects noisy in the grass? He bent back his head and screwed his eyes shut again. Didn't it all show what a devil of a fellow he was? Obviously, to touch Diana Kingsley-Pink at the junction of her own farm would be a grave tactical error but mightn't he take her hand and lead her quickly inside: he *understood* that she was worrying. Unfortunately, Diana was some distance away; an iron gate in the wall opened, clink. 'Okay?' her voice came in the darkness, but in such a brotherly tone, 'mind the stones. Don't trip.'

They walked up a curving path to an open front door with an inner glass-fronted door that was closed. There was, above the outer entrance, a very strong naked light bulb with heavy insects performing round it: not a naked bulb, as Moorman now saw, but a round naked light globe with a metal guard, reminding one of concentration camp perimeters. In front of the open door was a large mat which, as they trod on it, squelched, like bowel sounds. He wanted to say something funny about this but she was urgent to get inside.

Inside the open door she bent and pouted her lips in front of a mirror above a table, then rattled and pushed open the glass-fronted door, and threw her coat on a carved wooden bench. Moorman saw once again, the legs, the short pink dress with the purple band. There was no chance now of her hand.

There was a narrow hall with wood panels going straight ahead and a staircase to the right. Diana marched by the side of the staircase to a door which must have led to the servants' quarters once. She opened the door with a pull and had to lean forward, the blonde hair swinging forward, so that Moorman's heart quickened all over again, to loosen the catch on an unpainted wooden gate. 'Billy's put this up already,' she said. 'Heavens, he must be expecting about a hundred puppies.'

Moorman found himself in a little white-painted hall with faded red coconut matting on the floor. He felt slightly underground. Along the side of one wall stretched a deep-freeze which occasionally shuddered to itself. Several doors opened from the hall. Diana yelled 'Mummy', opened and shut one door rather fast. 'Nothing but an old crow,' she said. She tapped on another door, and pushed a third open. Moorman followed her into a kitchen lit by neon tubes so brilliant that he had to shut his eyes for a moment.

He looked at a white flash of light caught behind his eyelids, and then at a pretty little woman, very sunburned, who was leaning against the Esse cooker and drinking from a mug. She seemed to have been making clucking noises towards a covered birdcage on a stand. This was a very high-ceilinged room; a tall window behind the birdcage had a little plastic fan set into one of the panes.

'Oh, Dinah, you're here,' the little woman said in a hurry, but by no means crossly. 'I haven't got to sit through this by myself.'

When she said 'sit through', it came out as 'sit sroo'. 'And Billy's in the compound with my dear baby Honey now. I just know she'll hev a difficult con . . . confinement. I've shut Aunt Het in the schoolroom with a tin of petits fours.'

Diana's mother gave Moorman a charming smile. Her face was brown and a little puggy. She wore a blue shirt and trousers. He saw with surprise that the Formica-topped table was already laid for the next morning's breakfast.

She looked Moorman up and down—admiringly. 'Isn't he nice and (end) tall? How tall, six foot one, six foot two? Couldn't we find a part for Gordon in our next pantomime (pentomime)? Anything to keep those blinking Ince girls at bay. What was it like, the Y.C. do, children? Hev some tea?' She picked up a tinny-looking pot from the stove's black and put a stream of tea into one of a cluster of mugs standing there.

'She's bound to be hysterical, you know what she's like if you so much as touch that leg of hers,' Diana said, and pressed her backside against the Esse as if for warmth, hands behind her.

'Oh, Gordon—I can call him Gordon, can't I?—I seem to be fated with historical dogs . . .'

'Hysterical, Mummy—oh! she's off.'

'Hysterical, I mean. Remember (Shremember) Zola, Dinah? How she tried to bury her puppies? She thought (sought) she had done something (somesing) wrong; and yet Miss Maxey insists that labradors are the only ones wis brains.'

'Yes,' Diana said, with gusto, 'our other dog buried all her puppies in the garden. Mummy just happened to go outside and she heard these little squeaks and saw the ground moving.' Diana cradled her mug in her hands, 'Oh, we just saw your friend and mine . . .'

'Who's zat?'

'Miss Margaret.'

'Where was zis?' Diana told her: 'On the bridle path.'

'Going on the bridle path in Whitefield Woods at zis hour? Shocking. I suppose she was on her way wis old Ince's smock.'

Moorman, hoping to be languid, sipped his tea, which tasted vaguely of the thin metal pot. Diana pulled out a chair for him and then went to lean against the enormous old-fashioned sink, a very wide and shallow orange sink. Questioned by her mother, Moorman repeated the lie about being in business to earn money in order to write. This quickened her interest in him.

'Hev you read *The Bramble Bush?* Oh, it's very schrude but byeodifully written, I sink. I've got upstairs a little shelf of books that I call my Schrude Shelf. I've got'—she counted on her fingers—'I've got good old Lady C and *Peyton Place* and *Forever Ember*. Did you read Lady C when zere was all zat cufiffle about it?' And Moorman was able to deliver a neat reply: Leslie Langdon's remark about *Lady Chatterley's Lover,* and how it would have done perfectly well as a short story. He had not, in fact, read it.

Diana's mother heard a door open in the passage and gasped and ran out of the kitchen. She had a neat behind.

'Poor Mummy's almost going out of her mind,' Diana said.

He was about to say something about her mother's good command of the language, but checked himself. At least he always thought twice before saying something. That was why most of what he said was so brief and dull. He asked if the dog was very difficult by nature and in reply Diana turned her head towards him so that her hair swung forward again. He got up and leaned against the edge of the sink next to her.

Moorman thought: she's about nineteen.

Despite all that confidence and knowledge of cars and fluency, even the cackling, she's just outside of being a schoolgirl. He remembered the enthusiastic way she had turned round in the Mini van's driving seat, showing her pants. Her skin's like a baby's, and her lips have never received anything bad, or expelled it . . . he shifted his backside against the sink and at once crossed his legs because . . .

Her mother put her head round the door. 'It's schreally started,' she told them, her words scrambling in the excitement. 'Oh, and it's coming out the wronk way shround. I knew it! Dinah: just help Mummy by seeing that Aunt Het stays in the schoolroom. There's a darling.'

'Your mother calls you "Dinah".'

'Yes.' There was a pause as she strained her ears and Moorman pretended to strain his. 'I wonder if we'll hear the squeaks. It's all typically chaos—trust our Honey.

Mrs Gray at the kennels said Honey ought to have puppies for the sake of her health. She was,' (no perceptible pause here), 'mated with a beautiful big labrador named Gunner. Honey just turned round and stared as much as to say "what the flipping heck's he supposed to be doing"?' (Moorman noticed that she was introducing more and more funny voices into the conversation.)

'Poor Mummy—she'll go up the wall, I think, if Honey produces just the one. She's already promised one of them to the Inces, anything for nothing there! And then Mrs Gray has to have the pick of the litter.'

Moorman remained silent. He thought morosely of his small experience of dogs—Miss Toye's blind poddle, Mrs di Valvona's poodle with the underside medium rare and its unnatural interest in the curves of Uncle Grimaldi's arm. He thought he might tell her about John Close's little dog, or else remark that he always had preferred large to small dogs. He decided on: 'Where's the birth taking place?'

'Next to the schoolroom. That's why Mummy says to keep Aunt Het out of it.

'There's a long sort of cloakroom place full of old wellingtons and tins of Min cream, where Billy likes to keep some of his bits and pieces.' She cackled. 'When Mummy first saw it she said she wouldn't mind sleeping in there herself, 'cos Billy's such a difficult man to sleep with, you see. He'll sit up in bed and crunch an apple or eat a whole bar of Toblerone.'

Her mother looked round the kitchen door again and made another face as if she'd been stabbed in the back.

'What's happening, Mummy?'

'Only one little baby so far and—ugh!—it's got zis blue tummy. Isn't that just our luck?' The door closed and Diana shouted, 'Can we do anything?' Her voice replied: 'Just keep Aunt Het out of ze way.'

'Poor Mummy. She was so worried last night that she got a bottle of port out and we started knocking it back and putting it away when Billy came out of his workshop. After a few drinks Mummy puts on her little girl expression and opens her eyes wide like this.' Diana looked round at Moorman with an astonished expression.

He kissed her; in a flash.

The tempo of her voice didn't change, but she did blink for rather a long time. Then: 'We always have a rather special little go with the port on Christmas Eve: mince pies and the hymns from King's College Chapel. And a few tears as well.' Moorman forgot the kiss and its possible effect at the mention of Christmas; and in the anguish of imagining what limitlessly warm, amiable Christmases took place in this house.

'I think I'll have another cup of tea,' Diana said, with just the required hint of recovering her breath. 'Would you like a bicky?' She took an ancient circular tin out of a cupboard and poked her fingers around in it for a biscuit with cream in it. Moorman thought how embarrassed Mona Lisa was when compelled to put food in her mouth in front of him; how she pretended to pick at her food but, in reality, tore at it; he'd once surprised her with a piece of cake.

Diana's tongue came out after the crumbs.

'You mustn't get the idea that we're unkind to Aunt Het,' she said. 'I've told you that Mummy put pepper on her head to get her to wash her hair. But that was for her own good, wasn't it?'

Her voice quickened again, got into its stride. 'She used to be in charge of all the food here. She used to lock it all up and keep the key in her bloomers. Billy used to spy on her in the bath . . . Hel-lo.'

Her mother came back into the kitchen and leaned against the rim of the sink with them, her arms folded. This made Moorman feel rather important. 'Well,' she said, 'Sat's zat.'

'How many puppies?'

'Vun. A pig fetty one wis a blue stomach. Oh, trust my Honeybunch to let the Vicar down. How on earth's Mrs Gray going to hev the pick of a litter of vun?' Her face suddenly dissolved in smiles, a very attractive habit of hers. 'One thing, if Honey tries to bury it, it's pig enough to resist, isn't it?'

'Oh, Mummy, say "big" not "pig".'

Her mother widened her eyes like a small child. 'Oh, did I make a balls-up? But she *is* a pig, the blue tummy. Pig and *fet*. But zat's not as bad as when I said "listen to the smell" . . .'

They all laughed and it took hold of Moorman; he couldn't stop laughing; he shook with it.

'Silly old cow,' Diana said. He jumped, but her mother just went on smiling. 'Where's Billy?'

'He'll cut the cord and settle them down for ze night. Then I expect he'll retire to his den and go "zzzzzz" over the words and music, fest asleep.' She turned to Moorman and said: 'My husband gets so *cross* if anyone interrupts him while he's doing the words and music for our little amateur dremetic lark. You know, Dinah, that's only a week or two away now and we hevn't hed a proper rehearsal yet. Billy gets *fchurious* if we don't know ze words.'

'It's the Inces—no one wants to rehearse because no one can stand them,' Diana said, rolling her eyes.

Moorman suddenly realized that Diana's mother was eyeing him up and down; he felt like a pageboy being given the once-over by a roistering Duchess and it excited him very much. Surely she . . . 'I'm sure ve could find a part for Gordon, you know, darling.' She counted up on beautifully kept nails: 'Billy's playing Cassim Cursim and Miss Maxey's playing Al Boloni—it's a mixture of the Babes in the Wood, and the Forty Sieves, Gordon.'

'*Thieves,*' Diana said.

'You and I are the babes, sweetheart, and the Ince girls are the Forty—*thieves*—and ve need little acts for the third part of the programme. It's not acting, Gordon, just mucking around for ze over-sixties, and a little tea party afterwards, and ze Vicar's few words.'

Her command of county English, with comic-book German sounds, was extraordinary; it was continually exciting. Moorman found himself hanging on to her words. He also got an erection.

'I expect he works very hard at his job and hasn't got time to be in it. Hev you?'

Moorman, glowing, nodded.

'Vell, you could be a robber or somesing; I'm sure Billy would love to find a part for you. He's got a little dance all worked out for the robbers and the music's taped and everything; he *loves* it. "The Entry of Ze Gladiators" or somesing. Stay here a minute, children, while I go and make quite sure that my pussy dog is all right wis her blue baby.'

'Are you quite sure about no more tea?'

Moorman saw a grand opportunity to be a little boy. He said, as if confessing, 'Well, actually, I'm fonder of cold milk than tea.' In fact, he could scarcely remember drinking it in any quantity since the ritual third of a pint at school, with the occasional threepenny Festival of Britain bar of chocolate.

Diana smiled at this; her blonde hair swung forward

as she jangled the doorknob of a door next to the sink; a door impossible to open unless the kitchen door was shut. Moorman, looking in after her, felt a coolness in his face. He saw a very big stone-floored pantry with marble-topped shelves. He glimpsed brimming basins of potatoes and sprouts, enormous bread bins and stacks of cartons of Bonio. Diana picked up one of a row of pints of milk and filled a glass with a heavy base for him. After the first couple of draughts of milk, Moorman wished he hadn't mentioned it at all. His tooth began to ache violently. Diana offered him a biscuit and sorted round the tin again, as her mother put her head round the door.

'Oh, I sink it vill be all right,' she said. 'It vos just a very *pig* puppy.'

'Mummy! *Big* . . .!'

'Pig, big, who cares?' She went into the pantry and came out with two little oranges in one hand. 'I'm off to my little bed, sweetheart, to get vot sleep I can before Billy starts grumping and tossing around. Don't be too long now. Vy doesn't Gordon come over on Sunday?'

Moorman made an agonized movement; half grabbing an imaginary engagement book from his inside pocket, half covering up his floppy self at the thought of having to go into the pool. 'Oh, I ah, mm, love to,' he said almost inaudibly.

'That's fixed then. Make a day of it. Does ze poor darling vork on Sundays?' she asked Diana.

'Yes, he does.' Moorman was elated. Her tone implied that she'd soon alter *that*.

They stood interminably on the outside of the glass-fronted door, next to the mirror above the table. Outside the squelchy doormat and the insects dancing in front of the harsh bulb. Moorman didn't know which way to look: at her, at the glass of the door, with faint intimations of the red carpet on the other side, at the mirror. He panicked and said, 'Well,' and stepped down on to the noisy doormat. Pretending to stagger. 'Which way's civilization?'

Diana laughed and replied: 'Well, you just keep straight ahead to get to the way we came in. If you go to your right you come out on to our lawn and if you walk across that, you end up in the park – a rough park, you know, part of the grounds.'

'I see,' he pretended to be brief and sharp. 'And the pool?'

'That's at the top of the garden.'

She added: 'But you'll see that on Sunday afternoon if you can make it; please say if you can't.'

She was above him in the doorway; he below on the great wet mat. He pretended this was simply the beginning of a stylized farewell and put his lips to her cheek, which she immediately inclined. Then he moved his face up to hers. For a second it seemed that she might clamp her lips together, then she was moving them lightly; and Moorman felt cold and careful and so breathless.

He put his face up again and was received if anything, more cordially. Her lips, cool and mobile as if they'd never been touched before. Her head worked with a delight in kissing: Moorman felt like jumping up and down. He put his face up again to hers and a tiny end of her tongue pushed his excited teeth. Then he stood back, able to think of an assortment of fitting remarks.

'That was very sweet of you,' Diana said, first.

'Shall I see a lot of you?' He lowered his voice. 'Who else are you going out with?'

'Oh, no one. You see, I rather shock most people.'

'Well, you don't me.'

'I feel as if I've known you for years.'

He kissed her again, his hands skidding over the pink silk of her dress, and feeling the tight small of her back.

He felt giddy. He felt hysterical. He drifted his face upwards to hers *again,* and suddenly there was a disjointed whistle and the inner glass door opened. Diana straightened up.

A man in a double-breasted blazer and stiff-collared shirt (a man wealthy enough to be able to mess around the house like that) walked out, jingling money and keys in his pocket. 'Hulloa,' he said (not 'Hello'), 'excuse *me*' and he walked between them, jingling, and vanished down the path towards the iron gate. When they couldn't see him he called back: 'Keep that door shut if you can, because of the nits. There's any amount of them getting into the house.' He had a growling voice. The gate pinged shut after him.

'That was Billy,' Diana said.

'Oh.'

'He gets so worked up about little tiny things. The nits getting into the house, as if that could possibly matter. He never swears—never says anything more than just, "Damn, Damn." What does it matter if blinking nits get into the house?' She cackled (the doorstep scene was therefore ruined) and put her hand to her mouth. 'Oooh, I wonder if Mummy turned my bed on.'

'Your bed?'

'My blanket on.'

'Oh, a bed blanket.' (Appalling how he had adopted an expression of the di Valvona's.)

'*Bed* blanket, that's rather sweet. Yes, I have it on all year round, you *bet*. And wear my bloomers for most of the year—lovely!'

There was a car noise from the other side of the wall. 'He'll put his car away. *Then* he'll probably think of something he wants to do around the farm and go off with the big torch Mummy gave him, to look at the pigs. Then I expect he'll go back and write some more words and music and finally go to bed and wake Mummy up at about two o'clock. He thinks nothing of sitting up in bed and crunching an apple, you know, or a whole bar of Toblerone . . .'

'I'll try to come on Sunday.'

'Sorry. I do go on a bit and repeat myself: you must tell me if I do.'

'I won't have . . .'

'Mummy said—you heard her—come to tea and supper with us. If a growly voice answers when you ring up, just ask for me, all right?'

'I'll be in touch,' Moorman said.

He was getting ready to melt romantically away into the night. First: a last kiss, a telling, thoughtful kiss, the last kiss of a highwayman before he rides away into the insect-heavy night, his cloak flashing and blocking out the ghostly galleon of the moon, tossed upon cloudy seas. How odd that Mona Lisa di Valvona had been familiar with that quotation. Of course: Alfred Noyes. That was the author. He began a thought of Mona Lisa's dark head on the pillow, then thought of the soft kisses just now. Of course, he felt absolutely splendid. He looked up at her new, her nineteen-year-old face (he had got himself a *girl*—almost a schoolgirl) he put his lips up gently to hers and repeated—he hoped it was dangerously and hoarsely: 'I'll be in touch.' He turned to vanish into the warm black; her fingers light on the place he had kissed.

'Oi! Just a minute.'

She couldn't bear to see him go yet!

'You're going to have rather a long walk home unless I drive you there,' Diana said, and gave a cackle. 'Hadn't I better come, too? It's fourteen back to Springbourne.'

They kissed again, with knees pressing frantically, at the very top of Dover Street. He watched the van's lights halt and glow brighter at the corner. Was that automatic when one touched the brakes? God, he knew nothing. He walked down the steep hill and saw, to the left, the pier lights, and heard John Close's tram's dull note. A motor-cycle flashed past and then parked ahead of him; a light-noted Italian motorcycle, he recognized them, but the rider was no one he knew. He felt impatient, downcast, and superior. His tooth hurt, pleasantly. He remembered there was a Kit Kat waiting for him in his room.

10

Moorman at once began to devise methods of making a finer man of himself, in the eyes of Diana and her mother, an even more romantic figure.

This had happened once before.

At one of Mother's previous cafés, little Sheelagh Salter was among those helping with the washing up. She was really tiny, with a squeaky voice, and imperfect r's: still Moorman, the seventeen-year-old Moorman, was breathless in her presence, hot with jealousy at the prospect of old boy friends from the Secondary Modern's production of *Toad of Toad Hall*—she had played Mole—and tortured by the elaborateness of Sheelagh's life-plan. 'I want to marry a man with a long white house and a long white car and have a son named Ashley.'

Now Moorman loathed girls who altered the spelling of their names. He got in a temper when he thought about it. In the R.A.F. there was a Lynda and a Jacqui. He now, in maturity, realized Sheelagh had had what was best described as 'a sweet little body'. She lived with her aunt and uncle in Great Preston Road, Waterlooville, while for some inexplicable reason, her father, mother, and brother, lived in a prefab over the road.

The most exciting experience he shared with her was sitting on the couch in her aunt's front lounge, listening to 'Educating Archie', in darkness with biscuits and cheese in front of them. Her small brother kept entering for different parts of his toy printing outfit. This was not done maliciously; each time he did so, Sheelagh said, 'Out the light, Dave,' which Moorman had found wildly provoking: this readiness of Sheelagh's to be fingered all in the dark among burnt bubbled cream crackers.

So, to better himself in her eyes, he'd got the money—in fact, stolen £1 of it—to engage in a Charles Atlas bodybuilding course, which claimed to give him a remarkable physique in exchange for about £6 and ten minutes of his time each day. Of course, Moorman found the exercises both tedious and impossible. He couldn't bear, for a long time, to throw away the pamphlets, however, with their illustrations of Charles Atlas himself bending and pressing against a chair, looking like the strong man from a late nineteenth-century circus. Often, sitting up in bed, Moorman would re-read the initial literature of the course, telling him that he was of the stuff of which champions were made, for had he not had the pluck and enterprise to enroll in the course?

In addition to the following exercises, he should practise supplementary aids to clean living. He must not listen overmuch to 'Jazz or Ragtime': above all, he should try at all times to attend to his 'Personal Grooming'.

That phrase haunted Moorman still. His 'Personal Grooming'. It had nothing to do with the hours he spent drowned in shampoo and stinging soap: it implied stroking the back of beautifully-behaved hair with a tortoiseshell comb—possibly if one were an American officer in *A Bell for Adano*.

Even so, for Diana and her mother, try he would again to improve his 'Personal Grooming'.

Thorough, painful, nose-squeezing washes, a hot flannel to get the blackheads out, new and flashy pyjamas when that could be afforded instead of these shabby ones, his red, dishonourable helmet sliding out of the folds. A new bar of soap and tube of toothpaste. His mind ran and romped into ideas of the new clothes he would like: a light-coloured checked suit, a pair of dark, burnished shoes from Russell and Bromley, a rust-coloured pullover: on the Sunday morning after the dance he spent an unnatural while in cleaning his bedroom sink, trying to melt the old chips of soap and force them into the plug. Then he turned round and jumped in the air, for joy.

No more finger up his backside either when he sat in bed eating chocolate and reading *Mr Polly*. Wash hands after the lavatory. His cavalry twill trousers had been to the dry cleaners and were back. The bag was under his bed. Moorman, tucking a red disgrace back into his pyjama folds, ran and pulled them out; they had a slight aroma of rubber chemical and were shiny along the raised side seams but there was still a hard crease in them, a good day's crease. His heart leapt as he remembered that neither Diana nor her mother had seen him wearing the trousers. He laughed. He thought, so long as he could laugh at himself, he'd never go quite mad. From the window he saw a very dull morning, the pier going out silent, deserted, obviously not much of a day for swimming or playing tennis. Moorman screwed the dry cleaning bag into his tiny wastepaper tin and, last of all, cleaned his teeth fervently.

Suddenly it was difficult not to run downstairs leaping across the three intermediate landings. On the second floor, the plaque on Mona Lisa's door, 'Mona's Room', confronted him reproachfully, a 'mute, voluntary sacrifice' (where had he read *that*?): but oh, he did feel glorious. *Now* he did—on first waking Moorman's first sensations had been excitement, grinding his fists up into the pillow to keep off his erection. And horror at the sight of crumpled pound notes on the dressing-table's synthetic doily. Then, when he reckoned it up, he found he had spent quite little the previous night, about 30*s*. There had been, for example, none of the taxi-hiring back from impossibly remote villages that used to characterize his R.A.F. social life; sliding about on plastic transparent seat covers, being fought off by spectacles with flyaway rims, upward.

Moorman was anxious to see Leslie: to tell Leslie about his conquest and perhaps put in a momentous few hours work. Mrs di Valvona came out and caught him.

'Och, Gordon, I'm *that* excited.

'Some of ma relations are getting married and I just sent a note congratulating them on it. They're to hire the entire ground floor of the Royal Springbourne. Isn't that lovely?'

When she was really pleased about something that involved a great amount of spending, Mrs di Valvona wrinkled her nose and flattened her voice to intimate refinement.

'The groom is named Gino. Do you know the very tall, handsome boy who comes here sometimes on his Lambretta? Och, that must be the best-dressed man on the whole Island. He's a second cousin of Joe, Mona's Uncle Grimaldi, and he's to get married to Philomena, who happens to be related to our cousins in Ventnor, them that own the hamburger bar, the Mayfair.

'Gino falls for her soon as he sees her photo in a solid silver frame in their front room in Ventnor when he was riding round the Island on his Lambretta. He says to ma cousin, "Well, I have feelings for that girl, and I'm certain she'll feel *identical* when we meet." And now, Mother o' Mercy, Sister Michael Joseph's been to tell me they're taking the ground floor of the hotel for a sum said to run to three figures.'

He asked how Mona Lisa was.

'Och, I don't know. I don't understand. When I telephoned, they said she'd been leaking from some cause or other—nothing serious, but leaking she was. Adhesions, they call 'em. She's going to ring you from the trolley, she said. I've had enough of that nonsense. I'm fetching her home Monday. I'll get an Austin Westminster for to bring her.

'Och, I've been thinking (her voice sounded drowned in marge): It'd be a byeotiful surprise if you could announce your engagement, you two, with ma Mona sitting up in bed wi' her shawl; and we could take a wee photo with ma Instamatic and all.'

Moorman babbled unwisely that he was fearfully occupied at present with the idea of installing self-service equipment at the Pavilion. At that Mrs di Valvona's pale little lips compressed but she said nothing: she had a genuine respect for the improvement of catering premises, especially if large sums were hinted at. Outside the Tredegar Guest House, in a comforting grey Saturday morning, he began to dream up the connected story of the previous night for Leslie's benefit.

And the thought of kissing Diana upwards, under the light, made him want to stride along and really get busy. He almost bumped into one of Mrs di Valvona's lodgers, an Italian strongly resembling Anthony Quinn who suddenly raced round the corner from Dover Street carrying a *Sunday Mirror* and a large bar of Cadbury's chocolate, the bag held closely around one half of it. Moorman, with thoughts of Diana, forgetting the cackle, gave the slightest of smiles to him, and was rewarded with a murderous stare.

Leslie smiled and listened to Moorman's lies about being asked to take the lead in some amateur dramatics, and told him to go along (giggle) and enjoy it. As the tram took Moorman to the Esplanade the next afternoon he saw that there was a seagull perched vigilantly on each knob of the pier's brave Victorian railingwork. He started his walk to the top of the town feeling tickled by the double life he was leading; but arrived out of breath at Springbourne station; even, for a moment, mad with irritation at having to go all the way to Hemingford Priory. From the booking-hall, the bang of John Close's tram was scarcely audible. Nor could he hear, thankfully, the clicking noises of the rest of the town coining money.

Moorman bought a four and sixpenny return ticket in a booking-hall as hollow as a church and hung with pale yellow and blue travel posters of thirty years previously.

The train had a wide running board. Its way seemed to lie entirely at the foot of a steep, brambly bank, close to trodden-down iron railings. Just after leaving the red back-elevation of a secondary modern school outside Springbourne, Moorman saw, almost in slow motion, a railway employee creeping along the foot of the bank, carrying a big stick. He wore the regulation serge waistcoat and high waisted trousers of the porter and, underneath that, a Fairisle pullover. The train moved so gently that further along Moorman saw the out-of-season hen pheasant the creeping man wished to bludgeon to death.

He was half an hour too early at Hemingford Priory Station. He looked through the unoccupied ticket barrier, over the road gravel and through the gateposts, the lines of poplar trees vanishing into the distance. Then he walked round the station yard, trying to step over the shadow of himself that the weak sunlight produced; and eventually he felt too hot.

The station pub, The Sultan, also looked deserted. It was painted in the same colours as the station: yellow and brown. The licensee was said to be a certain Jonah H. Jellyman. Moorman walked out of the yard and over the sharp little hump of railway bridge to his right. From the top of this he was able to see the roof of Diana's house and the glitter of the hothouses. He observed that the railway line cut through two large paddocks. In the one nearest the farm stood a number of shanties that from time to time produced, squeezed out, a large pig. Moorman was unspeakably bored and thought of walking the other way up the road, towards the village. The thought of Diana and her mother sweeping along the yellow road in their van, late back from a smart pub, deterred him: they would see how hot and inefficient he really was. This drove him back to the station platform, where he stayed for another quarter of an hour, close to tears at the thought of Mona Lisa's discomfort, yet feeling the beginnings of ungovernable rage that he should propose to her in the spirit of a get-well card.

Another train with a running board arrived, the train Diana intended to meet him from, and Moorman went through the barrier mixed up with a great number of old women in print frocks and light purple, beneficial stockings.

He saw Diana just coming out of the farm entrance. She wore an orange striped dress, flat-heeled shoes and a straw hat trailing an orange ribbon. He pretended to stand still and wait for her. Diana walked straight up to him, not in the least abashed. He pretended to bow, she laughed, and they crossed the road. Moorman decided to be rather aloof and amused at the thought of taking an afternoon off. 'There's never any traffic along here except the occasional combine, and they have to give twenty-four hours notice to move,' she said.

By the iron gate she turned round and kissed him full on the mouth: cool and tasting of Polos. The gesture seemed half passionate, half a warm greeting. As they stood there, the sun came out strongly, and for a moment his legs were covered by hot pipes; then dull clouds came over and remained. 'I did so hope it would be a nice day,' Diana pretended to wail; but in the dullness, Moorman felt recklessly secure. His confidence swelled up again, until they were on the other side of the gate. It swung slowly back—chink. A complex rubber-band arrangement made it shut itself. From the garage regions at the back of the house came a regular Belp Belp Belp sound, and she explained: 'That's Billy taking it out on his new trailer. Something at the hospital upset him this morning.'

They didn't continue up the path to the entrance with the inner glass door but walked round the side of the house.

Suddenly Moorman faced an enormous lawn, shut off

from the gravel by tangles of brown netting for the tennis. There was a dome winter garden built on this side of the house, in useless proportions very like those of the Pavilion: white, sun-bubbled paint and a thickness of ferns and red flowers inside. He was also certain of the presence of an old lady wearing a hat, but as Diana plainly had no intention of acknowledging this person, he tried hard not to look. It occurred to him that life often consisted of trying not to look, or listen, as some female was in the lavatory. Diana said that her mother slept for two hours every afternoon; it was the only way she was able to cope with a household like theirs. She added—rather loudly and unnecessarily he thought—that her mother generally awoke in a bad mood.

They went through a gap in the nets and up one side of the lawn. The grass ended in a low rim, then there was a ditch and an area of rough land with cattle moving about. She, following his gaze, said, 'There's the park and Billy's cattle. *Some* of Billy's cattle. That was the original way in, through the park. I think of all the carriages coming in, and Aunt Het standing there with the key to the larder round her middle. Brrr, old witch.

'She insisted that they built an air-raid shelter in the park, with what she calls a Funk Hole. I think that sounds jolly rude: Funk Hole. I wonder if there's a bull about. Billy's bulls are always named Thomas.' Moorman braced himself for the first cackle of the afternoon and it came. He felt irritable. He hated the way in which the lawn was almost completely given over to tennis. He stared at his chukka boots, wondering if the hole on the grass between them had been made by a mole.

'You're standing on the clock golf,' Diana said, 'but we only use it when Billy lets the village have a fête here, so don't worry. We've got a croquet set, too, up in the swimming hut Billy made. Ho, yes, we got the lot.'

Moorman had caught sight of her lovely long legs, how brown she was; and had begun to prepare an amusing remark—no subject yet but at least he felt himself in action. Diana startled him. She stopped and pinched her sides and exclaimed: 'Oooh, I *am* getting so fat. Isn't it *disgustipating*? I was taking Honey walkies in the park last week and I just happened to jump over a fence. I heard this noise, a sort of slurping sound. Do you know what it was? The tops of my legs slapping together.' Cackle.

The swimming pool stood on its own grassy plateau at the top of the garden. Moorman wanted to say: 'Listen, you can only hear the silence,' but she was still talking busily about being too fat; he was petrified to say anything in case it should introduce his own large size into the conversation. The water was about five foot at the pool's deep end. Diana said: 'Just a sec',' and vanished behind the varnish-coloured hut. Back she came with the biggest shrimping net he had ever seen, to skim the dead leaves and a fallen beetle from the surface. As she did this, Moorman thought involuntarily of Mona Lisa when well: her hair compressed in the petal bathing cap, her leonine features creased as she prepared to walk off the springboard at the Blue Lagoon. Diana threw the net on the grass.

'Well, would you like to strip out?' she said. A cold hand was laid on his faint, flabby heart.

'Pardon?'

'Do you want to strip out, because I'd like to. It isn't cold, just dull.'

He said he had no bathing trunks.

'Don't worry about drawers, as Billy and Aunt Het call them. There's a pair of Billy's old ones inside the hut. You could have a little laze around in those if you wanted, but please yourself.'

Inside the hut Moorman drew in his stomach and prayed it would stay there. He stumbled about on more old nets, two or three deckchairs, a fully-inflated Li-lo, a big case made of plain wood which must have contained the croquet set. Everything smelled of dark varnish. Everything was expensive but undusted: he was painfully, elaborately cheap. Moorman found the trunks rolled in a clean towel and he felt flattered. There was, on one of the beams, a scrap of looking glass, and he saw a perspiring red face. He tore at the knotted laces of one chukka boot realizing what it was that generally held him back from choosing new clothes with care—the reflection of his sweating bulk from three or more sides in the outfitter's mirror. Already he could hear someone moving in the bushes behind the swimming hut; to his horror, Diana banged on the wood; in a frenzy Moorman pulled his trousers and pants off together thanking God that the inside rim of the pants was still unmarked. He pulled up the Doctor's trunks. They felt clammy, like a cold shopping net.

Outside he discovered that Diana had got changed in the bushes: a blue two-piece costume, not really brief enough for a bikini, and her hair tied up by a thick rubber band, giving her a severe, slightly patrician look. An erection arrived. Moorman turned away from her, pretending to be drinking in the cool air. Diana scampered past him into the hut and returned with the Li-lo which she bounced down on to the grass. She walked towards Moorman saying, 'Of course, if you'd prefer a

full-length deckchair left over from the Mauretania . . .'
Standing right in front of him. Would she cackle and draw attention to his large, ungainly body? She was dreadfully candid about rolls of fat, even her own imaginary ones. She widened her eyes as her mother often did. 'Oh, I say,' she breathed. 'I say. What a beautiful silky chest.'

She ruffled the hairs. 'Can I please touch it, Mr Man?'

Moorman pretended that it tickled. He was covered in confusion. The *years* he'd spent concealing himself from women!

'Why didn't you say in the first place that you had such a lovely silky chest? I had no idea, did I?'

Moorman replied to this in a plummy, affected voice which he at once modified for fear that it sounded homosexual. 'Well, I mean . . . I mean . . . how could I come up to a pure young thing, a lady I'd never met, and tell you I was hairy? I mean, whatever next?'

'Believe me, I'm not pure,' she replied.

Moorman went on his knees beside her on the Li-lo. He drew himself, with infinite care, into a lying position on the blue rubber beside her; taking care to keep his stomach in, to keep his legs spread out properly, since purple bits of testicle had a habit of peeping through the ends of unfamiliar swimming trunks.

She lay back and his head went on to the pillow beside hers: they just lay next to one another on a single person's rubber bed.

Moorman sat up in alarm. 'It's quite all right,' Diana whispered, 'really it is.' The end of a yellowish block of bushes concealed them from the house: the red house with the tall white windows and domed winter garden. Diana's legs went apart as they began the kissing very gently, moving as if to please and reassure one another.

Moorman rolled on to her, staring down into her closed eyes. The cold wind was on his back, and the cattle moved dully over in the park. He slipped his hands under her behind. How different its peach formation from the other mass he preferred not to touch, the iron-work that yielded not a millimetre at the back of Mona Lisa. He pressed Diana up to him and she said 'Oh': very simply, a remark in absolute agreement. Underneath him she seemed to melt warmly and this phrase Leslie Langdon had once used to describe a certain conquest flickered in his mind, exciting him the more—'thighs wilting in animal pleasure.' Right at the back of himself Moorman felt the start, the dry-mouth stage, of losing it. Oh, but God, these were the Doctor's trunks. She mustn't know: he mustn't collapse afterwards: should he? There was no help for it. Diana's tongue was in his mouth, a hand ran down his back and he'd discharged it—he nodded once or twice deep down inside the Doctor's copious yellow trunks and then made gallant attempts to continue pressing down on her. He straightened his shoulders from which all the stiffening of his life seemed to have been removed. There had to be a slackening now and Diana seemed to sense this. Her eyes came open. Moorman lay back on the Li-lo, one leg crossed acutely over until the damp patch on the Doctor's property should quite disappear.

They were talking—softly, with no undue noise or mirth. He began to love it, stretched half out on the wintry grass, pretending to fall into the pit of the sky.

'Why did I ask you to dance? Oh, I dunno. Well, I saw you there on your own: I'd *seen* you before. I thought, there's someone at least int'resting. So many nits live around here and turn up at the house and try to attack me.

'I know it's a bit peculiar talking like this, because we only met the night before last and I've never even been "out" with you, as they say. I know: I'm supposed to be all coy and give nothing away. It's just that I feel I've known you for such a long time, Gordon.' This free use of his first name flattered him.

'You looked, well, int'resting and a bit cynical at the same time. I suppose a bit sad as well.'

That was a good line then. The sad past.

'Mummy rather raved about you after you'd gone on Friday night. "I think that fellow's so nice," she said. She agrees with me about your being—just int'resting: well, in comparison with people like that fat Wilde, fascinating.'

(He'd test the value of the sudden ingenuous compliment.) 'I like you very much. You're very pretty.'

'You're not so bad.'

Her tone got busier. 'Mummy was very keen to invite you out today. And get Billy to ask you to be in our thing. It's only mucking about but it's fun. Mummy usually does a dance with a life-size doll of Aunt Het's: pretends to smack its arm away from her bum. You know: a lot of men think Mummy's a sort of dragon but she honestly isn't. She loves parties and getting in a party mood, dressing up, that kind of thing. She's perfect for Billy in many ways, although there's so much about him that's peculiar.'

'When did they get married?'

'Seven or eight years ago. I was just eleven at the time. I remember coming here and Aunt Het making a little speech about it, saying, "Little girl, I hope you'll be happy living with us." But secretly, you know, Aunt Het's got a real thing about Mummy, especially about her sleeping with Billy—sleeping in the same bed as her

Billy! She went white at the thought!

'In many ways, Aunt Het's been a bitch. I didn't see a lot of it because Billy paid for me to go to Overstone and I was away for a lot of the time. She hated the idea that Mummy was running the house, because she'd always been the one who dished out the sherry.'

A dazzling fact swam out of Moorman's brain.

'She was a *châtelaine*, was she?'

'Shit-what?' Diana cackled. 'Oh, oh, Kingsley-Pink's off again.'

He pretended to roll back slightly; he tried to talk with an edge of affront. 'In fact what I meant was, a châtelaine was the woman of the house who carried all the keys to the larders . . .'

'The real devil for food is Mummy's Mother in Duisberg—Mutti, that means Mummy.' Diana interrupted without the smallest contrition. 'Mutti's got this thing about never having much to eat at meal-times, this old-fashioned idea that ladies aren't supposed to be greedy. When she came to stay with us here, Mummy discovered a great *hoard* of stuff under her bed—gherkins, sausage, all the rest of it. Then when Mutti went home, all Mummy's brothers and sisters in Germany sent these ratty little notes saying "Why didn't you give poor Mutti enough to eat when she stayed with you?" And she ate her head off and Billy bought her a pair of warm boots . . .'

He managed a neat change: not pushing her off the subject but still drawing attention to himself, his faint buccaneering quality.

'Do you think your stepfather will approve of me?'

'Approve of you. How d'you . . .'

'And, for that matter, do you think your mother will approve of me?'

Diana rose perfectly to it, lifting herself on one elbow and looking worried. 'Why ever shouldn't she approve of you?'

The following had been slightly rehearsed during the hours in the Amplifier Room that morning. He was, after all, a bit of a rough diamond. He had a slightly dangerous past. He'd 'been around'. His world, he implied was tough and cut-throat: he didn't want, he suggested, to upset her with the tough, cut-throat detail of it. Her eyes were very wide and pale blue-green. During his rubbish, Moorman had a flash of disbelief that this girl should ever look twice at him. 'I was wondering if perhaps we shouldn't go too far with what we've started . . .' He shook his head and tried to grin a perplexed, strong man's grin, Gary Cooper very much in his mind as the model.

Diana leaned over and waited until he was quite certain she was going to kiss him before she did. This was the most exciting thing about her; the deliberate actions. 'Don't be silly; I fancy you, dun' I?'

'I couldn't help thinking about it. I think quite a . . .'

'Oh God, you're not broody are you?'

Moorman felt himself bridling like a middle-aged woman, like Al Read's impersonation of a middle-aged woman. He realized how carefully he must choose his words. He thought of the expression 'weighing his words'; with *his* words in mind the phrase suggested shop-soiled jellybabies.

Diana leaned over and kissed him again, steadying his shoulders with one warm hand. 'Listen,' she said, in a lovely soft way, 'I wouldn't care what you were—even if you were a. . . a lavvy cleaner, I'd still find you super.' (He hated 'super' because, to him it was a word from another planet, but about himself it was rather different.) 'And if I wanted to see you, I would. And I happen to want to, if it's all right with you.' She repeated 'silly' like a kiss and put her forehead in the hairs on his chest, which, to be perfectly frank he'd never noticed before, being too busy hiding himself from view. He pretended to look sadly up at the grey sky and over at the cattle in the park, the broad lawn with its rim and moat: when Diana looked up, she'd see his eyes wide open, as if recalling some enormous sorrow. He felt marvellous.

He almost got used to being in swimming trunks, except that his breathing suffered. A few spots of rain fell so they changed again and Moorman's stomach, allowed to come out to its fullest extent, felt as if it had been enclosed in some punishing device, a bobsleigh that was too tight or a dreadful garter. They walked, holding hands (although he felt nervous about that) round the side of the house where the front door had been, facing the park gates. Moorman remarked that he could just see the carriages arriving; 'landau' was in his mind but he didn't know how to pronounce it. They went through open french windows to a gloomy dining-room. So far as Moorman could discern, it was full of china cabinets, small sliding rugs and paintings with a light above each one. In the very darkest part of the room was a cabinet gramophone with a crudely made extra loudspeaker which Billy had built and rigged up for their parties, she said, as well as taking it to other people's parties and provide their pantomime music. She put a record on: 'Runaway' by Del Shannon, which came out when he was twenty-two and made him forget about how he looked and felt now; he almost wanted to dance. Then she put on an LP from the Supremes, and Moorman couldn't stand it. Girls singing gave him an erection and the miseries simultaneously. Diana began to jig around on the spot as if unaware of his presence. And he was petrified at the volume, booming and braying; shaking the atmosphere directly under what Diana referred to casually as 'Aunt Het's slimy little pit'.

To his relief they turned off the radiogram and went through the hall, in at the door beside the staircase; her hair swinging forward as she attended to the latch on the dog-proof wooden gate. They looked in to see the new puppy and its mother in the cloakroom, behind a barrier of sacks and newspaper. It seemed a perfect situation—girl and boy and sweet little puppy. But the mother spoiled it by jumping up and pinning the puppy to the floor as it squeaked madly. The air rang with Diana's shouts.

'Honey. *HO-NEY*. Stop. At ONCE. Brrrr. Bad dog. NAUGHTY.'

The mother slunk to the rear of the compound and the puppy put its paws on the edge of the barrier. Diana was soft again. He was on the point of telling her he loved her as she said, 'Oh, I can't see how Mummy will bear having to give her away.' It was the perfect moment to put an arm round her, touch her neck and wrists, take in the delight of new hair and baby powder; she, however, twisted free from him saying in mock panic, 'Oo, come on. Let's get out before Honey starts gobbling up its little sausages!'

They had tea under the beech trees close to the park gates—plates of cucumber sandwiches like stamps, triangles of currant loaf, two cakes with unfamiliar centres that tasted of apple and of custard and were, he gathered, from German recipes. Aunt Het did not appear for tea. Diana's voice had become rather loud again. 'She has her Earl Grey tea and a rusk in her room. And her blooming Patum Pe-whatsit muck all over it. Leave it Mummy, I'll take it up. Brrr, she's always on her thunderbox.' At the worst moments, Diana's conversation seemed entirely dominated by the lavatory. When he dominated *her,* he'd soon correct that. While she was away from the table her mother, who hadn't awoken in at all a bad mood, remarked, 'I bet she will come down for supper in some floaty little number because she knows Gordon is here; she can never schresist a nice-looking young man. Wait till she finds out you are here, Gordon.' And when he refused a third piece of the custard and apple cake, though his body was agog for it, and a fourth and fifth, Diana's mother said, 'Oh. You are not a pig eater at all.' He glowed.

Moorman sat up in bed the following night with his Kit Kat beside him; his lovely day at Diana's still letting off fireworks and trails of golden dust in his memory; thinking not about Mother or fish and chips but of a lovely day. Even after a Monday spent in boiling heat and cavalry twill as Leslie outlined a plan for converting the Pavilion to a self-service cafeteria, he was thinking of Sunday, saying to himself, 'I had a lovely day,' like some over-privileged private school boy.

There was still the faintest bloom in his mouth of spring onions and strawberries. They had had supper in the winter garden, a kind of summer dimness caused by the string of coloured bulbs above them, left over from some past garden party. By that time Moorman really had been confident. He'd even deserted his agonized listening post for mention of Diana's boy friends. His dread of the talented Doctor, her stepfather, was also much diminished. They'd been talking about famous Spoonerisms. Moorman believed he had quite won the Doctor over by pointing out that the reverse of 'let the flag be hung from the tower' was 'let the hag be flung from the tower'. At this, the Doctor growled 'wha-at?' and a grin moved slowly across his face, showing one gold-capped tooth and a hole in the centre ones, then he giggled helplessly with laughter.

'"Let the hag be flung from the tower." That's very nice, ve'good,' he growled.

Most of the conversation went over the head of Aunt Het, whose ancient square-neck dress had an area of buff vest above it for modesty's sake. She carried a valve portable radio everywhere, waiting for or reflecting upon Sandy McPherson's Chapel in the Valley and the Archers. Diana pulled a variety of different faces and made a pepper-pot motion above her when she cleared away the old lady's plate, but Moorman made a thing of talking to her; they all admired him for that as well. She said, in a voice like thin bread and butter. 'Some time ago they did an operation. I always say they had to take in a tuck in me.' And: 'I had a lovely cat named The Bogey Man. Oh, he was a beauty. An Egyptian head. When they were painting the winter garden the Bogey Man ran right the way to the top of the ladder, but he's passed away now of course.' Diana, behind her, pretended to buckle at the knees and faint with pleasure at this announcement. Aunt Het wanted Moorman to walk up with her and see where the Bogey Man was buried. He was in with both of them.

Best of all, most splendid: no swimming or tennis. There were an awkward few moments when the iron gate chinked and the vicar's two plain daughters walked boldly around the side of the winter garden, hoping to be asked to have a swim. But they just stood around, in freshly dismounted stances, sweating from their cycle ride. Moorman looked at the sweat stains in their dress armpits and wondered how Leslie's mothering manner would go down with them. Presently they drifted off again to the accompaniment of curses and threats sotto voce from Diana and her mother—'Oh those girls are tiresome! All zey are good at is jumping over plinking hurdles. Always somesing for nothing. And Billy has let them be in our pantomime—I could kill him sometimes.'

That recalled another beautiful moment during supper. The Doctor in his blue Aertex shirt was still giggling like dragoons on gravel over 'let the hag be flung from the tower', when Diana's mother leaned over the table and said to him: 'You know, we must hev Gordon in our little effort. He's a *netural.*'

Diana drive him home at gone eleven o'clock at night. 'Come and see us whenever you like. Oh, you must be at the rehearsal in the pub on Friday,' her mother said.

On the way through the wood, where they'd seen Miss Maxey jumping across the road with the Vicar's surplice, Diana backed the van into the beginning of a rough track and Moorman took down the top of her dress—she had changed into one that was mottled dark blue—and she undid her brassière hooks for him and then let the straps fall over her slack shoulders: he discovered dear little fine, ripe breasts and dared to make them crinkly with his lips. His hair was being stroked by her hand but not in the way that put his teeth on edge. Then she just put one finger in his crotch and kissed him with her mouth opened as wide as it could be.

'I want to give you all of myself,' she said. 'Do you

want to?'

Numb. 'I—I want to.'

He couldn't believe he was here, doing this.

'I—I,' (be careful), 'I haven't got any . . .'

'Little rubber insurance policies?' she said.

'No. No.'

'Do a bit of shopping, mmn?'

He would, he almost groaned to himself in bed. Leslie always had some. Meantime . . . sit on the fearful heat, the tempting tickle. Pretend Diana and her mother are watching continually through the window. He opened *The History of Mr Polly* and looked for the meal scene at Mr Polly's father's funeral to look at while he ate his Kit Kat. He wolfed two fingers, bit a third, and heard a noise outside his door. It broke through a weight of unease that had suddenly come over him. At first he didn't hear the knock. Guess who had returned that evening, still with a worrying leak, from hospital, prematurely discharged and discharging?

11

Mona Lisa's knock was repeated with an impatient nightie rustle; and what was Moorman to do, how was he to behave? He experienced a familiar kind of panic—that of being disturbed while at one of life's shameful acts, washing his hair, or eating banana split with bread and butter. Never in his life had he sat up in bed in front of a girl. He suspected that he might grip the sheet over his chest: a startled nymph.

The knock woke him up with a jolt. He'd been worrying so hard, so suddenly, concentrating so much on the sudden worry, that the print on the page of Mr Polly faded. He'd become shut away from the snatches of song from the Esplanade pubs far below his window, with 'You' always sung as 'Yeeew'.

The worry was Mr Starkey, whose presence at the Pavilion had somehow been confirmed that afternoon, when he mended the Allwyne de Luxe. He coughed a lot. He reminded Moorman of the actor who always played the fat man part in old Dickens films—Mr Bumble, Mr Pumblechook. For this reason it was difficult not to look at him, or hang on to his words, with the cigarette jumping as if taking part in some limp conspiracy.

Mr Starkey had been in the Pavilion a great deal; Moorman, obviously, was at first too excited by the thought of his own double life to notice how much. Mending the Allwyne de Luxe that afternoon had somehow resolved his status, no longer merely that of Leslie's friend, a useful contact, a man who could mend machines instead of printing Out of Service cards. As he wandered about, Moorman overheard Leslie talking obsessively to Mr Starkey about military history; he stirred his tea at the tea bar; he said, 'Oh, that's top hole, it really is,' when Mr Starkey righted the Allwyne de Luxe so that the ball trundled out of the hole to the place where the hammer would strike it. And not a word about involving Mr Starkey in the business. No 'Er, I've been wondering, stop me if . . .' Moorman flushed angrily. He remembered early days in the Amplifier Room when Leslie had fed him milk and brought him a bag of pears.

Why hadn't he got a dressing-gown? In a leap Moorman was out of bed to grab his soiled underpants from the floor and shy them to the back of the curtained clothes tomb. 'You bloody stinking piss, Starkey,' he screamed to himself. Mr Starkey had slyness and malevolence in his twinkling eyes and sober manner. He wore a double-breasted suit that was still and yellow in places, wrapped up in it, the jacket seemed to have bars and folds like a schoolmaster's gown. Moorman flew and leapt back, hump, squeak, and then called: 'Who is it?' with an elaborate inflection—the young scholar disturbed at dead of night in the tropics.

'It's me, darling. Darling?' The doorknob began urgently to rotate. This was a very tricky door, especially in the morning when one was sweating already in one's trousers. The mechanism had to be scrabbled about.

'Come in.'

She managed it: the door struggled open and Moorman, the remaining Kit Kat finger under his pillow, pretended to screw up his eyes to see who it was. He pictured himself—the young man reading alone in his room, shadows thrown on his face by a venetian blind, everywhere the orchestra of a night in Casablanca instead of Springbourne, with distant snatches of song from the Esplanade pubs down below his window.

Moorman had been for a drink and discussions about the self-service idea with Leslie and this Mr Starkey: it was less of a business discussion than a forum about military history. He'd returned to the Tredegar Guest House at ten-thirty and absolutely forgotten she was home.

Round her Mona Lisa clutched a garment of ribbed blue towelling; below a pale blue nightdress foamed and flared out, below that her legs seemed mottled, perhaps with tears, before vanishing into fluffy blue mules. She wore her charm bracelet and her hair was stiff and glossy: she must have had it done in hospital.

She stood in the doorway shivering—pretending to shiver? It was obviously meant to be the posture of an uncertain little girl but amounted to that of an overweight, eye-made-up hunchback.

How had he *ever*? At the same time Moorman's heart dislodged with pity for the big girl. She'd looked forward to coming home and seeing him. He thought of her dark head on the pillow, perhaps tearful, and said to her tenderly: 'Ought you to be out of bed? I was going to see you in the morning.'

Mona Lisa pulled the door shut behind her. When

it made insufficient contact with the frame, she turned right round to wrench and jiggle it. In the trial of strength her little girl stance was forgotten; he saw just a broad blue towelling back and, with her obvious beefiness, some of his discomfort went away, he felt less anxious about her. She faced him again, a prey to dry, quaking sobs.

'Are you in very much pain?' He remembered a kind woman saying to him once: 'Have you got a lot of pain?' and repeated that to her as well. Mona Lisa pressed herself against the bedroom door.

'Please say something,' Moorman whispered. 'Tell me what the trouble is, mmn?'

The words barely came.

'Don't shout at me.'

'I'm *not*, I whispered. Look, come over here a minute.'

'I won't. I won't,' she bellowed.

'Well,' Moorman spoke in a normal, level voice which she would naturally construe as pitiless, 'I can't hear a word from there,' and her face dissolved, fell apart, great fissures opened and the monsoons came into the rich, black earth of her eye-liner: whole, abrupt tears trickled down her cheek. He was so alarmed by the noisy lowing that accompanied this that he jumped out of bed, remembered only at the last second to draw his pyjama folds together and pull in his stomach. He went on tiptoe and put an arm round her shoulder, drawing her to the end of the bed. 'Oooh, be careful,' she said, 'I'm still leaking.' He reversed back into bed, careful not to sit on the end of the pillow because of the chocolate underneath, feeling to make sure that no vile helmet had been revealed when he was outside.

Mona Lisa sat all hunched up at the end of his bed. He wriggled one set of toes under her behind as a friendly gesture but she only shook herself and began to weep soundlessly into the crook of one arm. Moorman raised himself up helplessly.

'Did you say you were still—leaking?'

Mona Lisa looked up at him: the streaked eye make-up, the little wet paths down her cheeks. He felt dreadful about it. 'Aye I still am,' she said. 'Do you know how many pints of pus they took out?' She paused for optimum effect: *'Two!'*

'I expect it had to come out,' he answered weakly. 'Whatever was it caused by?'

'The doctor said it was adhesions.' Mona Lisa sniffed in a great, rending way. 'He sent some of it away for to be tested on the mainland and they rang up to say it was, um, sterile, but I didn't understand what he was getting at.' The details miraculously dried her eyes. 'But it's still coming out.

'You must tell me . . . you must tell me, darling . . .' His throat felt caught, but it was all right . . . 'Was I very bad when they took me away? I don't remember. I went out like a light. What I mean is, was I delirious?'

'No, you were a very good girl.' When he said this, Moorman couldn't help being struck by the intrinsic sadness of the expression. Despite her presence, a mountain of blue towelling, he thought of a small, gentle girl who always tried to please and to be brave, who deserved nothing bad, least of all to be deceived. He repeated: 'A very good girl,' very gently and unrehearsed.

'You looked out for me.'

'Did my best. It . . .'

'Och,' she said wildly, 'ah had to come up here and see you a wee while tonight.'

'What about your Mother?' Moorman was, to tell the truth, petrified by the thought that Mrs di Valvona might take her life in her hands and ascend to the topmost landing: might burst that tricky door open and occupy all of the doorframe: might say, not 'Mo-ona! Will you get back to your bed!' but, 'Well, this really settles it. Remember what I told you about ma Mona no accepting a ring for less than £250 (poonds).'

'Och, Mummy's away asleep. *She's* no well tonight. Her tummy.'

Mona Lisa's voice had levelled off, to Moorman's great relief. He felt they were now partners in a reasonable discussion about an operation. He hoped very much to steer the dangerous hanging crate of her emotions clear and away from talk of himself and his responsibilities to her. He felt it was time to be a little cheeky: 'When will you be allowed to get up then?'

'The Doctor says in a day or so.'

'You'll need a change . . .'

'What do you mean, a change?'

'I mean, it's tiring being in bed and lifting heavy sandwiches.'

Her face darkened again. 'Oh, don't be *hoarrible*.'

'I don't mean it: I was only pulling your leg,' Moorman whispered in desperation. 'Look, tell me what's the matter, don't keep it all inside or you'll . . .'

Mona Lisa shoved her fists into her dressing-gown pockets and hung her head. 'Nothing much.' Moorman tried to concentrate. His fingers tapped restlessly under the sheets. He couldn't help this: he was desperate for the remaining piece of Kit Kat. Even after the fourth finger, one had only just got the taste. Mona Lisa's head was still bowed. He could just hear: 'I'm going to get up tomorrow. Properly up.' He tried, he *did* try, to keep it light.

'That's good.'

'Of course I do. I'm delighted. What do you mean,
'Huh! You think so!'
"Huh, you think so!"? What a discontented voice to use.'

His elbow ached.

'Is it going to mean . . . No.'

'Mean what?' he demanded.

'Don't shout at me,' the tiny rabbit voice said.

'I'm not, really I'm not. It's when people don't finish off sentences.' He could imagine Diana's crisp voice cutting through whatever the matter was. He could more readily imagine Diana looking at Mona Lisa and giving one of her cackles. Or looking at *him* and cackling? He gripped the lining of the eiderdown. 'Please, what's the matter?'

'When I do get up . . .'

'Yes, what?'

'Is it going to mean that I see more of you?' This had clearly been thought out, but was delivered in a blotched, wet voice.

Moorman said patiently, with interior shivers: 'Look, I'm sorry if you've felt neglected. I came to see you as often as I could but then . . .'

'I know, you came as much as you could.' This was better. But—'I want to know what's going to happen now.'

'What about?'

'About,' she said, 'Us.' She made it sound like a large vehicle. Possibly a large double bed on mischievous unpredictable castors.

For the first time he noticed that she had a wad of paper tissues up her dressing-gown sleeve.

'I was so hot in bed, and uncomfortable.'

It made him sorry for her again.

'Never mind,' he said.

'It's all right for . . .'

'What for?'

'Nothing.' Had she gone off *us?* His heart quickened. 'I know for a start that ma Mummy's got fed up with me being ill.'

'Of course she hasn't, but you know what it's . . .'

'Och, she has!' Mona's voice, tear-thickened once more. 'She's been nothing but blooming irritable ever since Aldo Dinardo drove me home. You know wee Aldo—the one what looks like Anthony Quinn. He was taking some snaps of things under ma window later on. He got ma Mummy to have one with our dog and all she kept saying was: "Our Mona's loafing up the stair." Loafing!'

'She didn't mean it.'

'S'as if no one in the world has a blooming right not to be well except for her.' She unplugged some more tissues and began to weep more silently and carefully than she had so far. 'She does mean it. I think she hates me. She does, she does.'

'And in any case,' Moorman said, really making an effort to be bright, 'what does it really matter if you're going to get up properly tomorrow?'

'It'll be just as b . . .'

'Try to look forward, not backwards. Think of everything there is to look forward to . . .'

'Hah! Exactly! What?'

'You must try to think about getting better and not worse. It's not as bad as . . .' he foundered miserably.

'Tell me one thing,' her voice cracking. 'Oh, tell me this one thing. When I was lying there, was I in your thoughts?'

'Yes.'

'And . . .'

'What?'

'When I'm up . . .'

She didn't make it; let out an intimidating howl. 'Oh, what do I care? I don't give a bloody *damn*!'

'Please, *please*, don't do that.'

Mona Lisa turned round to face him accusingly, so that Moorman almost really did pull the bedclothes up in front of his chest. The tears glittering (his heart was being pushed and pulled about), she said: 'I've been sitting up there, pouring out pus,' (his heart recovered because that sounded so funny—Mona Lisa at the head of the table with a pot and a set of cups), 'and wondering all day if I can be sure of you or not. And I come home and ma Mummy's *hoarrible* and seven or eight nuns come in and keep on about how lucky I am and what a sweet mother I've got; and I feel hot, and I'm leaking and you're not there; and I'm just alone with ma thoughts.'

In fact, Moorman thought, compared to his—compared to the one that was formerly his—Mona Lisa's life wasn't all that bad. Here she was, high above the level of the fish and chip shop smells on the Esplanade and the drumming feet on the pier planks. She was bought all the clothes she wanted and could have a rest in the afternoons. What was she complaining about? His heart righted itself once more and he was able to speak a little more crisply to Mona Lisa di Valvona.

'You think too much, you know.'

'Eh?'

'You do. You think too much.'

Mona Lisa snorted and put her nose back in the crook of her arm, though now in passion rather than ungovernable sobs. 'Huh! Thank you very much. What a . . . what a *hoarrible* thing to, what a crool . . .'

'Um, I meant . . .'

It was dangerous. Her dry sobs began again and the blue mass heaved: he leaned right down the bed to try to put an arm round her shoulders. Mona Lisa moved forward, racked by a sob, and Moorman, his trunk caught in the tucked in bedclothes, felt as if he were being pulled in two. He patted her, trying to say soft things. She did at least shift further up the bed towards him, heaving and shaking, the words stumbling about.

'You haven't kissed me for ages.'

Against her ear he said: 'I have, I . . .'

'Not properly.'

That was true. He couldn't bring himself to put his tongue in the mouth of a body with a new scar, let alone a leaking one. He made attempts to rock Mona Lisa to and fro where she sat and was again struck by the pathos of it. Now, for some reason, instead of her dark head on the pillow, he could see her by herself, sipping a cup of tea and breathing back into the cup.

'You never say anything!'

'Say what?'

'You never say anything! About us. About what might happen and what you intend to do about me. Ma Mummy said I'd to have a little talk with you.' More rending sniffs. 'You're not thick, you know what about. Don't all the time use your education to get out of difficult situations: that's what you always do. You just got no idea of how it's been for me—even before I fell ill, and what they were all saying behind their hands.'

'Who said . . .?'

'Ma Mummy and everyone: Sister Michael Joseph, Sister Hoolican, ma Uncle Grimaldi—"What's the fellow about?" he says to ma Mummy. Aldo Felice, Pasqual and Elba . . .'

'Said *what?*'

'Don't shout at me.'

The small wondering voice. He felt irritated now. 'Just tell me what they've said.'

It seemed so unreasonable. He'd always thought that, when one plucked up the courage to propose, it was always a question of getting the parents of the girl to agree. This needling and prodding. He felt the beginnings of temper, even against her tears—they were just tears that the big entertainment had so far been frustrated.

'Didn't you realize why ma Mummy gives you them tickets for the Conservatives and Unionists' Dance at the Royal Springbourne?' Mona Lisa paused, gasped and gabbled onward. 'Well, she was going to get me a dress from Pettifords and invite Uncle Grimaldi and some of the nuns in for a wee drink before we set off, looking nice, and we were, we were going to, to, to go off to the dance as an, an, an, engage, engage, engaged . . .'

Mona Lisa shut her eyes and toppled down, to put her head on his shoulder. Moorman, highly irritated, got out of the way so that her head landed on his pillow, turned away from him. The bouffant, swept away from her neck, exposed a number of freckles and pimples. In all, he was reminded of the forbidding hump of Mr Polly's wife Miriam. He made up his mind he would die rather than submit to marriage with her; remembering Mr Polly's fearful and joyless dyspeptic existence. Mona Lisa was still talking but he could hear only snatches of it. 'Go on . . . tell me now, get it over . . . say goodbye and we'll always be . . . why don't you get it over.' Then, he could tell, she pretended to go limp, as if cried to sleep.

Moorman got close to her ear. He knew that in the ensuing speech he must not make even the most oblique reference to a marriage or an engagement—it all had to be to do with 'making promises'. He was fortunate in being able to use the large, all embracing word US—each time he did he thought about Diana Kingsley-Pink and was certain that he wanted to have nothing to do with this large machine US. He said he couldn't afford to make her any promises. There came a faint reply to the effect that, 'Ma Mummy would see us all right, she says.' He said he couldn't be sure of his own feelings, he had an unhappy childhood to blame for that, and he wouldn't risk hurting her. He couldn't take that risk. He was terrified of being involved and of letting people down. He made a mental note to bring out the unhappy childhood at an early opportunity with Diana. There was then a long silence.

Moorman now felt tired, drained, and was quite sure the worst was over. He patted Mona Lisa again, and she sat up, her back to him, strands of hair all over the place. He laid a hand on her back and she immediately snapped it into her armpit, so that he recoiled. She turned round, the ruined black eyes and sequins falling from the lids, and Moorman said: 'Let's have a talk about it all when you don't feel so . . .'

Without a word she stood up. Moorman leaned back on the ruined hot pillows. What had become of the Kit Kat finger? All he could think of was getting Mona Lisa out of the room. She opened her mouth, standing on a level with the mean little green distempered chest thoughtfully provided by Mrs di Valvona. Her arm went sweeping across the top of it.

There was very little to knock over: a few old Pan books wedged between one of the mirror supports and a Scotty dog wearing a Tam o' Shanter, made of the plaster that is normally esteemed a prize at fairs; Moorman's hairy comb, three of the white bone collar-stiffeners from his new shirts, the piece of paper on which Diana had written her name and number (he was never going to part with that) and a brown plastic tray bearing a collection of mean objects that rather summed up his life: a tarnished cuff-link, a Bic biro clouded black, some Polos in just the silver paper and an old Mint Imperial. These fell to the lino and scattered.

It was the violence of her gesture that made him leap up out of bed terrified, shoving back the helmet into his pyjama trousers. He went and grabbed Mona Lisa by the shoulders and she clung to his neck, pressing to him with such fierceness that he shouted: 'Oh, do be careful of yourself, mind yourself. The bloody stitches!'

Then he crouched down and chased with his fingers the things from the chest-of-drawers, his fingers pinching at the grey Mint Imperial.

Mother, when he was about seven, had brought him a box back from somewhere: even then he had been so unspeakably pleased and touched. He'd kept the box, with one sweet left in it, on his dressing-table at the other flat, until the white mint was yellow. He kept it to remind him of Mother. She found it, hit him over the legs and threw it out. Moorman picked this one off the lino and debated whether to put it in his mouth. Mona Lisa crouched down beside him, weeping again. 'Darling—leave it all and I'll do it, I'll pick it up, I'll pick it up,' she repeated, obstructing him from getting at the collar stiffeners, repeating, 'I'll do it.' He grabbed two of the stiffeners and was about to put them on the chest-of-drawers when he knocked his hand and they and the Mint Imperial fell down again. The Mint Imperial went skidding under the bed. Moorman hissed: 'Look! Cut it out! I'll do it.' He tried to shove her gently.

She banged her head on the lino. Deliberately. She beat it deliberately against the floor, a rhythmic thump thonk thump. It frightened him but even with his hands cupped round her neck, he couldn't stop it. 'Go on,' she said between bumps, 'Kill me. Do it.' He raised his hand to see if he was capable of hitting her, but she cowered away as if accustomed to this. They struggled and finally she stood up in time with him, grabbed him tightly round the neck and slobbered a kiss all over the front of his face. That finger of Kit Kat was still under the pillow. 'Why don't you ever kiss me properly?' She pulled him down on to her on his disordered bed. One of her knees, quite accidentally, caught him in the genitals: a dark, purple, muscular sort of pain like a black eye on the heart. He succeeded in rolling off her, into the cruel glare of the bedside light. He wondered how many dormitories of Italians throughout the Tredegar Guest House had stirred to the rhythmic thunkings of back-combed hair on linoleum. She lay there, miming sobs, composing the front of the blue dressing-gown.

He was quick: she'd know he was strong.

'Look, I'd better walk downstairs with you to your . . .' he began, giving the ribbed material a forgiving squeeze, and Mona Lisa screamed: 'Aaaaagh! That's done it. Ma wound. Ma stitches. I'm leaking again. I heard a thing pop. Mother o' God, it broke.'

'What? What?' His mind and body stammered with terror.

'You pinching me opened up ma wound. It's all leaking. It's started all over again.'

'I didn't . . . I . . .'

'Oh, get ma Mummy quick. She knows what little bowl and dressing to bring.'

'Can't you go back to your . . .?'

'Och, I *can't,*' Mona Lisa gasped. 'And trail it all down the stair and probably never stop it. Ah have to keep still.' She eased herself on to his pillow (the Kit Kat!) and looked sideways at him: this was difficult as her chins bunched up so.

She started to cry.

'I want ma Mummy. I want HIC! ma Mummy. Go and get ma Mummy. Oh, please, *please* do it.'

Sighing with exasperation, fear; was anyone ever so put upon? Moorman tore back the plastic curtain. Why hadn't he got a dressing-gown? He supposed that Miss Toye could have produced any amount of them from old gentlemen who'd died, the pockets full of green hankies and old nutshells, but what about a new dressing-gown, a camel-coloured one with braid in two shades of brown? That was something else to make a better man of himself in the eyes of Diana and her mother. For agonized moments he high-stepped around in the corner, putting on his old suit trousers and, for positively the last time, his new Ivy League Rael Brook shirt. Turning back to the bed he saw Mona Lisa lying with her face to the wall. Her hands pressed into the blue dressing-gown exactly as her mother pressed hers into the dangling heads and tails of the mink cape while describing some species or other of diarrhoea. Quavering, 'Hold on,' Moorman wrenched and jingled his bedroom door open and went down to the middle landing, uncertain what he would do when finally confronted by the plaque on the door. 'Mummy's Room.'

As Moorman walked along, searching for this landmark, another door opened. A small figure edged out, fully dressed in beautiful pullover, tapered cuffless trousers and buff slip-ons; one of the lodgers, the one who looked uncommonly like Anthony Quinn. Moorman hoped he smiled reassuringly at this observer, who stood and watched as he examined the line of doors closely. There were distant, rumbling Italianate snores all round him.

'Mummy's Room' was now in front of him. Moorman was now breathless with fear that the poodle would fly off the bed at his throat; that in the gibbet of light through the open door, Mrs di Valvona would shriek and clutch her throat, perhaps dying of frightened fat. Supposing both of them should die. He looked wildly back along the corridor to see the watcher silently withdraw, and the line of his mouth and of his moustache clamped in displeasure, and the door closed soundlessly.

Moorman tapped on the door to 'Mummy's Room'.

He did it again. His fingernails were too long; he would have to borrow Leslie's clippers before seeing Diana again. There was a sprawling noise and, 'C'min.'

Pushing it open he could see directly out of the window: the pier with the retreating tail light of an all-night fisherman's bicycle, the black band of the sea, and then the mainland's yellow industry glow.

Having been brought ceremoniously to view Mrs di Valvona's new O Sole Mio blanket, he knew that her bed was right next to the door: to speak to her he must, therefore, push the door to again, shutting away most of the light from the passage. In the half dark he could see the mass of her double bed. He whispered, 'Mrs di Valvona,' realizing as he did so that this was the first occasion on which he had called her by name.

Moorman bent, gently so that the sleeping black poodle wouldn't wake up, and addressed the point where he estimated his landlady's head, with the arrangement of chins, would repose.

'Mrs di . . .' He heard stopped breathing and saw the eyes wide open. 'Gordon? Is it? Who's there? Gordon?'

'Um, look, I'm sorry . . .'

Two arms, dimpled at the elbows and letting night cheese out from under themselves, sprang up and caught him round the neck. 'No, I'll do it!' Moorman said, forgetting where he was. His face was borne down, scuffed by the foamy lace and bows around her shoulders—she used a skin preparation named White Shoulders—and it came to rest, boiling hot, in the Stilton valley that lay closest to her excited heart. A wedding ring knocked urgently at his testicles. A voice whispered to him: 'My dear—this is madness.'

12

Leslie's and Mr Starkey's plan was as follows:

(Moorman, true to the spirit of grinning guilt, wanted to put it right out of his mind; to pretend it wasn't there, like Pitman's shorthand. Like Leslie's deepening joy in Mr Starkey's company and their discussions about Tel E Kebir, Omdurman, and the sacrifice of Private Kavanagh at Cawnpore.)

Where the money was to come from, Moorman had no idea. He felt relieved that he didn't know, yet provoked at being left out. Had they got enough, he once tentatively asked. 'Oh, ye-es, just about, I dare say,' Leslie replied. During the week that led up to the rehearsal at Diana's, Moorman would arrive at the Pavilion and try not to see the sacks of Colman's powder potato, which Leslie had at once ordered, standing just inside the doors. Similarly, he would try not to attend to Mr Starkey's banging and belping at the wall behind the tea bar, or his bag of tools spread flat on the ground.

Leslie said they ought to move the sacks of potato powder to the back of the pierrot stage: Moorman's heart leapt, he felt flattered once more to be involved in the Pavilion, even though the moving operation meant a dreadful perspiration up his legs and his back and backside itched like flames. Leslie's collar-stud buttocks stuck out as he tried and struggled with what were nothing but fragile great paper bags. 'We *are* being wise virgins in the long run,' he puffed (to Mr Starkey), 'you know, Mr S., I was terrified that that naughty little boy would come along and kick holes in them, or empty a cup of water on them. Believe me, I've seen what a cup of water can do to a tin of candy floss powder.'

To start with, Mr Starkey was to convert six chests-of-drawers into a form of self-service countering, joined by a Formica-topped tray running-board of his own design.

They (he and Leslie) arranged to buy a large second-hand hotplate and a lot of second-hand knives, forks, spoons, cups and saucers and thirty-six old sun-roof tables which, Leslie discovered, had been stacked in an ante-room of the Springbourne Town Hall since the burning down of the Seagull Restaurant in 1953, and about a hundred wooden chairs which were no longer needed by the Vine Hotel in Totland since termination of their Skiffle Nights. Unfortunately these had been joined together by wood battening in blocks of ten to prevent individual chairs from eagerly being smashed by the dancers; un-joining them would be a further job for Mr Starkey.

As to meal trays, Leslie had pulled off something of a coup. By telephone he obtained one thousand small round trays free of charge from Littlewoods Pools Ltd, each one bearing a picture of a firm handshake. Their only disadvantage was that they could be crumpled in the fist of quite a small child.

'Incidentally, I know you're head-in-the-clouds and thinking ill of no one at the moment,' (his nasty tone put a sudden blush on Moorman's face), 'but that little boy hasn't abandoned us,' Leslie warned. In a new matelot-striped jersey, he looked comically severe. 'This morning, before you arrived, he was having a little scout round the pierhead, pretending he'd just come down with his fishing-line, but I met his eye. Later, I saw Ned Uncles leading him away by his ear.'

Would Meatball come and attempt to plunder their self-service cafeteria?

Moorman found the term 'self-service cafeteria' enormously satisfying. It seemed to imply thick creamy ices mixed with various deep gravies; but, in fact, the beginnings of their cafeteria would be most modest. The 'catchpenny', as Leslie called it, was a special two-shilling hot lunch—sausage, powder mashed potato, and peas, with tea or coffee. And if this caught on they might do pasty, mash, and peas, or even, Leslie said, 'unassuming salads'.

He was very bright about everything, even the notion of having to hire two women to cope with the serving, a lad to clear away the dirty plates and possibly a cashier. 'What we do have on the credit side, as dear old Nell will agree—won't you, dear?—is the urn, the Jolly Jackson urn. *And* a reasonable little sink out at the back.' Mr Starkey began by cutting and drilling a small hatchway through from the tea bar to the room behind it; and Moorman and Leslie stood watching, eating Nell's flint undersided cheese rolls in the banging.

He'd forgotten what Diana looked like. Had she forgotten what he looked like? Now it was only Wednesday. Was her mother trying to keep them apart? He was tortured by the memory of his telephone conversation with Diana late the previous afternoon. Again, the Doctor's growly voice broke in: 'How are you getting on? Have you nearly finished?' Diana remarked: 'I've got the extension thing for the phone in my room. I was just having a tidy out. Mummy's just brought me a mug of tea.' Moorman, foolishly, had replied: 'Swallow some and let me hear what it sounds like over the telephone.' A cackle out of the receiver almost made him feel sick. 'Swallow some! Oh, don't be a booby!'

He'd spent the £7. 17s. 6d. he had in the bank on a gold bracelet for her which looked far more expensive. This instead of the dark brown square-toed shoes in Russell and Bromley's.

'Honestly,' Leslie Langdon said, 'it's tragic. Loneliness is, you know.' Moorman felt relieved at the warmth that seemed to have come back to Leslie's conversation with him. 'I feel quite sad sometimes thinking of the lonely. Poor girl came up to me a couple of days ago, after you'd gone off to your blinking whatsisname . . . your garden rehearsal at Miss Italy's, and asked if I'd go to the Recreation Ground with her later. "Come on," she said, "I don't care if I have children." I said, "No, dear, you find a friend of your own age: I'm too old for you, Christine."

'Then she did find herself a feller for a brief while, but I think he's made off now into the blue. She was buying him crisps, cups of tea, whatever he wanted. I shouldn't be surprised if he didn't fleece her of all her pocket money. He couldn't see a thing without his glasses on, and Christine kept taking them away; pretending it was all a game, you know, but all the time quite serious. I think it's a rotten shame for her to be so lonely, poor old soul.'

With his mouth full of sharp-edged bread, Moorman suddenly felt sick with shame at the memory of asking Diana to swallow her tea over the telephone, and with good old pure nausea at his brief descent into his landlady's bed. She had not mentioned it since, but called him 'darling' now, even in front of Mona Leaker.

He tried to speak: 'Bi widn't pithe bumberstamb begsackry bot bam Pharkey dbuth.'

'Mr Starkey? What that man Starkey does? Well, he's first and foremost a joiner. Invaluable man. I now find, as everything else, that he once worked for our mental,' (he meant 'mentor'), 'and teacher in S'Lots of Fun; all of which convinces me that what we want down here is Mr Starkey as a Consultant. Mr Starkey now enters the story, eh?

'In fact, I met Mr Starkey through dear Mary, bless her. You see, Mary used to work in Springbourne years ago, just after the war. She played a Hammond organ with one hand and a grand piano with the other down in the Albany when they were quite famous for the sing-songs they had there. Anyway, the proprietors decided to get rid of the grand piano, which was all broken anyway and looked horrible, Mary says—they'd painted it to match the organ and that did it no good.

'And Mr Starkey threw it away for them.'

'Threw it away?'

'Yes,' Leslie said, and pealed with silvery laughter. 'He did. He brought it up here, according to Mary, on one of those motorized luggage trucks you sometimes see about and then plonked it into the sea and it floated . . . away . . . away it went bobbing and floating into the great shipping lanes. It was last seen off Bournemouth.

'Anyway, Mr Starkey is far more useful to us than a thrower-away of difficult objects: I mean, I wouldn't go so far as to ask him to throw Ned Uncles Rock Shop away for us. Incidentally, old Ned's come quite all right about that . . . that business, you know, outside, and wants to forget it and bury the hatchet. He thinks he can persuade his bro-in-law to agree, so that's nice, isn't it?'

A section of light and relief flooded into Moorman who, nonetheless, had forgotten all about the summons from Softytop Ice Cream ('None Nicer' Brand) Ltd. He bit into his cheese roll, a huge bite.

'Where was I? Oooh, yes. Mr Starkey's powers of chucking away. No: the first thing about him is he's got this place at the top of St John's Lane which he says would be ideal to keep this little lot in,'—Leslie waved a hand to indicate the Pavilion's machines and the rifle range which they had decided to close down and sell back to U Need Us Ltd, Funfair Suppliers.

Leslie took a sip of his tea and sucked air in noisily. 'Gor! Warm! Nell, in future I'd like it all saucered and blowed.' Old Nell Sumption's rosy face dissolved in pleasure.

Moorman bleated: 'But couldn't we try to sell them while they're standing here?'

'Not really,' Leslie explained patiently. 'You see it's more a question of our paying someone to take them off our hands, and it's going to put whoever it is off properly, isn't it, if they come down here and see them? Like viewing bankrupt stock, no? Be a lot neater to have them stored away like a treasure trove.'

'How much do you think . . .?'

Leslie said: 'Fifty, seven-five, if we're lucky. It's the time of year.'

They had paid four hundred for the machines.

'The real problem we've got to overcome, what with resources stretched the way they are, and new staff to find,' he continued happily, 'is actually shifting them to Mr Starkey's; shifting the machines out. It would be nice if your friend Mrs di Valvona could help us there. I suppose you couldn't ask if she knows of a task force, whatever that is in Italiano.'

Mr Starkey, using a Black and Decker drill (how wonderful Moorman thought, to earn one's living with one's own gleaming set of instruments), had marked out on the wall behind the tea-bar the size of the new hatch in drill holes. It reminded Moorman of the V.R. that Sherlock Holmes used to shoot in his wall in Baker Street: how he wished he could be *there*, in the warm lamplight. He was certain that Diana hadn't meant any of it. Or had she known about his disgusting performance inside the Doctor's yellow trunks? Was that why her mother, for all her charm, was trying to keep them apart.

Now Mr Starkey chose wrenching tools and began to pull away the dull green plaster that Mr Vernon, the previous lessee, had chosen for his skating rink. Moorman and Leslie put down their teacups and went behind the bar to watch: a ferry came in and departed while they were watching. Underneath the green was revealed a garish wallpaper of the 1930s, made up of lists and diagrams for different cocktails—'Rhum Frappé', 'Melotone Melody'—behind that there was hardboard and then a piece of bar-mirror which Mr Starkey shivered to pieces with a chisel before he realized. And behind that, in between the layers of the far wall, they found a hollow filled with the bright new wood shavings the carpenters had thrown there years before. Leslie poked his finger among them and uncovered an ancient green bottle with a green glass marble caught in its neck, and two stiff and yellow bits of newspaper.

'I'll take that beautiful bottle if no one else wants it,' Leslie said. 'It's lovely. See how they used to pinch in the neck whilst the glass was still wet so as the little marble wouldn't roll back and block the flow of pop. "Block the flow of pop." How's that for poetry! See? Oh, and the cuttings are both about casualties in the Kaffir War of 1875.'

'An unremarkable conflict,' Mr Starkey said, 'except for the loss of the troopship Birkenhead,' and resumed his hacking.

The moon was sharp and bright, rushing over the top of the Mini van at sudden turnings.

'We ought to practise,' Moorman said, loudly, above the gear changes.

In the village pub after they had read through a pantomime in rhyming couplets, he'd just elbowed his way forward: what would all of them have? They had gins and rums and vermouths and crisps and a tin of nuts. The round was 22s. 6d. Almost a new shirt. But Diana had stood next to him—it was as good as if she'd taken his arm. Even better when Miss Maxey cornered them both told them a funny story as if, as listeners, they were indivisible. The story was about a maidservant who'd stuffed a Christmas turkey rolling about the floor, drunk, and afterwards discovered that she had put in her dental plate as well.

'Let's practise our words.' He remembered a lot from the play and began to declaim them. 'Oh, Eustace, we have come so far/the landscape's getting unfamiliar.' Diana laughed and concentrated on her driving. 'Now softly do I hear a crackin',' Moorman insisted, 'the sound of brigands crawling through the bracken/brandishing swords and uttering fearful *oaves* . . .'

'You've got a very good memory,' Diana said.

She'd noticed.

' 'Tis plain that they are brigands by their *cloaves* . . .

Oh, sister, 'tis a pity that some children haven't got any/ Pleasures like ours in studying birds and . . .'

'That one puts all my teeth on edge. Especially when . . .'

'Botany.'

'Ugh, yes. Did you notice how Jo Ince said her lines. That bit about, "What's this, me one-time pal turned traitor?" '

'Stay here till I return, I'll kill you later.'

'Yes—God, you have picked up a lot. You should be playing the lead. Billy gets so uppity about everyone else being word perfect, then he always forgets his own things.' She hurried on to what she wanted to say—Moorman noticed this happened a lot. 'Did you see the supercilious expression on that Mrs Appleby's face? She really can't stand amateur dramatics, you know. She just can't bear to be left out.'

How did he get her to stop the van without actually suggesting it? How did he find out if she'd meant it?

'At their house, they throw *cold sausages away*.'

Moorman patted the flat packet in his breast pocket and the hard box in his left-hand jacket pocket. He suddenly realized that he was about to ruin the trouser creases of his suit even more.

'Mummy makes marvellous hash-ups; she just slings all the leftovers in and covers them with baked beans, onions and tomato sauce—mmm, scrumptious! Another lovely thing is her firework sandwiches on Guy Fawkes night, and we always get Billy to . . .'

The enchanting spread of her legs on the driving pedals gave him the courage and the volume. 'I suppose we couldn't stop somewhere for a little while?' The ends of her hair swung round at him and she smiled.

'Well, if you're very good, I might take you and show

you the Wild Wood for a little while.'

Moorman snuggled against the locked door: he was being driven off to the woods by a blonde girl.

A moment later Diana stopped to allow another car past. Then the bonnet of the van dipped alarmingly down and shuffled into long grass at the side of the road. 'Do you think you could nip out and open the gate?' she said. Moorman plunged into the deep grass to struggle with a gate that also had a supplementary wire fastening. For a dreadful moment he thought he wouldn't be able to manage it, but he did and she drove the Mini van down a track full of sun-hardened ruts under his feet as he followed the tail lights.

She turned carefully into a space in a line of trees which looked directly on to a moonlit field. All around, the wood was of the very thinnest kind. When cars passed on the main road, their headlights blazed in the van's interior and Moorman jumped.

They sat in silence for a minute or two. An abnormal squeak outside made him jump again. Diana said with a little laugh: 'I used to be firmly convinced that it was rabbits doing that.' Then Moorman swung his knees across, striking the handbrake, and Diana seemed to slide to meet him, so that the first kiss was equally a collision.

He was being swallowed by her mouth. His own jaw ached with the extravagances of his mouth-figures; he'd never kissed or been kissed quite like this, with a sensation of touching the rough, ribbed places right at the back of one another's throat. Moorman tried to look at her, to see if her eyes were shut tight with pleasure, but they were open wide, looking beautiful and normal underneath that unusually shaped forehead and the band in her hair.

His nose on her forehead, he was at once assailed by dreadful fears. Had he looked stupid and girlish just now with his own eyes shut? Did his breath smell? He drew his mouth back hoping unobtrusively to pull out his lower lip and breathe experimentally into it, but she followed and closed her mouth over his lips. They went on kissing roughly, like tonsils, her head back on the rim of the driving seat. She worked her knees under Moorman's legs. He moved over and over until he was actually seated on the handbrake. Later an amusing remark about that but not now. One arm came across and spread out on his chest, trying to rub through to the hairs. Then, so out of his mind with excitement that he managed to move as if rubbing against porcelain, Moorman turned in mid air, feeling his knees chaffed by the rubber pattern on her driving mat. Her legs spread out wider and he pressed one knee between them, pulling her slightly up from the driving seat until that point of light, that beginning right at the back of him warned Moorman to be careful. He drew back from her and knelt over her on the driving mat. Her eyes were closed now and a half smile was on her face. His arm was round her shoulders at the back of the seat. She smiled and still didn't try to move or start again. Why? He tried to make his eyes bore into hers. Why had she stopped? Cold? Had enough? Irritation began, then he realized that his arm was trapping her long blonde hair. She'd said nothing, to prevent his being embarrassed. He moved his arm and Diana opened her eyes and shook her head fractionally. 'I've got a little rug in the back: a Hunting Stuart tartan thing that Mummy got out of the Harrods catty.'

Whatever Moorman said he knew would be hoarse and choked by spit. He opened his door of the Mini van and his foot moved in grass that was so long and dry that it lay almost horizontally. Again, the thin wood was lit up by a car passing along the road, and instinctively he ducked.

He walked round to the back of the Mini van, on his way kicking a rear tyre, since it seemed the right sort of careless gesture to make. Diana had spread the rug out and was kneeling on it, her eyes looking up at him, that delicacy of her forehead and dark hairband accentuated in the poor light.

It seemed he had to make only the most ambiguous stepping movement and he was lying on top of her, scarcely believing it, his hand inside the rim of her jeans against what he took to be faded blue old school pants—these excited him very much. He pushed her jersey upwards with one hand, then pressed his face downwards: he was rubbed and quite astonished by the knobbly character of the brassière she wore. The knickers were so simple. His hand went round to her back—purely bravado – he had no idea of the scientific loosing of a brassière. Diana, at this, sat bolt upright, slipped the jersey over her head and before he'd made a further move, unclipped the rear fastening and sat up straight, hanging her head so that the ends of hair swung forward, trapping the bra straps under her arms. Moorman was now faced with a prospect he'd often thought about in bed at night and in the morning: a slim girl with a bare top and long, tight trousers. When he closed with her again, she had a new sort of openness and coolness. He suddenly wanted to roll over and over with her, as if they were playing in a sandpit and, for a miserable moment, wondered if this could be a sign of old age.

Moorman was getting ready to go into his accustomed heavy sweat, killing it all by heaving and sweating, and then apologizing with his head in his hands; saying this was a sign that he really cared.

Instead, she had barely gathered him in, he had scarcely put a hand out to feel that the rim of the thing was still up tightly, when she began to laugh breathlessly, gasp uproariously then a yell one could tell belonged to a la-de-dah voice.

The cold wind on his behind, the rabbits (no, they'd be squirrels) noisy in the wood and the pale dominoes of straw lying over in that field, from which they were, of course, perfectly visible . . . Moorman suddenly felt conversational. Now hold on! Now just a minute. Steady! What's this? A yell in a la-de-dah voice? That's not the idea—one is supposed to sweat and heave and push and pull, possibly rolling down a steep bank with sharp twigs pricking. One is then supposed to apologize. He wanted to say 'Isn't that interesting?' He really wanted to talk about Diana's suddenly voiced inclination to yell in that rather rich posh way. He felt as if his nose were again touching the rear of her tonsils. He felt as if that unpredictable card his erection might vanish simply from the interest of the situation.

'Are you all right?' he said in a perfectly level voice which must have sounded to her absolutely in command. Quite accidentally so. 'Oh, yes, oh, yes, my darling,' he heard. So he pushed and pulled and spread himself about like the illuminated peacock's tail, surprised to find that he was in no peril whatever of firing until absolutely meant to. But in a few seconds, possibly thirty minutes, her mirth was up at the very top note again. Full of high style, feeling himself to be a devil of a fellow, Moorman thought about her with her trousers on. His mouth went dry. She sounded like a crowd at a gymkhana. For a moment he felt nothing—a terrific nothing that curled his toes in, and then all his interiors opened long windows, banged them and opened them and banged them again.

He hoped he didn't smell sweaty.

The wood squeaked.

The wood gave a squeak.

Diana said: 'The rabbits . . .'

A car's headlights from the road lit up the van and her forehead and headband. 'Mmmmm,' she breathed in, and held her breath. 'That was—aaaah, absolutely beautiful.'

He threw the helpful little cocoa skin into the grasses with an awkward overarm: Heads rabbit . . . He lay back as if the wood was an airbed and he could have replied wittily but tolerantly to anything on earth. The Pavilion seemed a warm, gentle occupation. Nell Sumption's cheese rolls were bendy-fresh. The season was bound to pick up. Mother meant well. Mrs di Valvona meant well. Diana's mother's phrase 'He's a *netural*' rested agreeably on him. 'I can't think of a nicer way of shaking hands,' he said, not knowing why, it was entirely unrehearsed, but certain that it was witty and exactly appropriate.

Diana laughed and blew air out, almost a raspberry, she rolled and lay on top of him flicking his mouth with her tongue. 'You are sexy, Mr Man.'

He let a smile wander about. 'Me?' Gently deprecating but not contradicting. Then: 'Excuse me for asking, but it *did* work out for you . . .' She giggled: 'What do you think?' 'Well,' he pretended to sound modest, 'I do like to think of it working out for the lady,' and Diana said clearly: 'I think that's a sweet thing to call us instead of crumpet or something.' He continued superbly—he did this all the time but never lost his gentle humility—

'I suppose I'll even risk asking the wrong question at the wrong time just to find out . . . you know, if it worked out for the lady.'

Diana was silent. Thinking, he supposed, of all the other girls he had treated like fine china. That was fair exchange for the moment (it had worried him) when at the rehearsal, she said: 'Billy's blazer buttons are Hawks—from Cambridge,' and he wondered to himself how many gay, lean undergraduates had flung their legs over her.

She said: 'I suppose I'm lucky in a lot of ways.'

'Lucky?' Every way seemed to glow in soft neon, erected as a tribute to himself.

'Oh, lucky that I'm not, well, frightened of it.'

'Why be frightened?'

'Those Inces often hop into bed with people at parties but they never let anything happen. Mummy said to me, "Never be a prick-teaser".'

The neons became a little more garish.

'I think I was lucky in the first place that I didn't have this dreadful thing of being scared of it hurting the first time, because I'd had the little operation, you see . . .'

He didn't. 'Ohmmm.'

'You know: when you have your womb sort of scraped out to stop you getting tummyaches when—you know—at certain times.'

'Yes.' His niceness was slipping away. He wanted a warm dish of compliments, not references to womb-scraping. He experienced a yearning to be played lovingly with: her hands cupped him but seemed to be pinging him about in the most conversational way, a gesture to accompany talking. When she cackled, did it strangle?

'I suppose you've done it thousands of times.'

'Not that many.'

'Oh, come on.' He thought this was a bit better; her tongue jumped out again and touched his cheek and she kept her hand still.

'Well,' he said, selecting a nice phrase, 'I haven't just come down off a Christmas tree.'

A mistake. Oh . . . the cackle sounded through the wood. Moorman opened his eyes, the last of the Ovaltine feeling gone from the testicles, and he said desperately: 'How about you? I mean, have you?'

'That was last summer and wasn't very nice. I met this fellow when we were staying with Auntie Marie, that's a Polish schoolfriend of Mummy's, near Cambridge, and a gang of us went to the Midsummer Common Fair. One of the men drove me back and we had a nifty stop at his brother's flat in Cherryhinton Road on the way. I remember, all I could think of was that he had absolutely ice-cold balls.'

In the ensuing cackle, Moorman attempted a last stand by saying was she cold.

'Not in the least—you kept me warm.' He'd managed it! Then she said: 'But I'm starving though,' and cackled. 'I've just remembered. I've still got the apple from today's lunch in the van.'

She tore deliberately at the apple, chewing it with her mouth open, so that he wanted to grip the linings of his genitals, pockets being out of reach. He lay with his eyes closed as his rosy view of everything sorted itself out—the tearfully complicated business of self service at the Pavilion, the money, the Italians, a ruined Daks suit, and three new shirts that needed washing. He wondered if he could put up with apples eaten like that and cackles like man-eating gulls. He forgot about giving her the bracelet.

13

He was numb with the failure of the weekend that followed. The thought of Sunday sent the same blast of chilly fear and embarrassment down his throat and out of his fundament that he recalled from assorted incidents at school—as, for example, when a sarcastic geography master sniffed the air and said 'Who's been having chips in here? Whole place reeks of chips.' Or when, out of 240 boys in three ranks, 240 well-washed faces, correct grey school shirts and properly combed heads of hair, only one boy had a blazer that was black not blue (it had come via Miss Toye from an old gentleman who'd died) and only one blazer didn't have a badge.

The sun shone at Hemingford Priory, the wasps murmured in the nettles round the station yard. When it was quite plain that Diana would not be coming to meet him, Moorman walked, sweating, down the farm roadway, nearer and nearer to the pat of tennis balls and excited shrieks.

Round the supper table, in company with five or six

dark-haired, chin-cleft agricultural students with dazzling smiles, Diana came out with: 'What I really like doing (cackle) is getting at the soles of my feet with Mummy's big serrated kitchen scissors, getting a nice hard lump of skin, pulling it off and eating it; mmmm, a nice feed of skin.' Moorman was sitting nowhere near her. She scarcely looked in his direction. She sat on the far side of the table. She displayed no partiality for any of the agricultural students but, he thought—sweating—there was something teasing and long-legged and permissive in the way she let two of them try to shut her between the folds of the air bed on the lawn, shouting 'Oh you pig!'

She played tennis with them long after the sun had gone in. Moorman sat on the heat-blistered bench against the winter garden looking at all this in passionate blurs through the tangle of the boundary nets. Diana's mother came out and sat beside him for a little while, wriggling her toes in and out of her exercise sandals; he thought, darkly, that she was trying to cheer him up. 'Weren't zey all impossible at supper time. But it wasn't *schreal* bad menners was it?'

Then Diana ran off the lawn—straight past him, through the french windows to the dining-room where the gramophone equipment was kept. The agricultural students joined her in a pack. The noise, Cliff Richard and The Supremes made Moorman feel on the edge of a white madness. They were *all* as slim and as good looking as Cliff Richard. They had tiny bottoms, like collar studs in taut white jeans. Moorman found himself unable to look down at his own trousers or at the point where his trousers joined his shirt. He looked straight ahead and remained on the bench. Quite an impromptu party developed in the dining-room; even

Aunt Het came in with her valve radio to watch, wearing a black choker. The Doctor and Diana's mother quick-stepped with a pump handle action. Moorman eventually stood at the door, trying to look tough. It was true that Diana came over to him, took his hand (he thought, patronizingly) she squeezed it and he snatched it away from her. 'Please come and do the Hully Gully for me,' she said and he, spit-blocked, said 'I'm not a bl—essed dancing freak.' Her reply was burned on the soft part of his brain. 'Oh, I made a mistake then.'

Everyone but him was happy, casual, drying out after a swim, with ends of hair curling up over towelling shirt collars. Moorman wished they would disappear—so hard that he saw streaks and liver bands before the eyes. They finally all did, except the one who had kindly volunteered to drive him back to Springbourne. Diana's mother collapsed on to a footstool, kicked off her sandals, worked her exciting brown toes about and said, 'Oh, oh, zose children are schreal breath of fresh air.' Moorman had thought he'd got the part. How about 'let the hag be flung from the tower'? The doctor brought out bottles of red and white wine for the students but gave Moorman scarcely a glance. He'd forgotten all about 'let the hag be flung from the tower'.

On Monday evening Moorman stood in the flesh-smelling Gents behind the King Lud, his hands behind his head. He thought he had recovered from the sorrow of Sunday at Diana's; he strained at his fountain to get it across to himself that he would *not* put up with being ignored or made to hang about during tennis and swimming or have 'let the hag be flung from the tower', his joke, his inimitable Spoonerism, ignored. He had drunk four or five Double Diamonds, warm and wet and tasting of his own existence. He had toyed with the notion of telling Diana to go to buggery. Then he felt sorry—even at the notion that this advice might make her face fall.

Mona Lisa, still confined to the Tredegar Guest House, was being a bother. This was why Moorman was still drinking with Leslie and Mr Starkey instead of going home to his Kit Kat and *The History of Mr Polly*. Mona Lisa waited for him round corners and outside W.C.s, like a love-drugged freestyle wrestler. Early in the morning she would wind her great arms round his neck, overwhelm him with her mother's *Je Reviens,* press her great bulk to his with whispers such as, 'You don't fancy me any more, why not?' A black cocktail dress with chiffon sleeves at ten in the morning. Moorman always tried to fend her off with an affectionate pat on the Mount Everest or a dry, clucking kiss on the cheek. She would turn round and, in that tiny, wondering voice, say 'Don't push me away.' Inevitably, too, Mrs di Valvona would appear and catch the performance's final few seconds. 'I hear you got a byeotiful new gurul friend,' Mona Lisa whispered: Moorman, terrified that her mother would hear, hissed back, 'Oh well, if you believe that, you'll believe anything.'

The next time it all happened, Moorman acted boldly. He manoeuvred himself out of Mona Lisa's rustling, crumbling embrace and adopted a businesslike tone, outlining to Mrs di Valvona the complications of moving the Pavilion's machines from the end of the pier to Mr Starkey's storeroom at the top of St John's lane. He wondered if some of her Italian tenants and friends might give them a hand. Mrs di Valvona raised a ceremonious hand and replied, 'Darling, let that be the least of your worries. The verra least. Och, I can easy get Uncle Grimaldi tae bring some of 'em in and all. Och, ah'm certain they'll co-operate.' She made a note of it in a gilt-covered notebook, pushing out a mitre-shaped tongue that turned Moorman's penis to jelly as he watched it. Then, squeezing his arm, she whispered, 'Not verra' long now afore you two can be together, eh? Gordon, believe me, believe me, night-times that girl *howls* for you. She howls.' It was quite plain—Moorman had no idea why and preferred not to think about it—that Mrs di Valvona believed the shifting of the Pavilion's machines to be the very last obstacle to her daughter Mona Lisa's happiness.

Moorman began to feel that time, before some terrible event, was running out. Frightened and depressed as he had been by Mr Starkey's hammering and preparations inside the Pavilion, he took to staying there late in the evening, until Leslie and Mr Starkey were themselves ready to leave. '*My*,' Leslie remarked, 'we are eager.' On Tuesday night the three of them walked down the pier together, towards the peacock's tail on the Esplanade. Moorman looked at the illuminations and was surprised to feel a strange peace, a thankfulness that he was getting out of *that* dodgy occupation. It was the lovely evening that did it, he realized later. He so seldom noticed lovely evenings. The sky was twirled, a long way up, with red and grey of such infinitely better quality than the Pavilion. There was just the sudden plash of an oar in the water close to the beach, as someone made fast the moored Pedalo boats; or the faintest breeze in the bells at the end of the all-night fishermen's rods, standing at the railings.

Mr Starkey left them at the pier gates and, as he walked away, Leslie stared after him with admiration shining in his eyes. They had talked about the Peninsular War for most of the walk down the pier. And Leslie seemed to stand around, consumed by reverence for Mr Starkey as the fatter man wrenched splintered wood away from the Pavilion's walls and doorways. Moorman stood in the crush of charabanc and taxi drivers, staring with true loathing at the rear view of Mr Starkey, as he was swallowed up in the human masses around the sea-front bus shelters. Then he had to turn away because a line of the most beautiful girls in short skirts walked together from the same direction. As they reached him he pretended to be deeply absorbed by the view of the other side of the Esplanade, as if trying to see a price ticket, perhaps, in the camera shop. He made his eyes go glassy. It was funny about passing girls he there and then began to love violently, in the street. When they were fifty yards away he was petrified at the thought of meeting their eye. When they were close enough to touch he pretended to ignore them, to be higher-class than they were, to have absolutely no time, even to look at them. He shivered with excitement and ignored them.

Leslie that night took him to see Mary playing the electric organ in a great, vaulted saloon bar, The Bodega, half-way up the main shopping street. She wore her accustomed sequinned top and full patterned skirt. She played the expected songs—The Railroad goes through the Middle of the House, In the Middle of an Island. She even had a small microphone on the top of the organ to enable her to sing. As she couldn't sing, she went 'mm-da-da' on certain notes in a voice that was intended to be smoky and mysterious. Moorman and Leslie stood against the bar and watched her. Moorman got fascinated by the tapping movement of her right leg on the bass pedal; indeed, found himself keeping time to it with his own. He stole glances at Leslie, whose eyes were shining almost as much as they had at Mr Starkey's disappearing bulk. Leslie looked back at him sharply on one occasion, then he appeared to pull himself together. He said, 'She's got a very bad ear, poor girl. She's taking drugs. She does too much.'

In the crush of pale ale at the bar, looking over a sea of opened shirt and dress fronts with red and freckles underneath, looking at the big fat, juddering arms and the trousers almost up to the ears, secured by braces, and the joke stetsons and the Babycham mats; looking as well at the youths in white socks and black side-buckled shoes, and the girls in pink, with crucifixes and white cardigans; looking at a hairy dirty man who did the serving and always brought customers' change on a tray swimming in beer ullage so that they couldn't possibly pick the sixpences up; looking over this sea of pleasure, this bowl of merriment, Moorman had one of those rare flashes of well-being that only came if he got in company with people he believed were worse off than himself. The same thing had happened on his few visits to London, riding the Underground. He remembered riding the Underground with pleasure, in spite of the filthy gales that blew his hair inside out around the tubes.

Moorman looked at Leslie again. His white shirt was opened to the waist and he wore a St Christopher medallion. For the first time, Moorman was even thankful he wasn't Leslie. He tried to imagine what happened in Leslie's caravan after dark, with Mary. He couldn't get out of his mind the foot that pumped the right-hand bass pedal on her Hammond organ. He could form, he felt, a much more accurate picture of what the performance was approximately like, thanks to his own encounters with Mona Lisa di Valvona in Bridewell Park. Leslie's romances were doubtless much the same; except there was a bad ear involved, and a fifty-year-old's vamp's voice which went 'mm-da-da', and a right foot that couldn't stop pumping. Moorman tasted Double Diamond and felt a violent shove from behind.

He turned and looked at a sea of faces, looking at him. They had the points of hair coming down between the eyes he remembered from the fourteen-year-olds who'd shouted at him at the end of the pier, between announcements to the ferries. And deep blue Saturday-night suits and white shirts undone at the neck, in an attempt to imitate Tyrone Power as a Mississippi gambler. Moorman's rust-coloured wool tie was suddenly grabbed and pulled tight. He hadn't even a clear idea of who was doing it, since the single spotlight that shone down on Mary at the organ was now directly in his eyes. He bumped the bar with the base of his beer glass and a sob of terror ran through him; he made out two scruffy, watery-eyed young men and, looking down, saw they were wearing the side-buckled shoes and white socks his eyes had rested on just now. 'You looking at me?' one of them said.

'No . . .' almost inaudibly. And by a squeak.

'You looking at *me?*' A horny thumb and forefinger came out and caught his cheek and pinched it, like a Victorian showing approval to a chambermaid.

'No.'

Leslie didn't even turn round.

'You looking at my bird?'

'No.'

'Lawyer.'

'How do you . . .'

'Don' tell lawyes.'

'Oi can take im, I can just manage 'n,' one of them said. It was extraordinary, a voice remarked at the back of Moorman's pale soul, that a customer in a public place could be cuffed and patted at the side of the face in the middle of a crowded bar. He stood transfixed to the spot. Fear made him totally ice-cold, though these odd, rational whispers kept coming: another one said thank goodness Diana and her mother weren't watching. 'You mustn't tell lawyes, it's naughty,' one of the voices continued in a wheedling tone, and Moorman felt a punch in the stomach, and another one in the stomach.

'You was looking at my bird.'

'I . . .'

'You *was* . . .'

'Wait till he goes or goes out to toilet,' the other voice cautioned; as Mary's voice, going 'mm-da-da' to Little Red Monkey covered the incident.

'*Oi* wants to take him here.'

'*Oi* wants to take 'en eytsoide.'

Leslie wasn't even standing there now; perhaps, said the coward's voice at the back of pure terror, he's gone round to the dressing-room with a bunch of flowers. In a tiny part of a second Moorman ran through all possible hints on dealing with a threat like this—talk reasonably, don't show you're afraid, try to laugh it off, buy them a drink, kick one in the testicles and another in the kidneys, wherever *they* were; but at the moment all he felt capable of was overwhelming friendliness. Deference. A brittle kind of courtesy. 'I'm sorry if I *did* stare at you,' Moorman squeaked through an African dam of spittle and terror, 'I wasn't thinking. I was just looking round . . .' Oh, if only he could say he was a talent scout for M.G.M. and wanted each of them for an important film part.

The faces grinned.

'Is 'e with you?' one asked the other.

'Noice in' 'e?'

'Ho hoi say, hanyone for tennis?' his friend said with a trace of irony. Another fist landed in the waistband of the cavalry twill trousers which, for all its hot thickness, was no kind of buffer. Mary was playing This old House is a gettin' Weary, and Moorman received another blow to the face and another to the waistband, thought of his boyhood passion for Rosemary Clooney, the subject of his first recorded wet dream. He saw Leslie coming back through the tables, looking peevishly about him. The yobs saw him as well: though he could scarcely be termed a threat, they might have thought he was a friend of the management. They punched Moorman twice more and walked casually back to their table just to the left of Mary's additional organ loudspeaker. They laughed and joked and took deep draughts from black liquid in stemmed glasses. Their fists had left, all over Moorman, an odd feeling of Bridewell Park.

Leslie asked him back to the caravan for supper. 'Mary can easily run up a bit of something, risotto or cold food,' he said; but Moorman, remembering the grey landscape of the last risotto cooked by the electronic organist, shook his head, said he was tired and wanted to go home. He was glad of the opportunity of slipping away without a glance at Mary's sequinned top and bad ear. He walked through the children who were collected anxiously and unhappily at the lounge door, watching their parents enjoy themselves. Despite the pressure of onion rings, the air on the Esplanade felt beautifully cool. His arms dried slowly, and he no longer had to keep himself from thinking about Diana and her mother. He couldn't think about them when he was hot, or on the lavatory: he imagined them looking at him.

He heard a slender rustle behind him, with the lights

of the Royal Springbourne showing through the ivy cover. He remembered walking through the side-door, watching his new trousers fly out in front of him. He was whirled round and knocked down; he hadn't realized that blows in real life did that. Moorman sat on the red pavement, brushing at his knees. Knees crashed him between the shoulder blades and another blow came that could only be interpreted as a box round the ear. His nose was pulled; his tie, once again was, so that sitting there, he wondered if he would ever be able to undo the knot. Then the two who had engaged him in conversation at the bar, ran off, laughing breathlessly, barging one another like dodgems in a game.

'Oi'm lookun' forward to me party,' he heard.

He sat there, trying to force Diana and her mother out of his mind again as the strolling evening holidaymakers stepped tranquilly around him, and the faintest snare drum came through the ivy of the Royal Springbourne, from the Stan Douglas Swingtet.

All the next day, and the next evening, he just wanted to go to bed and eat; to smell chocolate and fresh sheets together. Worry reached a certain matching level in Moorman's mind with guilt, and he simply craved for tuck. In the Pavilion he ate three Mars bars and a Milky Way. Leslie, with his new acidity said, 'I'm going to call you the Owl of the Remove.' Mr Starkey pushed and struck and wrenched the walls. Leslie watched, adoring.

Moorman at six o'clock went into the Esplanade grocer's from which the red-headed girl was mercifully absent, to buy three bags of crisps and a Crunchie. He noticed, however, a Cadbury's Easter egg which had failed to be sold the previous spring, reduced from eight and six to half a crown. Moorman loved the thin taste of Easter egg shell as much as he loved Diana and her mother. He bought the egg and carried it back to the Tredegar Guest House muffled in that enormous sports jacket of his, like a dagger in a blanket in a Kirk Douglas film. He saw Diana wearing just a pyjama top, kneeling and looking quizzically at him, her blonde hair swinging forward. He kept saying to himself, forgetting the cackles, 'she was such an adorable mixture of woman and little girl.' She was the nearest thing in real life to a picture in *Penthouse*. Against the jacket and Easter egg, an unhappy erection knocked.

His leg ached, his back and tooth ached, he was mad to tear into the chocolate shell when finally he walked up the steps, into the Tredegar Guest House. Mona Lisa was waiting in the hall for him, wearing the formal black evening dress with chiffon sleeves. She came for him like a wheeling squadron of old battleships, and Moorman, terrified for the wholeness of the Easter egg, turned away, trying to give her an affectionate peck on the cheek as if to say, 'Don't worry.' As the filmy arms went round his neck, fastening, Moorman put the rolled jacket to act as a buffer between them. 'And how are you tonight?' he asked with a jocularity not altogether natural.

'I've waited all day to see you,' she whispered, 'Why don't you fancy me any more?' His heart simply melted.

One of the facing doors crashed open and Mrs di Valvona joined them. 'Gordon, darling, is that you? It is you! "Is that you?" she says, and here he is in front of ma eyes. How're you? Ah'm blooming. Ah said blooming. So's she. The stitches come out tomorrow and the leaking's all better. She can do swimming therapy at the baths. And as for me! I tell you, Gordon, I'm that excited, I'm that worked up this afternoon. Guess what's happened . . .'

Moorman stood and listened, with Mona's dark eyes settling on him—cowardly, horrible, ugly-souled person, taking refuge in somebody's gossip—'After all these years, all the heartache has ended. As from now! Och, be happy for me, you two, and share ma great happiness.

'We're reconciled!'

'Who?' he said. The thought of Mona Lisa's head on the pillow made him stupid. Mrs di Valvona replied noisily: 'Who! Listen to'm playing about. It was in Pettifords this morning when I went up to get maself a wee something tae wear at the big wedding tomorrow. We both finds oursel' standing side o' the glove counter, her and me. And we just falls intae one another's arms. We just howled. The wee girl behind the counter didn't know what to make of us, I'm certain. Och, Gordon, come up the stair and get a wee drink tae celebrate all ma joy . . .'

'I'll just dump my . . .'

'Och, leave your coat. Bring it up to the room. "Jeannie," she says, "we've both bin so proud." I says, "Aye, proud. That's correct," with all ma damned eye make-up running all over the place and my wee dog and hers barking. She says, "Och, Jeannie, come upstairs and get your cup of coffee side of me," and I says, "Of course, but I'll pay," and she says, 'No, Jeannie, *I* will," so that we almost fell out again about who was going to pay for the coffee upstairs in Pettifords. And wee Kunzle cakes with it.

'Everything was sorta' strange at first, Gordon,' Mrs di Valvona said, handing him a tumbler full of Cinzano, 'but you know, I think she is real sorry for all the wicked things that she did and said; and you know me, you know me, I bear no grudge to no one. I says, "Let that be the least of your worries." She keeps on saying, "Och, Jeannie, I've been so *schoopud* and high-handed and independent." "That's all water under the foot o' the bridge," I says to her. Och, the Sisters are going to be that thrilled, Mona. Go and ring up the Presentation Convent and say if they were thinking of calling this evening, I might have a wee something tae tell them, something that'll interest them. I had to smoothe her over else she'd a had hysterics all over Pettifords coffee room: she was that sorry for what she'd done, and all the misery she'd caused.' Mrs di Valvona yelled: 'And Mo-ona! Ring your Uncle Joe up and tell him I want to see 'm.'

She sat beside Moorman on the black leather couch, her little knees peeping out.

'I've fixed everything up, darling,' she said, a caress in her voice. 'Joe's getting all the chaps he can for you this Sunday or Sunday week, is that okay?'

The machine moving. He put it out of his mind again.

'That's very nice of . . .'

'Not a bit. Say no more. Not one word more,' Mrs di Valvona said, holding up a selection of jewelled fingers. 'When ma daughter's happiness is at stake, nothin's too much trouble. Her Uncle Grimaldi said the same when I rang him up about it today. "When wee Mona's happiness is at stake," they was his very words. He's going tae come and lend a hand himself. It's got to be Sunday morning because most of them's off then. Ye don't have tae worry about giving them money neither. They all feel the same about our Mona. When her happiness is at stake, nothing is too much trouble.'

Mona Lisa came back into the room, limping slightly as she always did in front of Moorman. 'Sister Michael

Joseph and Sister Hoolican are on their way up the stair, Mummy.'

'Och, so I don't have tae keep ma news bottled up, that's grand,' Mrs di Valvona said, and began to hiss at Moorman: 'Hey, ye know the wedding's tomorrow afternoon. Are you coming?'

'I. . . I. . .'

Mona Lisa, her arms under the chiffon looking fragile, began to weep. 'Mummy . . . I'd like to . . .'

'Now you hush or I'll strangle you. If you're no well enough yet to help me around here, you're no well enough tae go tae weddings and wedding receptions. I want Gordon tae be there because there'll be people I want him tae meet. People,' she simpered, 'that he may be seeing a lot of once his wee caffy is under way.'

'I . . . I think I'll be . . .'

'Och, there's no need for you to come to the church, just come to the reception at the Royal Springbourne. It's to be a byeotiful do—a sum in excess of three figures has been named for the refreshments. The ceremony part should be finished by four o'clock. You'd be able to get away from your renovations a wee bit early for that, I'm certain. Just come and join us for the meal—a sit-down tea for eighty. Och, you stop sniffing, Mona! Will you cease misbehaving! I'll strangle you otherwise.'

The nuns came in: the tall, severe one and rosy Sister Michael Joseph who immediately sat back in the chair where Moorman's sports coat was rolled around his Easter egg. 'Och, Sister . . . and Sister, I must tell you before I go any further . . .' Moorman went behind Sister Michael Joseph, and, without thinking, put his hands down among the dusty folds that reminded him so forcibly of the black-out curtains for their school films. This made the nun sit bolt upright, her whiskers twitching. Moorman stammered his apologies and the nun, standing, looked compassionately as he failed to gather up the crushed box, and it fell on the carpet, where the poodle got it.

'What's that? What in the world's that? An Easter egg? Did you bring Mona an Easter egg, Gordon?'

What else was there to say but 'Yes'?

'Och, you spoil that girl. She's a very lucky one,' Mrs di Valvona said, 'Mother o' God, Sister, ah didn't expect to see her in Pettifords. It was an act of providence, so it was. Should I say, an act of God?'

'Say, rather, an act of God,' the taller of the nuns interrupted.

'Aye, that's what it was. He wanted to patch it up between us. He knew it was no Christian – sisters not on speaking terms. It was an act of God; this I firmly believe.'

And Mona Lisa knelt down, fighting the poodle off with her elbow, cradling the broken box with the clowns and circus animals all joining hands, the smashed chocolate shell in the mauve foil which she was kissing as she rushed from her mother's best room.

14

In a curious number of ways the Friday on which he had to go to the wedding *and* to Hemingford Priory reminded Moorman of sports day at school; beginning when he woke up fearful, as always, and much too hot.

An early haze settled over the beach below his window, and over the planks of the pier; transparent film on the sea, dimming the colours of the Pedalos, drifting into the sky and the white upperworks of the passenger ferries as they arrived, so that their yellow funnels appeared cast adrift just above the head of the crowd. Promise, to everyone bar Moorman, of a beautiful day. John Close's tram banged out of the mist and back.

It was also like sports day, this sensation of being without the proper clothes, having to walk a long way in a fruitless attempt to collect them, looking at his shadow in fear of being late for being last in the hundred yards and a disgrace in the medley relay. And after that, arriving and putting on his plimsolls, which cleaning with chalk had made even filthier: trying to hold in his stomach, while the lovely sisters of prefects, in blue-pleated summer gym slips looked with cool amusement at him.

The Victory Cleaners at the top of the town had a six-hour cleaning service. Moorman remembered their advertisement at the Scala the night Mrs di Valvona had paid for, or rather invested in him. At the time the information had been of no use whatever as he had given up trying to get the blue biro dust out of the pocket of his other suit. His *other* suit! Didn't that imply that he was the proud owner of a *best* suit as well? Moorman looked at an appalling charcoal grey suit in the Amplifier Room. One shoulder had in it an unsightly lump; the result of the Wild Wood he supposed. Moorman pretended to have to choose between lumping the other shoulder or never going with Diana to the Wild Wood again. He choose the lump in the other shoulder. There were also smears on one side of the jacket and on the trouser knees, stains which were sweet to the taste. The jacket pocket flaps were dog-eared.

When Moorman left to take this dreadful suit to the cleaner's Leslie looked at him in a funny way. With some justification perhaps: this was the second time in living memory that about half a Royal Naval ship's company had come in to play the machines. The entire dome sparked and rang with the jolts of the awakened machines, penny slides going in to the pin tables, competing with Mr Starkey's hammering. Leslie could hardly print 'Out of Service' tickets fast enough. As Moorman left with the suit, Leslie—searching in his pocket for change for one of the sailors, remarked, 'Don't tell me the bloody season's going to get cracking just as we're ready to pack up!'

Leslie swore so infrequently. It occurred to Moorman as he toiled up the scorching main street from the Esplanade, that in their 'grinning guilt' relationship, most of the grins had disappeared; Leslie was getting ratty.

That afternoon Moorman had to walk all the way up to the top of the town again to collect the suit, and it was still fearfully mist-hot. The suit wasn't ready. He had to spend half an hour slinking about under shop blinds in the old narrow quarter of Springbourne. He looked desperately into the paper-tulip interior of a sweet shop, kept by two sisters who wore violet-coloured smocks and seemed to have sweets in their mouths all the time. He froze when he saw Fred Wellspring's wife and daughter out shopping with their gentle alsatian. On his way down to the end of the pier again he looked into the dry-cleaning bag: the trouser seams were shiny.

He changed for the wedding at four-thirty, almost sobbing and washed with such vehemence that it made him sweat. One of his shirts, which had been hanging up to dry behind the pierrot stage, was still damp around the neckband. The trousers as well as being shiny now seemed a fraction too short: Moorman hauled them down over his hips and perspiration broke out all over again. In the good light of the Amplifier Room's windows he could tell that the Christian Dior tie had been a bad mistake, too. It wasn't so very different in design from the tie Mona Lisa had given him; not so unlike a black man's tie. Through the windows Moorman saw John Close pull up his lobster net and empty a hermit crab from it which he then threw with all his force back into the Triangle.

Moorman caught the tram; the still haze turned to a hazy hot breeze and blew his hair inside out through the open windows when he'd said he was 'off to the bean-feast' (one of Leslie's expressions), Leslie had simply nodded curtly, once. Again Moorman was walking along the Esplanade towards the battlements of the Royal Springbourne, past the line of cars with nice little secure worlds locked in them, gloves and tins of glucose sweets from chemist's. He pretended this was his first visit to the hotel; his suit was brand new; he hadn't asked Diana to swallow over the telephone.

The sit-down tea for eighty passed in a series of disconnected flashes, little scenes that jumped back to the face of his watch: he was petrified of missing the six-forty from Springbourne to Hemingford Priory. He looked at the wedding reception and imagined himself as one of the subjects. It was held in the same long room that the Conservative dance had been, with the long tables now arranged down the middle of the dance floor. Moorman stared at a lot of it without seeing anything; later he realized he might have been on the point of fainting.

Uncle Grimaldi, in his bootlace tie, pumping his hand and breathing onion into his face. A nasty little old devil getting up, steadied by many hands, and making a speech that referred directly to 'a lotta little babies, quick'. As orderly as policemen, a row of nuns having their tea. Bridge rolls with salami in them—Moorman found a great length of salami string in his mouth and didn't know what to do with it. Grace was spoken with some embarrassment by a surprise guest, the man who owned all the Pedalos and small pleasure craft off the pier who was, nonetheless, an ardent Catholic. Under the table children played and screamed in a foreign tongue. At the bottom of the table some of the Italian guests looked practically neolithic. At the top a handsome man in a terrible electric-blue suit displayed every sign of infatuation for a dumpy, ugly woman of about thirty, dressed as a bride, with whiskers.

Ten to six; Moorman was half paying attention to a story by Uncle Grimaldi opposite him, about the hand-made shoe he had removed and placed among the scraps of bridge roll and salami string on the tablecloth. He kept seeing Mrs di Valvona in the distance, pointing him out to one or other group of wedding guests or nuns. Then he saw her, sitting next to her sister Mrs Sangiorgio on the row of chairs at the far end of the room, where the bandstand was. Above them the box that illuminated the dances was dark, a room-full of painful memory. The two sisters were discussing something earnestly, their bruise-coloured petal hats close together; the paws and tails of their mink capes, even in this heat, studiously combining. Moorman, lightheaded with his efforts to behave naturally, seemed to see them at the end of a long tunnel; he turned back to Uncle Grimaldi; he looked at the sisters again and saw Mrs di Valvona's face wearing its expression of child's fury on top of all those dangerous chins; he turned back to Uncle Grimaldi and then saw Mrs di Valvona actually sitting on the dance floor, her stockinged cylinders stuck out in front of her, rigidly, as Mona Lisa's had been when she fell down four steps at the Scala. He saw Mrs Sangiorgio's face—the grizzled countenance that had so often watched him eat his banana split and bread and butter together in her cafè—was also perilously suffused.

Moorman *had* to go now to catch the train. He felt dizzy and still remote standing above her hat. Then her face lifted to him, the pale pale compressed lips saying, 'Och, I've had such *sorrow* tha' day, och, Gordon . . . that girl! That wickud, wickud girl; may God forgive her 'cause I definitely won't. I'll *strangle* her. With ma bare hands, I'll strangle her. Gordon, did you have your tea? Are you going tae see our Mona—aye of course ye are; she'll be looking for you. Och, ah wish ah'd never been persuaded tae come here and be insulted and . . . and . . . yoomiliated so; I'll strangle her; I'll strangle her so I will. Jesus strike me dead if ah *ever* . . .'

The evening was beautiful in his face as Moorman walked out through the hotel conservatory, moving this way and that for a moment in unison with a latecomer, an Italian guest with a cardboard folder under his arm: Odd, Moorman still a long way off thought, how like Anthony Quinn this guest looked.

Diana's Mini van scooted into the station yard. That cheered Moorman up. Obviously they were going for a little drive. He imagined himself giving Diana her bracelet parked somewhere along a farm track on the far side of the Wild Wood as the evening turned a soft grey around them. He closed the passenger door delicately, in case she was among those who couldn't stand doors to be slammed. Diana snapped, 'It's not closed, not nearly closed.' She leaned across Moorman as if he were a carcass to give it an almighty bang. She wore a tweed skirt, very short and a camel-coloured sweater with a round neck that made him long to press his nose into her shoulder.

'What have you done since I last saw you?'

Diana roared the engine, then turned round to face him before releasing the brake; and spoke as if ticking off items. 'Nothing very much really. Learning my words for Billy's little thing. Quietly getting fat. I made a few flans and fools at the Shire Hall. I asked Billy if he'd pay for me to do a secretarial course and he said he would. I'm going to a place in Newport, the Academy. Mummy asked him if I could go skiing and he said yes. Taking the bunny dog for a walk in the park . . .'

This ought to amuse her: how did he get into such comedies? 'I have just been to an . . .'

'Honey found a rat's nest this morning!' Diana's face dissolved and gave her a horrible double chin for an instant. 'Ugh! Uuugh! She was getting the little babies by the tails and chucking them up in the air. Their naked tails. Brrr, it turned me right up! Ugh!'

The Mini van struggled for a moment in the gravel deposit at the entrance to the station yard, then began again, pulling itself free. Diana drove straight over the main road and down through the poplar trees, past the farm buildings. As the ivy-coloured wall at the end flew towards them and Moorman panicked, Diana said listlessly, 'We're getting a student.'

Moorman blushed at his own lack of studentship.

'Billy's having one to help with the harvest; somebody in his last year at Cirencester College who wants to get a bit of experience.' The van tilted on the grass verge in front of the doctor's car and Diana hurled open her door. 'His name's Moller or Moyer or something. I 'spect he'll be a weed. The last one was: David Saltmarsh. He was just like a great big fat ugly Winnie the Pooh and everything you did for him, he said "Thanking yew".' She spoke in a fruity voice, as irritating as a damp shirt neckband. But at least, didn't cackle. She held the wrought-iron gate open for him with what amounted to a faintly long-suffering expression.

'You don't play cards do you?' she went on, crisply.

'No, waste of time.'

'Well all of us rather like it.'

'I didn't mean it was a . . . an . . .'

'And we're having a little game in the schoolroom this evening.'

Moorman struggled: 'I only meant that I hadn't got

that sort of brain. It's a good way to pass the time, but I meant that it . . .'

'I like Solo. I like keeping my eye open,' Diana said. Moorman wondered dully if her stepfather had printed the playing cards. 'And Billy made some sweet little rail things to put the cards on for people who can't hold them out in a fan, properly.'

Her voice was toneless. Moorman followed her, watching the soft part on the inside of her legs, filled with the desire to kneel and kiss them or see them rubbing together in pleasure at something *he'd* said; some joke or funny voice. They went beside the staircase, through the wooden dog-gate. Honey ran for them, creating a fearful noise. Diana bent down to make a fuss of her; and he felt insanely jealous. Then as he himself came through the gate the labrador jumped at him; he was still, despite its plain redundancy, fearful about mud marks on his suit trousers; he put his hands up but the dog's strong forelegs caught him full and ripely in the private parts, and he staggered back feeling the agony that is so specially evocative of a black bruise spreading all over him.

'Oh dear,' said Diana, a lightness in her voice. 'Did Honey get you in the wrong place?' and at the same moment her mother came out of the kitchen holding a mug of tea. 'Who's caught who in the schronk place?' Moorman could do nothing but try, with the dark bruise covering him, to smile.

He stood folding and unfolding his arms as the conversation proceeded without him, and the budgerigar from the kitchen said 'Kiss kiss'. 'Now Dinah sweetheart, Miss Margaret vill be here in about twenty minutes and Billy back from ze hospital maybe sooner, so I want you to help Mummy by doing the chream for tomorrow's lunch. I left a little bowl on a shelf by ze old wireless.'

Diana pretended to find it irksome. 'I ser-*pose* so.' Her mother bustled out of the wooden gate, holding the labrador back with one delicately shaped little foot and Diana turned on her heel and half-danced into the kitchen, giving Moorman not the slightest indication that he was expected to follow. He stood against the big sink, changing from one to another debonair stance, uselessly, as Diana slammed the pudding-bowl of cream on the table. He thought they must have glorious Sunday lunches here. He pictured onion sauces, three or four gravy boats with green rims, a baking tin of roast potatoes with dark and gold flecks in them. He'd eaten scarcely anything but salami string at the sit-down tea for eighty. He could have picked up the bowl of cream and drained it.

Diana coiled the lead off one of the hand-gun variety of electric mixers. 'These Phillips are good, aren't they?' he volunteered, and she simply nodded. Moorman's hungry mind turned and battered on the question: why was she so cool? Where had the admiration for his jokes and little voices gone? Was it simply because he had asked her to drink her tea so that it sounded over the telephone? Or, in the space of a week, had she become aware of every aspect of his fundamental rotten weakness? When should he try to give her the bracelet? She was warmer when she said: 'I really don't mind this job because I can lick all round the mixer afterwards.'

The instrument whizzing about, Moorman felt one of his angry, bored flushes. She was holding a conversation with the budgerigar. He plunged headlong into an exhibition of little boy eagerness. 'I've never used one of those mixers before, let me.'

Diana stopped it by means of a button at the side and offered it to him, dripping white. She at least stood beside him; she pressed the button again and Moorman pointed the vibrating gun into the cream, for the moment quite enjoying the solid waves and curls this created. He looked up to smile at Diana, who had her hands behind her bottom against the Esse, and she smiled too. He became intent on seeming like a small boy engaged by some fascinating new toy. He thought of a soft, 'Aaah, sweet,' hushing in her mind and felt much better, the ache in his testicles dulled to almost nothing. Diana said: 'That'll do, thanks,' and he withdrew the mixer: having neglected to switch it off first, cream flew everywhere.

In great splots on the front of his suit.

This really was the finish.

It hung in little beards and wedges from the gingham curtain that drew back on their old valve-type kitchen radio, and traces of it reached the budgerigar's cage, adding a bit of variety to the black-curling lettuce and spray of millet provided there. There were little trailing maps on the table and the kitchen's cork floor. Moorman held the spinning, creamy blades and looked at them. A big piece of cream landed on an open Esse ring, where it lay and sizzled, finally becoming a bit of rank meringue.

'Turn it off,' she yelled. 'Oh, you great booby, turn it off.'

He managed this. The blades died away with flicks. A last splash reached the front of that beautiful pullover of hers. He tried to brush it away but touched a shape of crinkly brassière, and also traced the smear down on to her skirt.

Diana began to laugh. Not the syllabic, well-kept

laugh that had welcomed some of his early remarks at the dance; this was a string, a conspiracy, a flaring tail of cackles at his expense, rattling, carping cackles. He said, obstructed by the furnace chimneys on each cheek, 'I'm sorry—I didn't know,' which, really, he'd said to a great many people in his time. She had taken a dry dishcloth from behind the taps and was dabbing about with it, laughing and shaking her head, mouthing, 'I don't know,' making no attempt to clean the cream from her own pullover. That was real wealth. Moorman went up behind her and pleaded: 'Look, I'm awfully sorry.' Hopeful of retrieving the situation somehow, he said: 'Can't we go for a little drive somewhere? Find a little pub?'

She turned round. 'No . . . no, of course, we can't. All Mummy's people will be here in a minute and I particularly want to ask Miss Maxey something.'

'Only a quick one.'

She looked squarely at him. 'Oh, do stop niggling on about quick ones. I've said "No." I never say "No" unless I mean it.'

'Let me give you a hand.'

'No, lea-ve it,' she said, extending the words in patience barely kept in check. 'It's all right. I know it was an accident, but it was so . . . I felt the tears run down my cheeks just now. You looked. In your hair . . .' She knelt down on the floor, the ends of her hair swinging forward, and cleared cream marks away with great encircling sweeps of the dishcloth, going 'Ugh.'

Moorman backed against the Esse where the piece of cream was still noisy on the hot ring. The phrase 'last desperate gamble' occurred to him. He took out the bracelet's red box. He crossed to the sink where Diana presented an adorable rear neatness, her gold hair parted to show a soft neck, she wrung the cloth out under the cold tap, which banged and juddered.

She turned the tap off. Moorman said: 'I wanted to give you this. It probably isn't the . . .' She turned round impatiently, and her face coloured at once with the most awful embarrassment.

'What?'

'I bought this for you.'

He'd also bought a packet of white cards in order to be able to put a single one with the bracelet. He had thrown endless cards away before inscribing one to his satisfaction, 'From Gordon with love', with loops that were thick and thin.

Diana snapped the box open. Originally the bracelet had been stretched taut over the velvety stuff inside but days in Moorman's possession had slackened the string responsible. The bracelet all lay at one end, a muddle of bright links. Her fingers spread them out until they could be recognized.

He heard: 'Oh . . . How gorgeous.'

Waiting for the soft arms round his neck.

And: 'I can't possibly take it, you see.'

He whined, knowing this perfectly well.

'It's just me, I'm afraid.' Diana spoke evenly and quite nicely. 'It's nothing personal, really. I think you're nice and . . . interesting . . . and Mummy's taken quite a liking to you. The trouble with me is, I so often plunge right into situations without thinking of the consequences. Then, after a little while . . .'

'You go off people.'

'Not that. I like you very much as a friend.' (After all, she was only nineteen. He'd better get rid of her as soon as possible. He hoped she wouldn't cry on her pillow.)

Moorman had the odd feeling that her remarks were

precisely the ones he would confect for Mona Lisa di Valvona's benefit. That Diana was desperately sorry at the thought that he might sip a cup of tea by himself, breathing sorrow into it, or might put a sad head on his own pillow. This was very interesting.

Diana kissed him on the cheek, a gesture which he didn't appreciate.

'I'm so sorry. I don't know what comes over me. It worries me. I start off gaily, thinking everything's lovely and then I start feeling trapped . . .'

'Trapped,' Moorman struggled out. 'You've only been out with me three blessed . . .'

'Oh, you know what I mean. I suddenly felt all intense and then I saw that you were feeling all intense and then I felt a lot less intense.' She tried to make it sound amusing, to lighten the conversation, just as Moorman could imagine himself doing. '*Please* don't feel intense or sulky or angry. You probably know a lot of far nicer people than me.'

'Are you going out with anyone?'

She admitted: 'I have been writing to someone for rather a long time.'

'How long?'

'Eight months.'

He stared up at the kitchen's strip lighting and then at the window, the gingham curtain in front of the wireless, the birdcage, letting the black bars of light from the neon dance in front of each piece. . . . 'What made you suddenly go off me?'

'Oh, I didn't, Gordon. It was just a feeling I got, that began, I suppose, at the rehearsal . . .'

'That I didn't fit in.'

'Oh, don't be silly, no.'

'But you went off me?'

'It was *me*.'

'Tell me when you actually felt it happen?'

He spoke as if it were purely of scientific interest, so she probably would say . . .

'Oh, I didn't *go off* . . . well . . .' Her eyes darted round as the wooden gate in the hall sounded. 'Oh, help, this will be Aunt Het downstairs. Oh, look, I don't want you to be hurt, I want you to be happy.'

He almost took her by the shoulder. What a mistake that would have been. At least he always thought twice, or two days, before doing anything.

'At least tell me what it was I did?'

'Was that the bell? I've got to keep Honey in. I told you, it was just me being silly. I'm cross with myself, not with you.'

'It was the cream, wasn't it? It was me spraying the cream all over the place. That was it, wasn't it?'

Aunt Het's face looked in and delivered formal greetings. Radio Newsreel music played, a long way off, from her portable wireless. The dog's bark and the puppy's yap and the budgerigar's chirp of 'Kiss Kiss' were all driving him mad. From here, Diana's mother's light footsteps could also be heard as they came down the main staircase. And the tuneless whistle and key-chain noises of the Doctor as he let himself through the wooden gate. Diana, fighting the reminiscent grin away, quickly said: 'Oh damn. Yes, I'm sorry. That did have something to do with it. The cream.'

Her mother, Miss Maxey, and a grey-haired woman in a windcheater, Diana and Aunt Het sat playing Solo in the place they called the Schoolroom. In this comfortable place the dog had almost ripped off the sofa cover and a large bone on the floor rolled under people's feet.

The Solo players sat at a table underneath a gigantic lampshade fringed with little red balls. Moorman was by himself on the dog's sofa, which covered his suit with pale hairs. 'We only use zis room for schrolling about in with ze dogs,' Diana's mother explained briefly over her shoulder. The schoolroom's only other furnishing was a television set with a little old-fashioned screen (possibly made by the Doctor) and a bookcase containing old *Girl* annuals and Enid Blyton stories.

Miss Maxey said 'Hulloa old chap' to him and then just concentrated on her cards. There was a great deal of helpless laughter and unspreading of failed hands. To drink, Diana's mother provided warm gin and French, which the Doctor had mixed up in a surgical looking jug with a metal handle; and there were dishes of small German biscuits and sugared almonds.

Moorman had to reach up to the top of the bookcase for his glass of gin and French. It tasted like medicine. From time to time the Doctor himself would tramp into the room, taking no notice of him, wearing heavy farm shoes, and stuck his behind out alarmingly as he bent down to look at people's hands of cards, whistling tunelessly.

Moorman looked through the *Girl* annuals. He couldn't bear to read the historical strip cartoons because they reminded him of Mr Starkey. He instead stared at *Pat Smythe Writes for You, So You Want to be a Nurse, So you Want to be a Hospital Almoner, Lettice Leefe, the Greenest Girl in School* and *Belle of the Ballet,* his brain heaving whenever he happened to turn to the inscribed frontispiece 'this book belongs to . . .' followed by 'Diana Kingsley-Pink' in large child's handwriting.

15

One way of dealing with this was to keep making wry and faintly cynical remarks out loud to himself—'God, you *do* get into some situations, don't you?' '*God,* life's funny sometimes.' 'God . . .' At best he saw himself as the sad, bruised hero of an L.P. sleeve of songs of heart-break. But he knew it was impossible to treat the loss of Diana Kingsley-Pink, the one scrap of Harrods life had ever offered, philosophically. Awful erections, like ghosts from a portrait gallery, accompanied the memory of the soft, cold arches inside her mouth; the lovely combination round his waist on the Hunting Stewart in the Wild Wood.

Another way was to square the shoulders (the suit was now ruined) and say—well, consider what you've got left, your health and so forth: this while his tooth and his heart were both streaked with agony and his nose blocked, and a suspicion of blood in the dislodging. It was true that, even in tears, Moorman couldn't help feeling relieved that he would not have to buy any more rounds of drinks at 22s. 6d. Then he remembered, and was comforted by the thought of his worldly goods, some 200 Edwardian penny-in-the-slot machines: the Allwyne de luxe, the Automatic Palmist, the Copper Mine, See Him Sweat, the Basketball, the Caley, the Grand National, the Uninvited, the Boxers, the Cup and Hat, the Gold Cup, Bedroom Scene—and a rolled gold bracelet looking rather more delicate and expensive than it really was.

On the morning after his final visit to Hemingford Priory, Moorman opened his eyes, not remembering exactly, to begin with, why he was miserable. He knew he was stiff eyed and prostrate through some immense tragedy, but couldn't collect the details of it. He'd been, in any case, a hopeless reporter. Then it all came back and he thumped his face into his pillow as the town hall clock struck a long way off. Diana's face in the green indicator light as she drove him back to Springbourne; and her efforts to keep things light; she even suggested again that they should wave to the fellow in the power station. She apologized briefly and scooted off, the van brake lights giving a last glimpse of warmth and comfort at the corner. The town hall clock struck five, six. Moorman lay in bed and wanted to drink fizzy lemonade until it ran down over his face. He went down to the middle-landing lavatory and stood over the bowl with tears in his eyes, wetting the blackened lino against the facing wall. The Tredegar Guest House was full of distant pig pens. He imagined vividly the scent of bubble-bath from between the legs drying on soft O Sole Mio blankets. He went back to sleep, his legs aching.

The town hall clock struck eight, nine, ten. With his eyes just opened, Moorman knew that outside was the sort of dull day that generally made him feel cheerful. He made up his mind to try, next time he woke up, to see exactly what it felt like the very moment one woke up. He felt for an instant, nothing but optimism and good humour, a return of the sensation of owning a new suit; then it occurred to him again that there was nothing in the whole world to look forward to. He had the aftertaste of a bad sugared almond from one of the bowls at Diana's mother's card party in his mouth. Then his bedroom tap ran cold *and* brown. From his window the Solent looked badly combed; the Esplanade and the pier seemed deserted. Only John Close's tram broke the silence, ba-bang, baa-ng and sliding to a stop at the end, where Leslie and Mr Starkey were already, he supposed, beginning another harmonious day. He left the Tredegar Guest House without a tilt with Mona Lisa di Valvona and presently sat on the tram, his nose pressed to the window, frightening himself by watching the creamy waves untop themselves through the iron pier supports. He thought of Diana's voice saying, 'What I especially love is jugged hare when Mummy does it with lots and lots of redcurrant jelly.' He sat for ages on the lavatory behind the pierrot stage as the wind moaned up the pan and the timbers of the pierhead shivered whenever a ferry touched the dock. He thought of the kitchen, brilliant with the strip lighting, and the beautiful lunch that was undoubtedly cooking there.

Moorman sat and examined the contents of his wallet. At least, if everything else failed, he still had his wallet, with pockets marked in gold for £5, £1, 10s. and stamps. How he would love to climb and hide away in the soft, breast-warm leather of his own wallet.

He turned to Mother's letter. By now it had been folded too many times, like a Spanish officer's credentials. The Canadian Brand paper was crisp in Moorman's fingers; the one fresh element to the day. Miss Toye sent her regards. The shop was doing well enough. 'Why don't you buy yourself out, dear?' And a blank cheque; at least he had a blank cheque to look forward to.

Leslie, or possibly Mr Starkey, had left behind the stage an old copy of *The Cruel Sea* in a Penguin edition. It seemed a snug thing to be reading on a wild, grey, cold day like this. At least (count your blessings) he wasn't at sea in a Corvette, or worse still in a life raft after the torpedoing of the Corvette, and with 'swelled, ruptured organs' thanks to V.D. The dreadful sensation as the icy Atlantic closed on them. He flicked the pages through to find other examples of people worse off than himself. He came across the bombing of a terraced house. The doorhandle rattled and he froze for a moment; he'd been in there over half an hour. The footsteps receded. Moorman found a passage about a high-class lieutenant who found his wife in bed with another. He felt even brighter and even began to read odd bits of the book in which people were enjoying themselves. His eye caught the end of one chapter . . . 'and following what seemed to him an excellent example, drank himself into insensibility.' How did one do that?

Leslie wore his blue V-necked pullover with no shirt underneath. He was tightlipped, and appeared to be fighting back a blush as he went over with Mr Starkey the plan for the removal of the machines into storage. He gave Moorman the impression that he, Moorman, had a right to know of the plan but was expected to play no real part in it. Since the Italian helpers preferred to lend a hand before Mass (Leslie had clearly been in touch about it with Uncle Grimaldi) the operation would have to start very early in the morning, if Mr Starkey could bear it, about 7 a.m. They had arranged to hire the truck and its nudging string of wooden trailers that took large consignments of ferry luggage from one end of the pier to the other. This would bring the machines as far as the pier gates. Then the helpers would carry them up St John's Lane to be stacked in Mr Starkey's store. Mr Starkey himself would drive the truck. 'You can pretend it's an armoured train crossing the Veldt,' Leslie said fondly to him and Mr Starkey replied, 'I'll watch out for Kruger's snipers.'

St John's Lane ran parallel with the main shopping street and, in fact, contained most of its tradesmen's entrances. When he came out of the lavatory, Moorman saw that Mr Starkey had already brought down two of the chests-of-drawers to be converted into self-service counters. As a rule Moorman and Mr Starkey scarcely said a word to one another; the latter was the kind of person who, confronted by someone, often pretends to look over his shoulder for someone else. His button eyes could on occasion seem as empty as the North Sea. But this morning he offered to take Moorman up to see the store and Moorman, wanting company, accepted. On the way down the pier, the wind buffeted the van—another van—and Mr Starkey gave him a résumé of the battle of Fontenoy which, owing to mismanagement and early morning fog, had ended in defeat for the British during the Marlborough campaigns.

Moorman sat in the van, his knees drawn up, as Mr Starkey importantly opened a small door in a large one, then pulled the entire front back, kicking bits of grass and stones out of the sliding mechanism, to show him the machines' resting place. This consisted of a clear area of concrete. Behind that, in the shadows was a great heap of blue and pink soft furniture with legs interlocked and castors hanging lifelessly; Moorman thought how marvellous it would be to sleep in there for centuries, his nose pressed on some old and sympathetic headrest. He found he didn't like Mr Starkey any better for the ride. He discovered, too, that Mr Starkey dribbled.

Early in the afternoon, Leslie Langdon said:

'Buy yourself *what? Out?*'

The wind had risen now, sobbing round the Pavilion, sweeping across inside as Mr Starkey opened a door to bring back a box of nails he had been to buy, up the town.

'When you decided to accept the . . . you know . . . I was over the moon. I was over the moon,' Leslie said, in a sort of weak dagger voice. He narrowed his eyes and put his hands on his hips. He pointed at Moorman. 'Do you know, I think you're the only person in the world who's ever managed to make me feel really vindictive. Normally I'm the mildest of men. If you take advantage of people, well, that's what you've got to expect, isn't it?'

Moorman couldn't find the words he wanted. He stammered and repeated himself and didn't want to go on talking. He tried to tell Leslie he was leaving Springbourne because of emotional problems.

'Oh yes, *I'll* bet. You think you'll just up sticks and push off. Gor blimey, well I wish I could say we'll miss you but we won't. Now just drop it. Leave it. Just leave it. I don't want a row or any unpleasantness about it but you can just take a powder as soon as you please, whenever it suits you. You'll be going home to Mummy I suppose.' Mummy! Who was that?

Moorman looked past Leslie, with his ring of hair standing out as if he'd just been read a ghost story. He made his eyes go expressionless as Mr Starkey did when looking at *him*. Leslie talked on and on about ungratefulness, his voice becoming unreal as well as more and more effeminate. Moorman was again counting his blessings. He thought to himself, so long as he could do that he'd never go quite mad. At least he wasn't outside in the wind; it held the weather cone straight and motionless on top of the little yacht race tower. At least he didn't at that precise moment want any chocolate; the thought made him feel manly and tough. 'Oh, piss off, Langdon,' he said.

'I should jolly well think I *will* let you out,' his partner replied. 'First thing on Monday morning when we've got the machine business sorted out all right. Mr Starkey's already said he's interested in doing the cafeteria with me. At least he knows his arse from his elbow. First thing on Monday morning. By the way you've got a great big black streak down the side of your face and a bit of snot under one nostril.'

'You can turn up tomorrow morning or not, as you please,' Leslie said, breaking the silence of the late afternoon. 'It would be a courtesy if you did, since they're all doing it to oblige you; in fact,' (spitefully), 'it's a sort of wedding present in advance, isn't it?'

Moorman was feeling quite pleasantly excited: this evening marked the end of his adolescent misery period, and the beginning of his Naval hero misery period: he had made up his mind to, in the words of *The Cruel Sea*, 'drink himself into insensibility.' Up to now, when he needed to count his blessings they had nearly always included the fact that he neither drank nor—save in the occasional effort to impress—smoked. But, what with everything, he might as well do both. He might as well drink properly instead of getting himself occasionally puffed out with Double Diamond.

On leaving the Pavilion he walked and then caught a

bus to the top of the town. The conductor was a student on vacation; which made Moorman feel uncomfortable. He went to the Scala cinema to see *Topkapi,* in which Peter Ustinov was an almost exact reproduction of himself; only Moorman didn't realise. Afterwards he returned to the Tredegar Guest House with his half bottle of whisky; no, half bottle of scotch sounded much better, much more heroic. It was Johnny Walker. Unfortunately the beauty of the dandy's clothes on the label made him miserable all over again.

But he liked his situation, as he prepared to drink himself into insensibility, sitting up in bed: a tough guy using the tough guy's method of forgetting an unhappy affair. If only Diana and her mother could be here to see it. He pretended to slop the whisky around in his tooth mug and slur his speech; he had not yet quite overcome the vileness of the taste.

Moorman took another drink and kept it pressed under his tongue. From the antler-horn table he took the old school copy of the book that had always given comfort to him. *The History of Mr Polly*: he took some more medicine, kept it pressed under his tongue again, and read the passage where the young Mr Polly is deceived by the little boarding-school girl. Quite often Moorman had wondered if he bore any resemblance to Mr Polly at all. He decided that he did not. Mr Polly was slim and had a beautiful soul. Mr Polly was bold enough to take to the open road, and because of that, came across the Potwell Inn and the lawns that ran down to the river.

Moorman burst into tears, then checked himself, remembering that he was supposed to be a Naval officer drinking himself into insensibility. He made quite a good recovery in fact, continuing to take the whisky like castor oil—he had to admire his own strength of character as revealed in the way he kept on at the whisky. Once his mind was made up . . . He also had to laugh at the number of improvements, for the sake of Diana and her mother, that had not been put into effect. Here he was still in his old pyjama trousers with a finger up his backside. What he really needed to drink himself into insensibility was a smooth pair of pyjamas, and a dressing-gown with a knotted cravat underneath it. His 'personal grooming' had still shown no evidence of existing. Had Diana told her mother about the business with the cream? He wondered if her mother asked why he wouldn't now be in the pantomime. He wondered if Diana, with cackles, had told the entire rehearsal about the business with the cream; if they had based an impromptu sketch on it to amuse the over-sixties. The slow grin crossed the Doctor's face, in Moorman's imagination, showing first the gold teeth, then the gap in the middle. Moorman discovered he didn't care if Diana *had* told them. Did that mean that the whisky was getting to work?

It still tasted as horrible as it had when he first sipped from the toothmug; as horrible as the glass he'd drunk at the Royal Springbourne dance to impress Diana. But now it was milder. He was able to hold a cheekful without a feeling of burning. This meant, did it not, that he was getting a taste for whisky; that sounded very good. 'I have been getting a taste for whisky.' This could be the basis for a set of new bad habits to sweep away the old, childish ones. The taste of whisky killed the craving for chocolate, absolutely. He began to do a sum in his head, comparing the cost of half crowns for whisky and sevenpence for Mars bars and sixpence for Kit Kats; but had to abandon it. He said 'God, I was pissed last night', and 'God, I got so *pissed* last night'; excellent conversational material.

'I was *so* pissed last night.' But he wasn't. He simply felt no fear. He was outside his marvellous memory and watching it *not* function. He poured the last lot of whisky into his cheeks, held it there—it didn't sting at all—then swallowed it with an exaggerated gulp. Well, he had drunk half a bottle of Scotch and had failed to drink himself into insensibility. He was sitting up in bed, scorning the idea of chocolate, collecting his thoughts perfectly, picking his arse and his nose, reading the bit of Mr Polly where Mr Polly lays about the bully with a dead eel. There was a knocking on his door, or another door somewhere. He disregarded it. He was not in the smallest degree drunk. He was, on the contrary, very comfortable. He was thinking how awful it would be if he didn't have this room to come home to in the cool of the evening. There was a kind of nutty, slightly cough-mixture taste in his mouth. His senses were sharp. That *was* Mona Lisa di Valvona's voice he could hear, calling and weeping outside. He was quite in command of himself, yet felt his mind somehow rolled back and at a distance from what he saw—like the curve of a highly carved balcony at the theatre.

The season, he thought, was only just beginning: August—months still remained in which he could swim and play tennis. He thought himself sitting at the end of a lovely white tablecloth tasting the whisky on everyone else's behalf, and nodding his curt approval. Soft fairy lights hung in the arches of the winter garden. Moorman felt the delicate warmth of new potatoes against cold pie crust without jelly, and spring onions tasted in unison with strawberries. He ate his supper, poised, beautifully dressed in a biscuit-coloured suit with cuffless trousers and a flared jacket. The trousers, no matter how languidly he crossed and uncrossed his legs, remained impeccably creased. He blinked at the others at the table, and smiled indulgently. They were on at him again to say it—please say it once more, say it, say it, say it for us, O please. He saw Diana say, O, please. He could have dived in between her lips when they formed, O, please. The others roared for him to say it again. O, please; and under the table all sorts of trim little legs brushed and pressed against his. They roared for him to say it again. Moorman held up a hand. The clamour ceased. He was squeezed under the table and, at the same time, right between the eyes. He had to close them. He saw blackness broken by flashes that formed themselves into ranks of hussars and dragoons, the extra coats on their shoulders swinging this way and that; a rhythmic jingle in his ears. He opened his eyes and looked down the table. How they all adored him. How they all wished they were him. He felt the cool material of his suit and the hot place that was being squeezed as Diana's lips shaped, O, please. Very well, he would say it just once more. The applause was deafening. The silence was also deafening. Now . . . 'let the hag be flung from the . . .'

The town hall clock tower struck a long way off: Moorman only heard four chimes but must have been subconsciously counting since he was absolutely positive it was eight o'clock. Moorman thought he would get up early and surprise everyone. He did not have to be down at the pier gates until an hour ago; oh well, he was an hour late but at least didn't have to wash or shave or do his hair. He got out of bed by means of a double somersault (it felt like). Some time later he was sitting on a window ledge, leaning right over the precipice of guest house gardens that stretched down to the canoe lake, shouting remarks at the people below.

He was also looking for a sock under his bed, holding in his teeth a pair of exceptionally thick cavalry twill trousers which had somehow acquired a faintly savoury taste. He blew all the fluff under the bed into his own face and laughed at the pleasure it gave him. This also had something to do with being fortunate in that he didn't have to spend hours getting ready to go out, he was ready in a moment; always casual. He did not even have to go downstairs to pee, having just done so out of the window. He had been greatly moved as the thin, thick, malty strand sailed down towards the Esplanade.

Moorman danced in and out of a bedroom one floor below. 'Aha! I've *caught* you!' It was really wicked of him to interrupt the Italian couple from Ventnor who, after their wedding at the Royal Springbourne, were honeymooning—at special rates at the bride's aunt's lovely guest house. But it was so interesting. The tall bridegroom his bottom high in the air, licking this recumbent auntie figure who, even at that moment was unwrapping a toffee, looking perfectly abstracted. The bridegroom leapt into the air and dived for his hanging cardigan. Moorman slammed the door (quick reflexes: that was another blessing to count), and neatly went to the side of a pair of outstretched fat arms on the landing.

They were all after him, the women, even the landlady's daughter. She had on a navy-blue tailored suit with white piping and a corsage of artificial gardenias, and carried a big white handbag. Moorman jumped all five of the bottom steps and was in the sunshine, thinking how interesting the ancient pagoda shaped pillar box on the corner of Pell Lane was. The big white handbag clubbed him but didn't hurt. 'What did you do that for?' he asked in a perfectly reasonable voice. 'I wasn't looking at you.' He kicked a dog in the pink place under its woolly body, and ran off.

'You never got your name in—not on the *Herald,*' he explained. 'Sometimes you got your initials on a play review or something like that. They used to say it was the best training you could get, but I disagreed, you see. All you learned to do was stand at a church door and take the names of the people who came in, and later on, make a list of the people who *didn't* come in.

'I think I'll make a list here and now. Have you got a piece of paper and a pencil, or a biro? What's *your* name? And can I have the initial as well, and any rank or style?'

Moorman was standing next to a small, thin, balding man wearing an ice-blue mackintosh underneath which he had a striped matelot T-shirt. He was holding, with some difficulty, a slot machine, the Allwyne de Luxe. 'Could you give me your name?' he repeated. But his attention was distracted by the bald man's reply by the confusion in which they were both standing. It seemed that the entire Esplanade was alive with men of the same diminutive build, many wearing moustaches, all wearing pointed slip-on shoes and carrying or helping carry slot machines with ball and claw feet. Moorman recognized ball and claw feet thanks to his acquaintanceship with Miss Toye, Mother's friend. 'Can I do that?' he said. To his surprise he kept sinking to his knees. On about the fourth or fifth occasion, a face wearing a jaunty peaked cap looked into his eyes and said, 'Been on the beer, mate?' Moorman got up with dignity, shook his head and felt his way along the side of a line of parked luggage trucks, loaded with cabinets with ball and claw feet. An iron sailor lay on its back, its arms outstretched. At the back of the last truck, three people, led by a man wearing handmade shoes and a bootlace tie, were heroically trying to unload a cabinet with the head and shoulders of a gypsy, writing attentively behind its glass. Out of pure devilment Moorman put a penny in. The hand holding an ancient penholder began to move to and fro. The cabinet had trapped the fingers of the man in handmade shoes, who screamed. Then a card dropped down to the pavement. Moorman sat down against the luggage truck to read it, taking no notice of what the man in the ice-blue mackintosh was saying to him. 'You are the possessor of unusual gifts,' the card read, 'but owing to your excessive modesty you have always been denied your true reward. You are kindly, temperate and steadfast but mask these virtues by your desire not to intrude in matters which you believe are none of your concern. You have wisdom, patience and tolerance, and the capacity to make lasting friends. Forget your diffidence, overcome your shyness and there are no heights to which you may not climb.' The face with the peaked cap was back. 'Been on the beer, mate, have you?' Moorman gave him a charming smile, and—because he believed the enormous crowd were not now looking in his direction—wiped some of the stuff from the corners of his mouth on his sleeve. 'Give 'n a cup of tea to settle his stomach,' a voice said. 'I'll see to it,' Moorman said firmly. 'I'll do it. Where is he?'

He was looking up at a set of lights arranged in different-coloured bands to form a peacock's tail, buzzing and flashing, spreading and withdrawing. 'Why did you have to come and show me up like this?' a reedy voice demanded from a long way off, a distant ice-blue mackintosh. Moorman wanted to reply that it had been it had simply been because he'd wanted to run all the way down the steep hill to the Esplanade. All he managed was, 'Bit sick.' He got up from reading the card from the Automatic Palmist and, beginning to feel not quite himself, went to the edge of the pavement where a wonderfully kept green sports car was parked. It was a big help to be a bit sick on the canvas cover that was there to protect the upholstery: well, it *had*.

Moorman stood and watched men he recognized as lodgers from the Tredegar Guest House and their friends, carrying slot machines over the road, through the taxi rank, on to the pavement in front of S'Lots of Fun and up the cobbled approach to St John's Lane; oh, yes, he was perfectly lucid. He noted that it took four Italians to move an electric pin-table but only two to move the iron sailor, who sat up on their shoulders like a hero at games. Moorman was seized by a violent desire to give all of them a hand. He grabbed the end of a cabinet from one of the luggage trucks. A stab of pain went through him. He looked in alarm at the black splinter at the end of his forefinger. It put him on his back again, looking into the chasm of the sky and the perplexed face of the ex-manager of the Club Marimba, Whittlesey, imparting a fine spray as he shouted noiselessly at his partner. It was important at this moment to warn Leslie (it was Leslie!) not to take into any business partnership the flabby aircraftsman he appeared to fancy so much. Then Leslie had gone again. Moorman was up on his feet and making for a cluster of Italians who were unloading another machine from the trucks; because he wanted to ask them *where* they got woollies in such marvellous colours. There was a cheering, applause from far away, busmen's peaked caps being waved. Moorman deliberately went and tickled the Italian who at that instant bore the entire weight of the machine: he stepped alertly out of its way, and the cabinet crashed down on to the pavement; so did Moorman; the pavement had a scrubbed yet thoroughly dog-arsed aroma.

He found he could lift his head up slightly and look right inside the machine. He could with one finger raise the drawbridge of the miniature castle and peep at the model of Hitler sitting on the pot, with the tiny paper turd threaded on to his underside. A voice he recognized as his remarked: 'You know . . . old Fred Wellspring was ab-sol-utely right. It was made by foreign prisoners of war! Look, you can see where they had to paint out the extra T in "sweat". Don't worry about the breakage though. I've got a blank cheque. I'll pay. I'll pay. I'll pay . . .'

He laughed at the two taxi drivers who were passing the tiny chamberpot around on the pavement with the toecaps of their shoes. The paper turd broke off its thread and blew away across the zebra crossing, almost between the rolled Turkish carpet legs of the one woman in the world he really and truly loved: she was here. He could feel the rough texture of her uncured lynx cape and the smell of her Swedish fryers she insisted made no smell. It was Mother, on her way across the road. From where Moorman lay, she seemed to have the peacock-lights in her hair, like the trademark for Columbia pictures. She held her hat on with one hand, and a veil blew out at an angle. He wondered where she had got the heavy gold Omega that was on her wrist; if it was from Miss Toye, he would accept one: in fact, was that not Miss Toye in the driving seat of the Austin Westminster at the facing pavement. If not, one of her Hungarian refugee friends, or Italian refugee friends; or was it Michael Holliday sitting there, or Anthony

Quinn, or another very like him?

Mother came up so close that he wanted to push his nose into her fur, to smell the mixture that reminded him of her: batter, mothballs and a touch of cologne. He started to tell her that she was absolutely right, he was positive, he would buy himself out at once. Then he perceived that she wasn't listening. Probably it was some historical novel she was anxious to get back to, by Margaret Irwin or Margaret Campbell-Barnes . . . in that case she ought to meet Mr Starkey, he said, because of . . . but he'd been very wrong about the Italian attitude to work, he continued. After all, they were a nation of workers. Look at the Moto Guzzi motorcycle. Four more of them were crossing the taxi rank holding an electric pin table like a ceremonial coffin. Really, it was about time he bought everyone a cup of tea, he interrupted, ignoring a faint slap across the mouth. 'I always think I'm going to be sick if I drink tea early in the mornings, unless I have a biscuit with it. Otherwise . . . but I'm never actually *sick,*' he insisted, dabbing with the sleeve of his charcoal grey suit at the fur cape, very sorry for what had happened.

Mother, for some reason, chose to put on a funny voice. Don't be ridiculous, he wanted to say, nobody talks like that. And he might hear the floating quality of Leslie's voice, too—he'd twisted his pocket linings in case Mother would hate him—or sometimes his head spun round and caught the eye of a crowd that seemed to be waiting to see a procession. He wanted to go up and address them, reason with them, tell them he loved them. Politeness, however, (he thought: 'politeness, however,') demanded that Mother should first complete her remarks. 'Complete your remarks,' he urged her, with what he knew to be a dazzling smile.

What, Moorman wondered warm and pleasantly, did Mother mean by: 'As God is ma witness, Joe, I'll . . . Don't you dare deny it, you, you nonentity. It's all written down by Aldo Dinardo, a close friend of ma family, in this folder. Buckshee kisses off some bleached-up bism at the Conservative and Unionist Buffy Supper! Hey!' That reminded Moorman of the 'Eh, sir, eh!' among jolly Pickwickian characters, the rosy-cheeked jugs, the rounds of beef, the hot toast . . .

What did Mother mean by 'Two-timing bugger!'

'Mother o' Mercy, look at you standing there. If ma Larry wasna' in his grave, *he'd* . . .' Moorman began in a rush to tell Mother that, provided the Swedish fryers were completely odourless, he would come to work for her . . . 'Lucky for all of us that wee Aldo's been eating his heart out, *eating his heart out* for that girl as surely as she, God forgive her, I'll strangle her when she's stopped crying . . . as she's bin for 'm.'

A grand tone: 'Have the goodness . . . have the goodness to remove your junk out of oor house at your earliest convenience!

'And if you so much as dare to look that girl in the eye again, so much as touch the hem of her garment, it's court for you, ma lad. Hobbledehoy! Gigolo! Lounge lizard (loonge lizurd)!'

What, precisely, did Mother mean by all this, he wondered.

Moorman believed he was following her, the heads and the tails going rhythmically, with beads of corn and tomato on them, across the zebra to the Austin Westminster, where Miss Toye, Anthony Quinn, or some such person, sat waiting for her, the collar of his red towelling shirt turned up at the back.

Moorman wanted to be enfolded in her arms. Provided

that, at night, she would leave his door open bumping the bed, provided that the Swedish fryers were really and truly odourless, he would be proud, happy, inflated with ridiculous pride, to help her in the shop. 'Where there's muck there's money,' he reminded her, thinking this at least would get a laugh. But little dimpled arms shot out of the fur—the whole day seemed to be furry, muffled by ranch mink or uncured lynx—and patted him backwards. It was so ineffectual a pat that Moorman noticed it. He ordered himself to get a grip. He came forward from his rolled-back balcony of the senses. He was on the Esplanade, interrupting the transference of the machines from the Pavilion to Mr Starkey's store in St John's Lane. And in front of him it was not Mother but Mrs di Valvona, smelling somewhat of sick, wearing an olive green costume and a fur cape, shouting to a great crowd of people including her sister Mrs Sangiorgio (they were reconciled!) about someone who by all accounts had deceived and shamefully misused her daughter, the stout Mona Lisa di Valvona.

At the same time the wind along the Esplanade strengthened. Moorman's hair blew inside out. He saw the huge crowd of taximen and holidaymakers watching, and tried to put it back, but it blew inside out again. Mrs di Valvona threw down an orange folder and the sheets of paper blew vigorously about: precise details, recorded in an Italian's night-school English: from the tryst with the grocer's shop girl outside the chemist's to the meeting with the girl dressed in an old bale of silk at the Conservative dance—this while Mona Lisa di Valvona lay at death's door (though entering might have been something of a squeeze).

A hockey machine stood on the paved rim of the taxi rank. The iron sailor stood at the bottom of St John's

Lane, and a wondering little boy in toddler's reins was trying to shake hands with it. See Him Sweat lay on its side. Leslie wrung his hands (people really did that in real life!). A pin-table stood outside S'Lots of Fun, like a workhouse boy looking in at the workhouse masters. Mrs di Valvona shouldered about the Esplanade, ordering the Italians to put down the machines where they stood and go away to Mass. Uncle Grimaldi got in the back of the Austin Westminster; Mrs di Valvona, with less facility, into the front. A crowd of yobs started the massacre. They clustered round the hockey machine and began a game. Then someone came out of S'Lots of Fun and put a penny into the pin table: it punched weakly against the electric noise from inside that fantastic treasure palace.

Moorman ambled (as Leslie would have expressed it if he were not so busy) over to the Austin Westminster as it drew slowly away. He started to explain to Mrs di Valvona—her head turned away from him like a Queen—that he *was* sorry; that he knew she would do anything in the world to prevent her little girl from being hurt and he himself would do anything to prevent it, but the one thing he couldn't do was the thing she wanted him most to do, namely . . . Moorman had the taste of whisky and metal and copper dust in his mouth. He turned away from the wind of the departing limousine and, once again, saw See Him Sweat lying where it had been dropped, the broken glass laid carefully inside the cabinet frame. People were playing his machines all over the Esplanade and a little way up St John's Lane. He heard the new style police alarm. On the far pavement he was not in the least surprised to see Meatball, taking from the pocket of his khaki shorts a screwdriver with a misty yellow handle, the kind that lights up when electrical contact is made. Moorman thought with some pleasure that his tears at this moment were tears of whisky: he felt desperate at the thought of Mona Lisa's head crying on her pillow, yet at the same time laughed so much that he got a stitch at the thought of Mrs di Valvona wearing only her vest. Although it was chilly, Moorman was too hot. Of the paper turd from See Him Sweat there was now no sign. Unless it was himself.